HARTSLOVE

K.M. Grant is an author, journalist and broadcaster. She is also the Royal Literary Fund Fellow at the University of Glasgow. Her first book, *Blood Red Horse*, was a Booklist Top Ten Historical Fiction for Youth and a USBBY-CBC Outstanding International Book for 2006. The sequel, *Green Jasper*, was shortlisted for the Royal Mail Scottish Children's Book award, and *How the Hangman Lost His Heart* was an Ottakar's Book of the Month and a *Sunday Times* Children's Book of the Week. She lives in Glasgow and can also be found at http://kmgrant.org/.

Also by K.M. Grant

BELLE'S SONG

THE PERFECT FIRE TRILOGY
BLUE FLAME
WHITE HEAT
PARADISE RED

HOW THE HANGMAN LOST HIS HEART

THE DE GRANVILLE TRILOGY
BLOOD RED HORSE
GREEN JASPER
BLAZE OF SILVER

HARTSLOVE

K.M. GRANT

Quercus

First published in Great Britain in 2011 by
Quercus
21 Bloomsbury Square
London
WC1A 2NS

A CIP catalogue reference for this book is available
from the British Library

ISBN 978 0 85738 187 3

1 3 5 7 9 10 8 6 4 2

Typeset by Nigel Hazle
Printed and bound in Great Britain by Clays Ltd, St Ives plc.

In memory of Kettledrum,
the real The One of 1861

PROLOGUE

Wednesday, 29 May 1861

In a silence feverish with hopes and longings, a scrappy pony, hemmed in by the pressing crowd, flattened its ears. Harassed beyond endurance, the man perched on its back raised a flag. As he did, ten thousand throats caught ten thousand breaths. Ten thousand fists squeezed ten thousand slips of paper. Twenty thousand feet raised themselves on tiptoe. The man's arm, rigid with responsibility, was jolted from below. 'Get them away, McGeorge!' The cry was taken up by others. 'Get them away! Get them away!' For a second, McGeorge hesitated and the flag wavered. Then he stiffened and held his nerve. Not yet.

Barely six feet away from him eighteen of England's fastest horses were poised, every nerve strung taut in bodies so sleek and lean they were almost transparent. Skin glistened and quivered as they rocked. Some shook violently like kettles on the boil. Some boiled over and began to reverse. Others had to be turned by their jockeys for fear of a false start. Soothe. Brace. Soothe. Brace. The jockeys were as tense as the horses. In the next two minutes and forty-five seconds, their places in racing history would be decided.

Amongst these sleek, boiling equine arrows, one horse stood out. He was not beautiful, at least not in the conventional sense. Where his companions were elegant, he was sturdy. Where they seemed barely strong enough to carry the designated weight of 8 stone 7 lb, he looked able to carry a fully armed dragoon into battle. His sixteen hands of height was matched by great depth of girth, arched loins and a large head which he carried poked out like a child who has suddenly smelled something quite delicious. Only muscular quarters, dropping away to a thick tail, betrayed any hint of real quality: those, and his deep chestnut coat, the blood-red broken by a white unfinished diamond, its edges almost touching both eyes before tailing into a narrow stripe running down the horse's long face and broadening untidily about three inches above a smoky nose. A white, sickle-shaped snip disappeared into his left nostril, and three white socks, two on his front legs and one on his nearside hind, gave him the look of a horse an artist has spoiled with one or two misplaced strokes, and afterwards, with regret, has decided not to bother finishing.

The horse also stood out because he was facing backwards

and chewing on an apple core unexpectedly spied amidst the straggles of grass. He seemed only marginally aware of the other horses or the crowd, and quite unaware of the challenge ahead. His head was lowered, his teeth were crunching.

McGeorge shouted. The crowd began to hiss. The horse looked up with mild interest. Somebody ran out and pulled him round to face the front. The horse was not pleased. He was looking for somebody else and was not sure what was wanted, which was unsurprising since his jockey was thirteen years old and befuddled in equal measure by fear and whisky.

In an open cart halfway up the course, five sets of knuckles and five faces under five wide-brimmed hats grew pale as they watched the horse lay back his ears and chew.

'Daisy should have ridden him,' murmured Lily, her skin as white as her dress.

'You know she couldn't,' retorted Rose. As the oldest, she felt that the looming catastrophe was her fault. Her short temper grew shorter.

'Garth's terrified. I can see it from here. What happens if The One never even gets started?' Lily gazed in despair at the horse. Hope easily deserted her, and it did so now. She drooped like a flower without water. Rose looked helplessly at Daisy, standing, feet splayed. 'Will he start, Daisy?'

'He'll start,' Daisy said, though her voice was grim. She

stopped twiddling the bracelet she had plaited from the red horse's tail-hairs three months before and began to pick at one of the ribbons from her hat. She hardly heard Rose. She was aware only of willing Garth with all her might. 'Count, Garth, count: one, two, three, GO; one, two, three, GO. Come on. We've practised so hard.' The bottom of her stomach was pitching and rolling.

'What's happening?' One of a pair of identical twins, the youngest members of the family, who were squashed in the bottom of the cart and could see nothing but backs and hats.

'Shhhh!' their sisters warned. Clover and Columbine subsided. 'It's our future too,' they grumbled. As usual, nobody was listening to them.

McGeorge was fast losing control of the crowd. Any moment, he would have to let the horses go. Still The One was busy with his apple. Daisy could not bear to look; she could not bear to look away. Garth was listing heavily to one side and it was only now that Daisy was forced to acknowledge what she had, up to this moment, refused to accept: Garth was drunk. Drunk, drunk, drunk. All the care she had taken to keep him sober had been pointless. Sober, Garth might just remember the race plan. Drunk, there was no chance. She crumpled and held out her hands. Instinctively Lily and Rose took one each, then caught the hands of the twins.

'Everything will be all right, won't it?' Clover whispered,

eyes huge with terror. They had never all held hands in their lives. Rose had never encouraged it. Before anybody could answer, there came a great roar. McGeorge had given in, the flag was down, and the Derby, the greatest horse race in the world, was underway.

1

Hartslove, nearly four months earlier

At the end of a long drive whose trees had once been planted with skill and care but was now overgrown and pitted with potholes, a skinny, mop-haired, thirteen-year-old boy, half drowned under a man's silk shirt, was staring at a 'for sale' sign. He was staring hard at the sign, whose freshly painted words, boldly inscribed with a cheeky exclamation mark, seemed designed to insult the crusted iron gates. It was hard to believe that only twenty years before the gates had been so grand that visitors would automatically sit up straighter in their carriages as they passed through. Now the gates sagged, the lock rusted and dropping off. The new year frost sparkled like fairy dust on the iron bars, yet there was no magic here. The frost just looked cold. 'For sale', the letters winked, 'though who would want *this*!' the unwritten addition.

'That's it. That's the end. Pa's a demon, a *demon*!' The boy swore loudly, using bad words he had heard Skelton, the groom, shout when the coach horses misbehaved and he thought nobody was listening. Not that there were any coach horses now, or, indeed, a coach. There was just Tinker and the vegetable cart. Garth had watched the last coach leave Hartslove two and a half years before. He remembered the day very particularly, not because it had been his mother's birthday, although it was, but because his mother had been inside the coach. She had never looked out. Like the coach and horses, she had gone through these very gates; gone and vanished.

And the 'for sale' dashed forever any hope that she might return. Lady de Granville was not like the de Granville ghosts. If Hartslove was sold, it was possible that at least some of the ghosts — the Dead Girl who hung around in an upstairs passage, for instance — would follow Garth and his sisters to a new abode, being of the same blood and all. But their mother was not a ghost: she was a cloud. If she returned to Hartslove and found her children gone, she would presume they had forgotten her and cloudily waft away again. The thought made Garth's bottom lip tremble. He pressed against the gate until the bars bruised his skin.

He was aware of movement and saw his father loping towards him, Gryffed, his ancient wolfhound, padding silently behind. Charles de Granville was shivering in his tattered black morning jacket yet he hummed as he slithered in the icy scum. Garth could just hear the end of a tuneless 'Yankee Doodle'. How familiar the song was,

7

even though, on this freezing morning and with the 'for sale' sign creaking, it seemed to Garth that it must have been another boy who, in a flurry of sisters, had once tumbled down the stairs, giggling and shouting as Charles pretended to be the feather in Yankee Doodle's hat and chased them around Hartslove's great hall. Garth waited until his father was quite near, then deliberately climbed on to the remains of the gate and forced it to swing. He longed for his father to scold so that he could blaze back. But Charles de Granville just settled his thin frame on his soldier's legs. 'Ah, Garth,' he said, thrusting one hand into a sagging pocket and dropping the other on to Gryffed's head.

With dogged fury Garth swung to and fro, wishing a terrible wish: he wished his father would vanish as his mother had vanished. Immediately he was filled with panic. The twins believed that wishes came true. What if his father did vanish? He swung faster. *That's not what I wish*, he thought frantically and levered his body up so that he was doing a handstand on top of the gate. He cartwheeled along the narrow bar, then whipped his legs over and vaulted to the ground. He did not know how he did these acrobatics. To an outsider they gave an impression of weightless freedom; to Garth they were an anchor. So long as he could control his body, he could make some sense of life. If he lost this control, as his sister Daisy had since her pony had fallen on her five years before . . . He gritted his teeth. He had avoided riding since Daisy's accident. The moment her legs had been crushed was a recurring nightmare. He did two backflips in quick succession. *I won't even imagine it. I won't.*

Charles watched his son vault and flip, then picked a sprig of berried holly and proffered it along with his most crinkly, twinkly, charming smile. His eyes were bright but not with drink as they usually were. Garth could recognise that special drink-brightness a mile off, just as he could recognise the drink-smile and the drink-laughter and the drink smell-on-the-breath. This was a different brightness though it was just as familiar. Garth's throat tightened. He ungritted his teeth. 'Father,' he warned, 'you haven't –'

'Hartslove luck,' Charles interrupted, and banged his left heel three times, spitting into the mess of winter weeds.

Garth choked. Now he knew exactly why Charles had come down the drive, and it was monstrous, MONSTROUS. Though the 'for sale' sign marked the final ruin of the de Granvilles of Hartslove, Charles de Granville was about to hand over cash to a horse-dealer.

This was actually worse than monstrous, it was hideously cruel because before everything had started to go wrong, the arrival of one particular type of horse had often been a special moment between father and son. This type of horse was not a riding horse; it was a horse chosen by Charles from an advertisement in a racing newspaper, and the horse was always called The One because, until it disappointed, it was always going to be the one that won the Derby. When delivery day arrived, Charles would call Skelton and the three of them would wait right here, Charles biting his fingers, Skelton smoking his pipe and Garth hopping from foot to foot. As the hour approached, Charles and Garth alone, without ever asking Skelton to join in – that was the best bit – would bang their left heel three times and spit. 'Hartslove luck!' Charles would whisper. 'Shut your eyes, Garth, my boy, and when you open them you'll see the next winner of the Derby.'

His father was whispering now, his tone pleading. 'This really is The One, Garth. Bang your heel and spit! Do it! Do it!'

Garth did bang his heel and spit. He banged his heel hard on his father's toe and aimed a vicious gob at his father's cheek. He also drew back a clenched fist. Gryffed prickled and growled. Garth let fly, missed, and before he could let fly again, there were hoof-beats.

There was just one horse – Garth could hear that – and instead of a light, steady beat, there was chaotic skidding. When the horse finally appeared, it was not being led by a man, it was dragging a man behind it. Charles sharply ordered Gryffed to be still and pushed Garth aside.

'This colt yours?' the dragged man panted. He jabbed at reins flecked with froth and crammed his bowler hat more firmly on to his head. Despite the cold and his loud checked suit, he was sweating.

'No!' shouted Garth.

Charles bit his lip. 'I believe so,' he said.

'Money?'

'I have it here.' Charles fumbled in his pocket.

The man snatched the wad of notes. 'I'll count it.'

Garth counted too. Ten, twenty, forty, sixty, eighty, a hundred, ten, twenty – Garth's eyes widened. Two hundred. Three hundred. His mouth dried. Three hundred and sixty, seventy, eighty. Four hundred. *Four hundred!* Enough notes to get rid of that 'for sale' sign. He turned to his father but for the moment Charles had eyes only for the horse. The man pocketed the notes. 'Guineas, wasn't it?' he said, and held out a bag.

Charles coughed and dipped into another pocket. Four hundred shillings, dropped in uneven handfuls, formed a mountain in the bag.

At last the man was satisfied. 'I'll give you a receipt.' He thrust the horse's rein at Charles and scribbled something on a dirty piece of paper. 'There,' he said. 'It's yours, and I wish you joy of it. It's hauled me all the way from Liverpool and I'm less fond of it now than I was when I first saw it and I wasn't that fond of it then.' He laughed sourly and gave the colt an unfriendly slap. It took no notice. 'It's a scatty thing. Three years old and no sense at all.' He turned to go.

Charles fiddled with the reins, suddenly eager. 'Drink for your trouble?' He was just putting off the moment when he and Garth would be left alone. The dealer knew it and gave a pitying sneer. 'No, guv'nor. I'll get something in town before I get the train. Oh –' the man clapped his bowler even more firmly on to his head just as the colt, jigging about, caught the top of Charles's arm between two large incisors – 'it bites.'

Garth wrenched the lead-rope from his father and threw it at the dealer. 'Take it back. There's been a mistake. We don't want it.'

The dealer did not catch the rope. Instead he jangled the bag triumphantly. 'Well, sonny, me neither!' He chuckled loudly and walked briskly off.

Surprised to find itself free, the colt walked swiftly after the man, and Charles had to run to catch it. There was a small tussle before it agreed to come back through the Hartslove gate, only to shy sharply first at Gryffed, who followed every move his master made, and then at the 'for sale' sign.

Despite Garth, and despite the animal being nothing like its advertisement – it was even the wrong colour, chestnut instead of bay – Charles's eyes were sparkling again. If drink was Charles's prop, racehorses were his drug, every fix bursting with promise. 'This *is* The One, Garth,' he burst out, holding tight to the rein. He really believed it. It was winter now, but as he smelled the sweet smell of the colt's sweat and felt the strength of its will against his own, he could already see the Derby course bathed in early-summer sunshine and a jockey wearing the red de Granville silks punching the air in victory. His heart glowed.

Garth could not contain himself. He swore and swore again. He swore until he could think of no more swear words. 'How many The Ones have there been already, Pa? Ten? Twenty? And how many have done anything for us except eat up money? You're a . . . you're a . . .' He had used up all his bad words so he kicked the gate until it threatened to collapse completely.

His father paid no attention. He was too busy running his hands up and down the horse's front legs and over its withers. 'See here, Garth, he's not much to look at but he's by Rataplan out of Hybla and his half-sister won the Oaks in '54. He's got the makings of a star.'

'He's a horse – a hopeless, bloody great rubbish horse!'

Charles stood back. He was smiling, and that was when Garth finally exploded, attacking his father with fists and boots and roaring as loudly as the bear whose head and pelt lay outside their father's room must have roared on the day it earned its title 'The Cannibal'. Gryffed's hackles rose. Had Charles given the word, he would have gone for Garth's throat. No word came so he stayed sitting, though he shook and his upper lip curled above his teeth.

'How dare you!' howled Garth. 'You're the reason we're having to leave here. You're the reason the girls'll have to go and live with Aunt Barbara. You're the reason I'll have to go into the army because where else is there for me? You're the reason for the end of Hartslove. It'll be as if our family never existed.' He was furious to discover that he was crying. 'Why don't you just DIE?'

The horse, terrified, reared. Garth did not care, he pummelled and clobbered until, in final desperation, he blasted, 'I suppose it was because she saw this coming that Ma went away.'

The words hit Charles far harder than any bang in the gut. He sagged, suddenly an old man. It was hard for Garth to keep pummelling after that and, despite himself, his punches died away, leaving him breathing in short, steamy puffs. Charles stood quietly for several minutes. Garth's heart jerked. He felt quite empty. 'Pa,' he said. 'Pa.' He no longer wanted to punch. Instead he wanted, quite desperately, to turn the clock back, not just half an hour, but back to the days when his father had never sagged and he and Garth had wrestled in fun. How reassuringly solid Charles had felt then, for all his spiky frame, and how Garth had loved him. He had loved his mother too, but even when physically there, she had never actually seemed very present. 'It's like being hugged by a cobweb,' Lily had once said, and the name had stuck. Indeed, after their mother had gone, the de Granville children wondered guiltily whether she had heard them calling her 'the Cobweb' and taken that as her cue to sweep herself away.

Garth swallowed. 'Pa,' he said again.

Charles swallowed too. 'Garth.'

Neither seemed to know what to say next and the colt was restive. Eventually, with an apologetic murmur and a self-deprecatory shrug, Charles began to urge the creature up the stable drive. There was crunching on the gravel. Skelton was striding down. Charles greeted him and within moments was reciting the horse's breeding. He already seemed to have forgotten about Garth.

The 'for sale' sign flapped and the boy's temper surged again. How dare his father? How DARE he? Doubling over, he found a pebble. Taking careful aim, he threw it at the horse's rump with all the force his anger could muster. It hit true. The horse grunted and spun round, whisking the rope through Charles's hand. It galloped straight back down the drive, with only Garth between itself and the road.

Garth knew exactly what he was going to do. He was going to step smartly aside and let the animal gallop through the gate, right back to Liverpool and into the sea if it damned well wanted. What did it matter? Four hundred guineas were already lost. He forced himself to watch with steely unconcern as the reins swung between the colt's front legs. 'Trip over. Slip on the ice. Break a leg,' he muttered, blocking his ears against his father's shouted alarm and stepping out of the horse's way as it swished past. 'That's right. Get lost.'

But at the gate, the animal hesitated. Which way to go? Two long chestnut ears flipped in different directions.

Two smoky nostrils flared. A tremor shuddered down its back legs and Garth could see where the pebble had made a small cut in its ungainly hindquarters. It turned, and two large, childishly expectant eyes peeped through a straggly forelock. The ears reversed their flip, then reversed again. Before it could make up its mind as to its next move, Charles ran past and it was recaptured. 'Thank God!' Charles said, unable to disguise the reproach in his voice.

'Too scared to catch him yourself, Master Garth?' Skelton, following close behind, knew just how to rile. It was something he practised with pleasure. Garth growled, glared, then fled up the castle drive, over the drawbridge lying aross the old moat, under the archway, across the courtyard and through the antique doorway into the Hartslove hall, where he stopped in front of a boy as furious as himself. 'I hate everyone! I hate everything!' he cried, though he got no answer, the Furious Boy being one of many pale life-sized statues brought to Hartslove by a previous de Granville from a Grand Tour of Europe. Garth turned right and ran into the dining room. A trestle from the servants' hall had taken the place of the original dining table, but the oak sideboard was still under the Landseer portrait of his mother and on it, between two stubby candles, was a bottle of brandy his father had left. With only the smallest hesitation Garth reached for it, pulled off the stopper and drank the contents. He gasped.

The taste was vile, but a fire ignited in his belly. His eyes narrowed.

Nursing the fire, he lit a lamp and, skirting the wooden lift that plied a creaky trade between the dining room and the kitchen directly below, he ran down stone steps, past the kitchen door, then down another flight of steps until he reached the old dungeons, now used as larders. He shivered. Even in high summer it was corpse-cold down here, and during the winter it was colder than the ice house. Spectral light seeped through the tiny, crusted windows, as though some very old animal was blinking. He bumped his head on a dead hare hanging in stiff splendour from one of the many bloodstained hooks. His heart banged but the brandy kept him going.

At the far end of the dungeons was a small door with a huge key poking from the lock. The key was superfluous since the door was never fastened. Nevertheless, Garth had only been through the door once before; this was his father's private territory. The door groaned open at Garth's push. He stepped inside. The air was so thick his footsteps were smothered in the gloom. To his right he could just make out a stone slab. He held his lamp up. Fuzzily revealed was an Aladdin's cave of bottles, all neatly laid between ancient round arches dating from the castle's earliest days.

The door swung closed behind him and his lamp flickered, but Garth did not retreat. Instead, putting the lamp down, he went to the wine section first, pulled out a bottle and with sudden, furious force, hurled it against the wall. The glass split and the neck of the bottle, still corked, rolled sideways, coming to rest in a dent in the floor. The noise was duller than he expected. He took another bottle and threw it. Then another and another. The wine did not spray; it trickled slowly down the wall like blood, and the rolling bottle-necks unaccountably reminded Garth of French aristocrats being beheaded. He got into quite a rhythm as he hurled and hurled. The stain spread. The smell was sweet and sickly. The floor grew sticky. Shards of glass floated on a thick red sea. He had to take care not to slip.

He saved the brandy until last, and when he pulled out the final bottle he did not throw it at once, but uncorked it and took six or seven deep pulls. The fading fire in his belly reignited with astonishing vigour. It was a strange, not unpleasant feeling, and as the liquor crackled through his veins Garth felt an extraordinary lightening. He took another gulp and the empty hole in his heart filled with blurry exhilaration. Taking one last pull, he hurled the bottle with all his might. It was done. His father's cellar was destroyed. He tried to pick up the lamp. His hand did not want to obey him. He found that very funny. Leaving the lamp, he squelched his way to the door and let himself out. His feet were wet, the sleeves of his shirt stained and soggy. The fumes buzzed around his head.

He swayed slightly, thinking he would go upstairs and sit with the Furious Boy, but he only made it to the dead hare before he sank down, closed his eyes and let the brandy burn the last memory of the good times clean away.

2

Daisy found him. She had been sent by Mrs Snipper, the only indoor servant to remain at Hartslove, to fetch the hare which, so Mrs Snipper said in her curiously emphatic way, would Do For Supper. Daisy disliked going down to the larder, but she never refused Mrs Snipper, who, unasked, had taken over the kitchen when Cook had left. First, though, she had to find the crutches which, since her accident, had become as much a part of her as her hands and feet.

Other people felt sorry for Daisy, but Daisy had long since given up feeling sorry for herself. Certainly, crutches were a pest and callipers an inconvenience. Certainly, nobody would want to marry her. However, Daisy did not care about marriage. She more than did not care. Daisy never wanted to leave Hartslove, and her lameness bound her to the place in a very practical way: elsewhere, she would feel a burden; here, she was part of the furniture.

Also, her accident bound her particularly to Garth, for Garth had dragged her from under the weight of the fallen pony, and when she was recovered as much as she was ever going to, it was his teeth that had scarred their nanny's buttocks when she had made Daisy cry, and it was his fists that had punished the grocer's boy for imitating her hobbling gait. Daisy knew she had a special place in the corner of Garth's eye and, in return, she loved him with unswerving devotion. This devotion had deepened since their mother left, particularly after Garth ticked Rose off for scoffing at Daisy's habit of saying, 'Goodnight, Ma,' to a cobweb that hovered above her bed. 'It's a very good idea,' Garth had insisted with such firmness that even Rose had not dared contradict him.

Daisy found her crutches at the bottom of the kitchen stairs, took a candle and clumped down to the larders. The acrid smell of alcohol hit her before she found Garth folded up on the floor. 'What on earth?' – she saw red stains on his sleeves. Horror seized her. She slammed down the candle, manoeuvred her legs to kneel and rolled him over, a scream gathering in the back of her throat. 'Garth! Garth!' Who had attacked him? Where were his wounds? She could see only hollow cheeks, dirty smudge marks and greenish skin.

Garth unwillingly opened his eyes and licked his lips. He had no idea how long he had been down there. His tongue was furred and thick and he could no longer feel his feet. When he tried to sit, he was like Clover's rag doll. It was when he slumped again that Daisy noticed the amber-coloured footprints leading from the wine cellar. The scream died away. 'No,' she said loudly. 'No, no, no.' She let go of Garth, clambered up, opened the door wide and found herself slithering in a ruby, glass-encrusted sea. 'Holy Moses!' she cried, sliding back and slamming the door behind her. The dead hare swung in the draught. 'Who did this?'

'Did it on purpose.'

'What?'

'Pa shouldn't drink. Now he can't.'

Daisy stared. '*You* did that?'

Garth tried to sit up by himself. 'Because of The One.'

Daisy paled. 'What on earth do you mean?'

'He's bought another The One. He can have his horse or his drink. Not both.' He smiled a brandy smile, a drink-on-the-breath smile, his father's smile.

Daisy recognised it and shook Garth until his head rattled. 'You're drunk, Garth.' She was appalled.

'Drunk as drunk,' Garth said gaily. 'Ma's gone off. Pa's gone mad. I've gone drunk.' He flapped his arms.

Daisy stood up. 'I'm getting you some water. Holy Moses, Garth. *Holy Moses.*'

Garth tried to stand. The world capsized. He did not feel so good now. His teeth began to chatter. Daisy hooked his arm over her shoulder and they both struggled up the steps into the kitchen, where Garth collapsed on to a chair. The range was unlit, but Mrs Snipper had laid the fire and Daisy put a match to it. She felt Garth's hand. It was as frozen as the hare. She forced him to drink some water but his teeth clattered so badly against the glass she was worried it might shatter. She wished she had not shaken him. There seemed nothing else to do except fetch more and more water until at last he sipped quietly. The blaze quickened. His clothes began to steam and his colour returned to something a little more normal. Daisy sat down opposite him. 'You were joking when you said Pa had bought another The One,' she said when she thought he could hear her properly. 'I mean, he couldn't have. We can't even pay Mrs Snips or buy any groceries.'

This last did not appear to be true since there was a side of ham, a basket of vegetables and a large vanilla cake with a bite out of it on the kitchen table. However, although all the de Granvilles knew that none of this food was bought, they never enquired where it came from. Mrs Snipper never told them that she had a son, Snipe, who, despite his bird-name, had the pulse of a fox and the same thieving talents. It was not that Mrs Snipper was ashamed of Snipe. Far from it. It was just that Snipe was not sociable. His only expressions were watchful, murderous and blank and his only human emotion was worship of Lily, for whom he often left gifts, their intended recipient clear from the lily invariably attached. Mrs Snipper did not worry about Snipe being detected as he lurked round the castle: he could smell danger on a dandelion head and never used the front door, preferring to creep along the dank, earthy passage which led from the deep roots of a chestnut tree in the field at the front of the castle to the back of the kitchen range. The bite out of the cake carried his teeth-marks. It would never have occurred to him to cut it.

Garth glanced at the cake. His gorge rose. He tried to speak but the brandy's skim was a foul coating on his teeth and his insides seemed filled with grease. He lurched to the sink and was violently sick. 'He doesn't care about Mrs Snips. He handed over four hundred guineas,' he said, wiping his mouth, 'and there's a "for sale" sign at the bottom of the drive.' Daisy gasped, dropped the glass and felt herself shattering. Garth knew as he spoke that he should have been more careful, but with the brandy gone he felt cold and even emptier than before. 'At least if Pa goes on selling things, there won't be much of anything left to move,' he said in a vain attempt at humour.

'It's not true.'

'It is true.'

Daisy sat down heavily.

'I'm going to the Resting Place.' Garth was suddenly short of air. He staggered out, his stained shirt sticking to the bones in his back. Daisy got up and began automatically to gather up the slivers of glass. She was giddy from the news and hardly noticed when she dropped the glass again. Though she didn't want to be a nuisance, she didn't want to be alone. She left the glass, hobbled up the stairs and through the hall, automatically grabbing a cloak for Garth. It was perishing outside and he would never take one for himself.

What the de Granvilles called the Resting Place was not a place so much as a tree. It was, indeed, the chestnut tree amongst whose roots Snipe's tunnel began. The tree was so old it did not grow or spread; it simply was. Gnarled and twisted, its branches nothing more than sapless ropes, it nevertheless retained a mystical dignity, in part because around it, half buried and weathered into strange shapes, were three ancient tombstones. Set against the prevailing wind, parts of the stones' inscriptions could still be felt by careful fingers. Nearby, and clearly part of the group, was a flat stone whose inscription had been worn away entirely apart from an H too deeply etched for even the harshest wind to obliterate. The de Granvilles had always been told, and had no reason to disbelieve, that the remains of their crusading ancestors were buried here, and Daisy knew instinctively that the flat stone belonged to a horse. She did not know how she knew, but this belief was reinforced by the shadows that occasionally flitted over the field even under a cloudless sky. Sometimes the shadows were armed men. Sometimes they were horses, snorting and whinnying on the edge of the wind. Sometimes they were girls dancing. There was no pattern.

Daisy found Garth leaning against the tree. She knelt and scraped the frost from the flat stone so that she could trace the H with her thumbnail. The feel of it steadied her. 'Nobody will buy Hartslove,' she said decidedly. 'Why would anybody want a tattered old place that's half falling down and so filled with us? And they'd have to have Mrs Snips! I mean, she's nowhere else to go.'

A hard nut formed in Garth's chest. 'Don't be silly, Daisy. Some rich mill owner'll buy it, stick Mrs Snips in a workhouse in Manchester and hire retinues of cleaners to scrub us out. And when the place is pristine, they'll clear all these stones and make a golf course. It'll be as if we were never here.'

'It won't,' Daisy said fiercely.

'It will,' said Garth.

Daisy could not bear to argue. Instead, she hooked the cloak over Garth's shoulders, huddled her arms round herself and gazed at her home.

In the eight hundred years since the first foundations had been dug into the small, rocky hummock set bang in the middle of a moorland valley, Hartslove Castle had undergone many transformations, none of them fashionable, for the de Granvilles never had enough money to employ a grand architect to tear down the old fortress castle and start again. Instead, over the generations, the family had waited until bits fell down naturally, and then employed the same silvery stones to rebuild as best they could. The effect was peculiar, as though the castle had occasionally shaken itself and, when the dust settled, was surprised to find itself slightly differently configured. Above the old keep, flatter than when initially built and now forming the third wing of a square courtyard, hung a large flag. The flag was draped listlessly today, but in a breeze a red horse at full gallop was revealed, along with a black raven, wings closed, perched on a chestnut-and-silver plait in the shape of a crescent.

In the autumn, the ivy that completely covered the ruined fourth wing turned flame-red and was host to strange rustlings. They were not the rustlings of ghosts. The rustlings were Garth, flipping and tumbling. Sometimes the girls would watch: Rose tightlipped; Lily terrified; Daisy thrilled and envious in equal parts; Clover and Columbine crowing and clapping. Garth himself heard nothing. He just leaped and flipped, boneless as a fish, performing some private, high-risk air-ballet to which, though all his sisters provided an audience, they were not invited – or perhaps only Daisy was.

Her throat tightening, Daisy turned towards the narrow river. Amid the skeletal winter branches on its far bank she could just see a small grey church and the outline of the churchyard wall. The church was not used, although the bell was still rung randomly by a young priest who had made it his home. Since he had never offered his name, the de Granvilles called him Father Nameless.

Valley and hill, river and wood, castle and church: this

was Daisy's world. It was the only world she wanted. She forced herself to look down the drive towards the gate. Thankfully, the 'for sale' sign was too far away to see. She stood up, her chin set. 'We can't leave here,' she said.

'No,' agreed Garth, getting up too. 'I'd rather set the whole place alight and burn with it.'

This was not an idle fancy: Daisy knew Garth could do it. Her fists crunched into a ball. 'Garth –' A crash.

Skelton was forcing The One along the carriageway from the stables and the horse, jibbing, had smashed into a fence post. Daisy pressed her shoulder against Garth's. He pressed back.

The horse and Skelton skidded to a halt in front of the drawbridge, the horse sweating and his eyes foolish with fright. Daisy said the first thing that came into her head. 'That's not a racehorse!'

'Oh,' said Garth with heavy sarcasm, 'don't you know anything, Daisy? It *is* a racehorse, and not just any old racehorse. It's The One. It must be. Pa says so.' Sneering did not suit Garth. Daisy did not smile.

The horse bucked and kicked out with his back legs. He tried to gallop off, but Skelton's weight dragged on his tender mouth. The cause of this particular upset was soon apparent. A saddle had been strapped to the horse's back, the girth tightened under his stomach. Though he was well past breaking age, this was his first experience of the saddle and he did not like it. More than that, he would not have it. He did not recall that he had had just the same reaction when the steel bit was first pressed between his teeth. The bit was now so familiar he hardly noticed it. This saddle, on the other hand, with its flaps and buckles, was certainly an enemy.

Buffeted by the horse's antics, Skelton was chuckling. Animals had to learn. 'Unbelievable! He's not even used to a saddle! Just wait until we get a boy up,' he joked, swinging harder on the reins as the horse reared. 'Master Garth! You're light enough! Come and be jockey!'

Garth paled.

'Ignore him,' said Daisy. She began to walk towards the horse, leaving Garth behind.

'Ah, Miss Daisy,' Skelton said, doffing his cap in mock respect. He glanced at her legs. 'I'm afraid you won't do.' Daisy coloured. Skelton liked to remind you of things you would rather forget.

The colt was blowing hard, the skin on his shoulders ridged with dirty froth and his long chestnut ears pointing in the direction in which he was hoping to fly. He launched himself into the air again. Daisy was forced to duck. Skelton swore and whacked the horse with the reins. The horse reversed at speed. 'Take care!' cried Daisy as two hind legs slithered on to the drawbridge. 'There are holes!'

'Damned animal,' roared Skelton.

Attacked from the front, with his hind legs scrabbling and the horrible saddle still on his back, the horse became wilder than ever. He tried to gallop forward, dragging Skelton with him, but his mouth was too sore. In the end, quite suddenly and amid a shower of saliva, all the fight went out of him. His head drooped. He panted.

Daisy approached him again. 'Miss Daisy . . .' Skelton warned.

She did not reply. She manoeuvred her legs to crouch down. The horse blinked miserably. 'Can't you take the saddle off?' she said in a low voice. 'He hates it.'

'Not until we get back into the stable yard,' Skelton replied. With the horse temporarily quiet, he took out his pipe and clamped it between his teeth. 'He should have been saddled months ago if he's to race this year. He's got to learn to carry a rider as well.'

'But he's only been here a few hours,' Daisy argued. She wished she had Rose's authority or Lily's defenceless frailty, or even the twins' cheekiness. Skelton might take more notice. As it was, he just struck a match on the bottom of his boot. At the flash, the horse flicked his head briefly, but he was beaten and he knew it. His lower lip quivered.

Daisy remained where she was, though pins and needles prickled her feet. Gradually the horse stopped panting and they observed each other more minutely. In the horse's white-rimmed eye Daisy saw herself, and in Daisy's eye the horse saw his own darkly reflected. The reflection reassured him. He allowed her to touch the snip on his nose.

Skelton chewed his pipe for five minutes more before

bending down and knocking it on the gravel. As he did so, Garth came to inspect the horse, first on one side then the other. His fingers moved at lightning speed. The horse breathed sharply. Garth helped Daisy to get up. He had a strange expression on his face.

Skelton finished with his pipe and tugged on the bridle. With a last, desperate flourish, the horse twirled round quicker than the groom was expecting and pulled the reins from Skelton's fingers. Free for the second time that day, he trotted off, then quickly broke into a canter.

At first he chose to canter down the drive towards the main gate, but changing his mind for no reason at all he executed a small pirouette round the largest of the many potholes and returned, bypassing Daisy and Garth at increasing speed. Skelton shouted and tried to block his path. The horse skittered away round the old chestnut tree, his unkempt mane banging this way and that. Surprised by the flat tombstone, he leaped over it, whereupon, to his enormous and evident joy, the saddle flew into the air and hung, birdlike, for an instant before landing with an inelegant splat on the grass. Daisy laughed and clapped. Relieved of his burden, the colt slowed to a trot, then a walk. He passed the saddle and stopped to sniff at it. He put out his tongue and gave it a tentative lick. *What's this?* he seemed to ask. He appeared to have no idea that only moments before it had been the enemy on his back.

Skelton dived, caught the reins, and with bad grace

picked up the saddle. The girth was not broken: it was missing entirely. He searched the grass. He stared at Garth and Daisy. They stared right back. It was Skelton who carried the saddle to the stables.

As soon as Skelton was out of sight, Garth produced the girth from under his cloak. 'Garth, you genius,' said Daisy. Garth grinned and with one accord, he and Daisy ran on to the drawbridge, Garth slowing so that they could keep pace together. When they got to the middle, Garth tossed the girth into the moat with a grandly romantic gesture and they both watched it disappear noiselessly into the slimy thicket. Daisy made to follow Garth as he ran into the castle, then hesitated and went back to the moat. With great difficulty she scrambled down the steep bank, her callipers catching in the tangled reeds. She pushed her way through, grimacing as her shoes squelched and her skirt stuck to her knees. Eventually she saw the girth and picked it up. It was leather and expensive, and though the horse did not like it, if he was to race he would have to wear it. Hating herself for being so practical, she struggled out of the moat. Then, not knowing quite what else to do, she wiped the girth down and left it where Skelton would find it.

3

The next morning, the children held a council of war. Rose sat under the portrait of their mother. In repose, their faces had a similar faraway look and Daisy was sometimes frightened that Rose would disappear too. However, Rose was no cobweb and she wasn't often in repose. Rose barked and snapped. She did not look like their mother at this moment. She was grim-faced.

There had been a scene earlier. The destruction of the wine cellar had been discovered the previous evening and Garth had owned up at once, defying his father with bloodshot eyes. It had taken until breakfast for their father to react; half outraged, half apologising. That was the way with drink: wanting it and being ashamed to want it. Fuelled by the bottle he kept in his room, Charles had ranted about the extra work clearing up the cellar meant for Mrs Snipper. Garth had said nothing. In the end, Charles had closed his mouth and walked round and round the dining room. The children had sat tense on their chairs. They knew what was coming next. With a sudden dart, Charles had wrenched from its hook a picture of Sir Thomas de Granville painted in all his early-eighteenth-century finery. Tucking it under his arm he had hurried off, calling for Skelton and the vegetable cart. When the front door had slammed, all the candles in the castle had blown out and refused to light again.

Rose, Lily, Daisy, Clover and Columbine were now trying not to look at the empty space on the wall. Garth was poking the fire. He tossed five glowing embers into the air and began to juggle, defying them to burn him. Not even Rose liked to tell him to stop. Garth's behaviour had become so erratic. Any moment now he might throw the embers at the curtains. 'Another ancestor for the sale room,' Garth said, tossing the embers higher and higher. Sparks cascaded. He allowed them to smoulder.

'Our ancestors are abandoning us,' whispered Lily, eyes glued to the sparks.

'No,' Garth corrected her. 'Pa's abandoning them.'

'Don't,' Lily begged. She could not criticise even a character in a book for fear of hurting their fictional feelings. She stroked the lily she had found threaded through the handle of a cage containing two white doves.

'You shouldn't have smashed the bottles,' Rose said, eyes also glued to the sparks.

'Smash them, drink them – what's the difference?' Garth retorted.

'When they're drunk, they don't all go at once,' Rose said. She gestured at the portrait behind her. 'Next time he might take Ma.'

Two embers dropped. 'You idiot!' Rose cried. They all leaped up, scorching the hems of their dresses as they stamped out fiery flakes. Garth threw the rest of the embers back into the fire. He was sorry and not sorry, just as he was sorry and not sorry for smashing the bottles. A mocking 'Yankee Doodle Dandy' pulsed through his head. He wiped his hands on his shirt and shoved them into his pockets.

Wisely, Rose moved to the more important point. 'We've all seen the "for sale" sign. Now we've got to decide what to do.'

'Will Aunt Barbara even be able to have us all?' For Lily, the thought of being separated from Rose was worse than the thought of being separated from Hartslove.

'I don't know,' Rose said, trying not to sound impatient. 'I really don't know why she would want *any* of us. I wouldn't, if I were her.'

'Couldn't you marry somebody, Rose?' asked Columbine. 'You're old enough. If you were married, we could live in your house.'

'I'm not getting married,' said Rose, blushing furiously.

'But you *could* marry,' Columbine insisted.

35

'She'd have to find somebody to marry her, stupid,' said Clover, 'and that wouldn't be easy.'

'I think Mr Rose would do it.' Columbine was dogged. 'I mean, he looks at Rose like Gryffed looks at his dinner.'

'But Rose couldn't end up as Mrs Rose Rose,' Clover argued, 'and anyway she doesn't have fancy dresses or a corset or a crinoline or anything. She just has the Dead Girl and the statues and the Cannibal and Father Nameless, same as the rest of us, and I don't suppose they're much use if what you're looking for are normal things like fashionable clothes and hair that's pinned properly. But it doesn't matter,' she added hastily, seeing that Lily was about to cry. 'Aunt Barbara will take us. I heard Mrs Snips say so.'

'You shouldn't eavesdrop, Columbine,' Rose snapped.

'I'm Clover,' Clover said.

Rose glared. 'I don't care which you are. You shouldn't eavesdrop.' She had been very touchy on the subject of Arthur Rose, the young veterinary surgeon, since Father Nameless, in terrible distress, had brought an injured thrush to the castle. Arthur, dressing a hunting wound of Gryffed's, had invested the bird's dying moments with grave importance and even officiated at the burial service for which Father Nameless had tolled the bell. For some reason that Rose herself did not quite understand, the bird's death had reduced her to helpless tears and Arthur had set himself quietly to comfort her. Rose was not a fool. Though Arthur said nothing lover-like, she knew he loved her. She knew because whenever he was called to Hartslove, he looked for her even before his patient. She knew because he was always happy to walk down the drive in her company. Most of all, she knew by the way he said goodbye. It was this that had captured her heart. He said goodbye as though, above everything else, he wished he was saying hello.

Arthur's love for Rose had been obvious to all after the day with the bird, and Columbine and Clover liked to make sly references to it. It was not so much the jokes that Rose hated, it was that Clover and Columbine were right: the de Granvilles *were* too strange for anybody normal to marry, and Rose resented this. She loved Hartslove as much as any of them, but since their mother left, both castle and family felt increasingly like a shipwreck to which she was forced to cling whilst the great steamer of the world forged on without her.

She jerked, just in time to hear Clover or Columbine say, 'Anyway, it wasn't Mr Rose who made the offer.'

Lily breathed, 'Enough, enough.'

Yet that was true too: Rose's only offer had not come from Arthur but from Arthur's employer, Mr Snaffler, who, last Christmas, had impudently declared to Charles, in front of them all and Mrs Snipper, that 'despite everything' – this accompanied by a disparaging gesture at the castle, its ancient peculiarities and its dusty contents – he would 'take your oldest girl off your hands and without a dowry too. Best bargain of the day.' Rose still shuddered at the thought.

Clover and Columbine knew they had gone too far and quickly changed the subject. 'Couldn't the people who buy Hartslove buy us too? We could work with Mrs Snips. We could "work our fingers to the bone". We could "drive ourselves into early graves". We could "work until we could work no more and die at our posts, still in uniform".'

Rose recovered herself. 'Where on earth do you learn such phrases?'

'The dead people's section of the newspaper,' Clover or Columbine said, pulling the *Manchester Guardian* from under her seat.

'You spend far too much time reading those stupid things,' Rose said. 'We should throw them all out.'

The twins were aghast. The newspapers stacked in their father's library were their only source of information about anything. Their loss would be a calamity. 'Actually, I think it would be horrible, cleaning up other girls' mess in our room,' they said quickly and in unison, to distract.

'Better to live somewhere else, do you think?' Columbine asked.

'Don't be silly,' Clover rejoined. They began to argue.

'What would happen to Garth?' Lily was growing unhappier by the moment. The twins stopped arguing. The newspaper danger was past.

'I'd join the army,' Garth said. Silence. Only Rose, Lily

and Garth could remember their father going off to the Crimea, his sword spangle sharp and his boots shining. All of them, however, could remember his return, his sword broken and his boots cracked. That he had returned at all was a miracle, so their mother had told them. But an odd sort of miracle, because he'd looked so strange and thin, and along with spent shells for Garth, a horseshoe for Daisy and some peculiar Turkish hats and shawls for the others, he had also brought home his drinking habit.

'What about Father Nameless?' Lily's eyes brimmed with anxiety as one worry tumbled over another.

'Aunt Barbara wouldn't take him,' said Clover or Columbine matter-of-factly. 'He smells, and she's no bell for him to toll.'

'And the Dead Girl? What will happen to her?'

Nobody had an answer to that. Garth turned himself upside down. 'I know what will happen to Pa,' he said.

Five pairs of eyes swivelled towards him. 'He'll go and live with Skelton and keep on buying horses.' His bitterness was the sour, embedded bitterness of the old rather than the impetuous, passing bitterness of the young. Rose flinched and blamed herself. As the oldest, she should be able to make life sweet.

Daisy spoke without really meaning to. 'What happens if Pa's right about The One?'

Garth turned himself back upright, stalked out of the room and slammed the door.

'Don't daydream, Daisy,' Rose advised when the echo had died away. 'Pa's never been right before. Why should this horse be any different?'

'I don't know,' Daisy said, 'except that Hartslove's never been for sale before.'

'And you think that'll make the horse run faster?' Rose tried not to sound exasperated.

Daisy saw the horse's face again. 'It might,' she said.

Rose pressed her fingers together. 'Forget about the horse – except I suppose we could sell it.'

'That would upset Pa,' Lily said.

'He'd get his four hundred guineas back.' Clover and Columbine spoke together.

Rose pressed her fingers harder. Four hundred guineas. For a horse. She stood up, not because the council of war was at an end, but because if she didn't move she thought she might scream. 'I'll get a job,' she announced.

They all stared at her.

'Doing what?' Daisy asked.

'You think there's nothing I can do?' Rose was very sharp indeed.

'No – no,' said Daisy. 'I just meant – I just meant . . .' She shook her head. 'Pa will never let you.'

'Pa must never know,' said Rose fiercely. She sat down again. 'Mrs Snips will help me.'

'I could work too,' said Lily. 'I'd do anything so that we don't have to leave here. Anything.' It was unlike Lily to be so emphatic. Clover or Columbine began to bite her nails.

'Don't bite your nails, Clover.'

'I'm – oh, it doesn't matter,' said Columbine.

Rose was not listening. 'No, Lily. Your job will be to stay here and look after the others. That's the best way you can help.' Lily's relief was immediate and evident. The outside world was terrifying to her. Columbine and Clover were dismayed. Lily look after them! Why, she couldn't even look after herself. Clover opened her mouth to say so. Rose shot her a warning glower.

'You'll never earn enough money to save Hartslove, Rose,' Daisy pointed out, trying to be realistic. 'You'd have to be – I don't know – the prime minister or something to earn enough. And even if you were the prime minister, you'd still need to be him for a long time before you had enough money, and a buyer could come up the drive tomorrow with money in a sack.'

Lily gripped her chair.

'For God's sake, Daisy!' shouted Rose, losing her temper. 'I'm trying my best!'

Lily began to cry and the twins to clamour. Though she was sorry to upset, Daisy still had her question. 'But what if the horse really is The One? I mean, if he really did win the Derby, would Hartslove be safe then?'

'For goodness sake, Daisy! Clover! Columbine! Shut up!'

'But would it?' Daisy could not give up.

Rose tried to collect herself. It was not fair to be angry with Daisy. 'I suppose so,' she said.

The twins stopped clamouring. 'And if Hartslove was safe, would Ma come back?' Columbine had to ask.

There was a small gasp from Lily, Daisy and Clover. All faces were now turned to Rose. 'I don't know,' she said bluntly.

'But might it help?' Clover leaned forward.

Rose stood up very quickly. 'Why do you have to ask such things?' she cried. 'We don't even know why she went, so how can we know why she'd come back!'

Lily shrank into her chair. Again, Rose tried to collect herself. 'It couldn't make things worse though,' she said in her more usual voice. 'It absolutely couldn't do that.'

The council of war came to an unglamorous end. Lily was white as a ghost. Clover and Columbine scurried back to the newspaper hoard. Rose counted it a failure.

Daisy went into the hall. Somebody had slotted her crutches one under each arm of the Furious Boy. Despite the frost, she swung herself out to the Resting Place and sat on the flat stone. For once the Resting Place offered no comfort. Nothing stirred. The shadows were absent. Restless, she got up and swung herself to the stable yard.

Skelton had taken the vegetable cart on errands and The One was alone in the last of the six loose-boxes. He was looking out, but when Daisy called he took no notice. Nor did he seem to notice when she stroked all the way down his white blaze and traced his sickle snip. He was in a world all of his own. Leaning her crutches against the wall, Daisy unbolted the stable door, went inside and bolted it again. The One still did not move. Skelton had laid down straw, but the bed did not look comfortable. As best she could, Daisy began to push the straw into banks against the wall and to flatten out the rest. The colt still took no notice, not even when she straightened the woollen rug fastened loosely under his belly. She sat down, her legs out in front of her. 'I'm sorry you're alone,' she said. 'There used to be lots of horses here, but they've all been sold.' He turned his head to scratch, and only now seemed to catch sight of her. He cocked his ears and wandered over, clumsily scuffing the straw. Daisy was suddenly very aware that her legs were completely exposed. If he was careless, he would stand on one or both. She could try and pull them up or she could do nothing. He loomed enormous above her. One front hoof was raised. Daisy did nothing. The hoof came down, brushed her calliper, then veered to one side. A dark nose was lowered and two lips tickled. She was closer to the colt than she had been by the drawbridge. She could see the mixed red and white hairs in his diamond. She could smell the hay on his breath and see that the white tissue round his eye which gave him a look of permanent surprise was in fact the colour of mother-of-pearl. She also noticed for the first time the slight overbite, top lip folding over bottom, suggestive of the colt's rueful dismay at finding himself not quite as everybody had hoped.

She put out her palm. He took a finger between his teeth, more to hold, she felt, than to bite. He seemed shy. Daisy told him about his predecessors, at least those she could remember, and then about Hartslove itself; about Rose, Lily, Garth, Clover and Columbine, Gryffed and Mrs Snipper and the Dead Girl, and their mother, and everything else that was important to her. She did not speak of her father. She did not know what to say about him. The colt seemed quite gripped, and when Daisy moved, moved with her. He did not object when she put her arms round his neck to pull herself up, or when, seeing yesterday's sweat still ridged on his coat, she began to pick at it with her fingers. 'Skelton should have done this,' she murmured apologetically. After a bit she decided to take off his rug and give him a proper brush. He was too tall for her to reach his back so she tipped the water out of his bucket and used the bucket as a step. A shadow loomed. The horse started backwards, knocking over the bucket and crashing Daisy into the straw.

A scraping of bolts and Skelton seized the horse by the forelock.

'Don't! It was my fault!' Daisy shouted.

Skelton let go of the forelock and pulled Daisy to her feet. 'You shouldn't be in here, missy. He's a careless brute.' Skelton fetched a head-collar and tied up The One outside.

'You're not going to try the saddle again,' Daisy said quickly.

'No, Miss Daisy. Not today.' Skelton was running his eyes slowly from the tip of the horse's ears to the end of his tail.

Daisy could not stop herself. Unpleasant as Skelton was, he knew more about horses than she did. 'Could he be a good racehorse?' she asked.

'Good?' Skelton blew on his hands then crossed his arms. 'He's not much to look at, but he's got strong limbs and enough space for powerful lungs. So yes, if he buckles down and learns his job, perhaps he could be a good racehorse.'

Daisy's heart banged. 'Could he be The One?'

Skelton cast a crafty glance. 'Important that he is, is it?'

'You've seen the "for sale" sign,' said Daisy blankly.

'And you don't want to move?' Skelton walked round The One, slapping his rump as he went. The horse swished his tail. 'Don't you kick me, sonny,' Skelton warned. He returned to Daisy. 'I'd have thought you and your sisters would like nothing better than to live in a nice cosy house and have bedrooms that don't leak. This old castle's had its day. It's full of the past, when the future's what counts.'

'Hartslove's our home,' said Daisy stiffly, wondering how Skelton knew about the leaking bedrooms.

Skelton laughed. 'People move homes every day, missy. That's how the great big world keeps turning.'

'Not our world,' Daisy said.

Skelton sniffed. '*Your* world!' Then he seemed to think the better of his manner. 'See here,' he said in more respectful tones, 'his head and neck, well, they're too heavy. Too much muscle here' – he slapped the colt's crest before moving behind – 'and not enough here.' He slapped his rump again. 'As I say, he's got decent enough legs, strong bones and room for lungs, though his back's too short. A racehorse needs to be able to stretch and spread himself. And, of course, his coat's a mess, and his mane and tail are thick as Tinker's. Common blood in there somewhere.' Daisy gazed at the horse in silence. She was sorry she had invited the insult. The horse himself, however, was staring into the middle distance again. Skelton threw on the rug and fastened it.

'I'll put him back in his stable,' said Daisy. She wanted to apologise to the horse in private.

'I don't think so, missy.'

'I said, I'll put him back in his stable,' Daisy repeated.

Skelton shrugged. 'If he gets away again, your father'll be furious.'

'It's my legs that don't work, not my arms,' said Daisy coldly.

Skelton undid the rope and handed it over. Daisy waited until he was in his house before she moved. Inside the stable, she undid the head-collar and took the horse's long bony face between her hands. 'Are you The One?' she asked. He pushed her a little with his nose. 'Are you?' she whispered. She tightened her hands. 'I'm going to believe you are, and you've got to believe it too. We've got to believe it until it's not possible to believe it any more.' She wanted a sign – anything would have done – but no sign came and the horse drifted over to his manger. Daisy did not really want to leave him, but she was worried about Garth, and after a while went off to find him.

When she had gone, Skelton came across the yard. He opened the stable door, threw off the horse's rug and scrutinised every inch, tapping his fingers on his chin. He replaced the rug and went into the feedstore. Only two bins had anything in them: one was filled with oats and barley; and the other, into whose lock Skelton fitted a small key, was filled with bottles of brandy. Skelton counted the bottles with some satisfaction. Though he had paid for them himself, he was not tempted to open one. He had an idea in his head, though no actual plan was as yet formed. He relocked the bin and went outside.

The horse was staring over the door of his box. Skelton flicked the feedstore key at him, making him jump. 'Don't be a dreamer, laddie,' the groom counselled. 'There's been too much dreaming altogether round here. You can't live on dreams. The world's a-changing, boyo, and places like this with their ghosts and their tombstones need new blood.' He noticed that Daisy had left her crutches behind and toppled them over with the toe of his boot. 'Those girls! Might as well be living in 1261 as 1861! As for that boy –' he flicked the key again – 'he's going to be good-for-nothing, just like his da. Wise woman, that Lady de G. Got out while the going was good.' Whistling, he returned to his house and slammed the door with a loud and proprietorial flourish. He thought nobody heard, but the tombstones at the Resting Place rattled like teeth.

4

Though the castle was hunched under a blanket of mist and the roads treacherous, the first of the potential buyers turned up the following morning, unannounced. Charles himself had only just struggled back from the town, having been in a hurry to exchange Sir Thomas de Granville for three crates of wine, two of brandy, a small wodge of notes and a bag of change. He quickly carried the crates to the wine cellar, fearful of meeting his children. He could not explain his need of the contents of the crates to them or even, satisfactorily, to himself. He had sampled the brandy already.

Gryffed alerted him, and coming back to the hall, the last crate safely stashed, Charles found a father, mother and two pretty daughters, the father remarking unfavourably on the statues, the dust and the inadequate light. Rose, Lily, Daisy, Clover and Columbine had heard Gryffed's bark too and come running down. Garth was nowhere to be seen.

'Ah!' said the father of the daughters, 'good to catch you in, Sir Charles. I've had my eye on this place for years.' Without further introduction he began to outline the tremendous work that would be involved in bringing 'this old wreck', as he called Hartslove, 'up to scratch'. 'You must admit that it's a disgrace as it stands.' He waved a chequebook. 'Now, I'm a fair-minded man so I'll pay a fair price on condition that you're out in six weeks. We'll want the place thoroughly modernised before the summer. That ruined front will have to go. And the moat. All very quaint, I'm sure, but the Wars of the Roses are over, you know.' He laughed at his little joke and scribbled out a sum not quite as large as he might have written had he not smelled the brandy on Charles's breath. 'Take this, Sir Charles, and we'll consider the bargain sealed.'

Rose was shocked into paralysis. Surely it could not be this quick. Six weeks? Their father would refuse. He must.

Only he did not. Actually, Charles felt an extraordinary desire to laugh. It should not have come to this. Of course it should not. But it had, and brandy made everything very easy. Grab the cheque and it was done. He was going to exchange Hartslove Castle for a bit of paper. It really was quite funny when you thought about it. He stretched out his hand, but as his fingers brushed the cheque, the air was shattered by a scream so blood-curdling that Gryffed's every hair stood straight up on end. Daisy clutched her father. Lily clutched Rose. Clover and Columbine clutched each other. The buyer clutched his wife and children. The cheque fluttered to the floor.

The scream came from outside, and Charles, dragging Daisy, was first out of the front door, closely followed by Rose and Lily and Clover and Columbine, still attached to each other. The buyer and his family brought up the rear.

The first thing they saw was Mrs Snipper, one hand over her mouth and the other braced, palm outwards, as though waiting to catch something. They squinted up, as she was doing, and through the mist they could just see the top of the battlements. First there was nothing except stone, then there was Garth, now visible, now not, performing slow backflips, his feet only just catching the narrow merlons sticking up between the gaps in the castellation. Mrs Snipper was beside herself. 'Do something, Sir Charles. For God's sake. Master Garth'll kill himself.' She wrung her hands. Charles opened his mouth.

'No,' Rose said quickly. 'If you shout, you'll distract him. He'll fall.'

Charles's lips snapped shut. Over and over went Garth, his white shirt billowing, so that there looked to be no boy inside it at all. Charles ran back inside, heading for the tower staircase.

Daisy glanced at the visitors. Both girls were whimpering. She was frightened for Garth but it struck her, in a brainwave, that this was an opportunity. She hobbled over. 'I'm so sorry,' she said. 'The Spirits don't usually appear

51

during the day. Perhaps your father's upset them by not offering enough money.'

'What?' blustered the father. He had no idea of Garth's existence so was not sure what he was seeing.

'The Spirits,' Daisy explained, employing her most practical smile. 'They come with the castle, I'm afraid.'

'Spirits? Don't be ridiculous,' the man declared. But he could not take his eyes off the whirling white cog high above him.

'Please don't worry,' Daisy said. 'The Spirits are quite harmless.' She paused. 'Mostly.'

The mother had begun to shake her head and shove her girls towards the carriage. The horses were already straining to be away. 'Let's go, Wilbur,' the woman said. 'There's plenty of other places. I don't know why you ever wanted this one. It's giving me the creeps.'

The man resisted. His wife was adamant. They were still arguing as the carriage jolted off rather faster than the coachman intended.

Daisy forgot about them instantly. In the unearthly light Garth was like a bouncing star, except he began to miss his handholds. Nothing could stop Mrs Snipper calling to him. 'Come down, Master Garth,' she implored. 'Come down!'

But Garth kept on flipping, over and over, round the crumbling battlements, behind the keep, down the south-east wing and back. He was in a world of his own; a world of spinning and arching, where death and life were all the same because he was not just a de Granville, he was all the de Granvilles there had ever been, and he was standing with them against the enemy who these days might come in carriages with wives and daughters, but whose chequebooks were as dangerous as Saracens' swords. And there were other enemies. Garth named them as he flipped: drink – the thief who had stolen his father away; false hope in the shape of that horse; anger and sadness, both of which were eating him up. He thrust his body over and over. He would never stop flipping. Flipping was the only thing he had left. His feet slipped. The drop yawned. He did not care.

He heard his name shouted. Charles had made it on to the roof and was holding out his arms. 'Garth! Garth!'

Garth jerked, was almost lost. His father caught him and yanked him on to the flat of the roof, but Garth slipped through and flipped on, all the way down the south-east wing again. Only his concentration was broken. Now he was aware of the upgust of wind rattling through his shirt. His left hand missed the merlon completely. He was flipping on air – he was falling. For the first time, a tingle of fear. He did care. And here his father was again, again holding out his hands, those same sweet, kind, treacherous hands that held his children close even as they handed over money and opened bottles. Garth could not help himself. He clutched at them. Charles pulled him close and for a moment father and son were locked in a desperate embrace. Then Garth felt the smooth neck of the brandy bottle in his father's pocket. His fear turned back to anger, his anger to despair. He thrust away, leaving Charles once again with empty arms. 'Garth!' Charles cried. 'Garth.' Garth shook his head and ran to the edge of the ruins. Here he stopped and stood tall, his shirt draped like an angel's gown. He opened his arms and the sleeves were like wings. He was Hartslove; Hartslove was him. At the Resting Place, the gravestones shimmered. In the stables, The One stirred. In the wood, Snipe paused. Without a sound, Garth thrust upwards, arched, and plummeted into the dark.

Everybody was screaming now, everybody except Daisy, who swung across the courtyard and lurched on to the drawbridge, gripping her crutches so tightly her knuckles cracked. 'Don't take him,' she begged the castle. 'Please don't take him.' She held her breath, willing herself to see Garth tumbling over and landing in the soft sludge of the moat, willing herself to see him clambering out. 'Now,' she willed. 'Now, he'll appear now. Help him, Hartslove. Help him.'

A moment more, then she saw him. He was no longer an angel. He was a dirty, wet boy clambering up the banking and setting sail across the field towards the river. She watched him until she heard somebody running up behind her. She turned. Charles had rushed down from the roof. 'Oh sweet Jesus,' she heard him repeating. 'OhsweetJesusno.' When he reached Daisy, his legs buckled and he sagged against her. 'It's all right, Pa,' Daisy said, holding him tight. 'Garth's all right.' She held her father until his legs gathered strength, then helped him back across the drawbridge. 'Garth's safe,' she told the others. 'We've seen him.'

'Lord Love Us.' Mrs Snipper was still wringing her hands. Lily had fainted.

'I don't think the Lord had much to do with it,' Daisy said. 'Help Rose with Lily, Mrs Snips. I can manage Pa.'

Daisy left her father in the library and returned to the drawing room. It was impossible to believe that scarcely half an hour had passed since the intruders had arrived. The cheque was still lying on the floor. Daisy burned it whilst the others laid Lily on a sofa and sprinkled her with water. When Lily began to come round, Rose wiped her hands and tried to be practical. 'We must start packing,' she said, looking rather hopelessly around the room. 'Do you suppose people who buy castles buy the furniture and the tapestries? How do you take down curtains? Are they sewn on to the rails?'

Daisy turned from the fire. 'What do you mean, packing?'

'Don't be silly, Daisy. You know just what I mean,' Rose said in a tired voice. 'We can't stop people coming, and if Mrs Snips hadn't screamed, we'd be sold already.'

'Don't you see?'

'See what? For goodness sake, Daisy. See what?'

'That we don't have to go.'

'Oh, please. We've got to go, and that's that.'

'You mean you want Hartslove to be sold?'

'Don't be unfair,' cried Rose. 'Of course I don't! But living here costs money, and we don't have any.' Daisy blinked. 'And besides,' Rose carried on, recklessly allowing her worst fears to tumble out, 'we can't carry on living all bound up with stones and cobwebs and the Dead Girl and the tombstones at the Resting Place. Next year I'll be eighteen. Eighteen! Don't you understand, Daisy? Don't any of you?' She could not stop now. 'I want to have a proper life, an ordinary life, and how can I – how can any of us – have an ordinary life when nothing here is ordinary? How can we actually have any life of our own at all?' She could see the shock on her sisters' faces but she did not care. She could not, just *could not*, spend her whole life in a place so full of the past there was no space for anything else.

Daisy gulped. 'It needn't be like that, Rose. You can have a life. We all can.'

'How?' Rose asked, all her energy draining away. 'How, exactly, Daisy, unless we leave here.'

'Through The One.'

'Oh, Daisy!' Rose slumped on to the sofa next to Lily and buried her face in her hands. Lily was sitting up. 'Don't upset Rose any more,' she begged.

'There's no need to be upset. Don't you see?' Daisy said earnestly. 'The One's going to win the Derby. I absolutely believe it. And when he wins, everything'll be different.'

'Different?' Rose did not bother to raise her head. 'How different? Whatever The One does, Pa will still drink; the candles will still go out; the Dead Girl will still haunt Pa's passage; Ma still won't come back.' *And Arthur Rose will still marry somebody else*, she thought, though she did manage to stop herself saying this out loud.

Daisy shook her head. 'No, Rose. It won't be like that.'

'How will it be, then?' Rose could not fight any more.

'I don't know,' Daisy said. 'But it will be good for all of us, each in our own way. I just know it.'

Rose closed her eyes. 'Even if you're right,' she said, 'even in the hugely improbable likelihood that you are right, just tell me this: why on earth should this The One be different from any of the others?'

Daisy held her ground. 'I've never believed in any of the others,' she said.

Rose pulled herself together. Daisy must be made to face the truth. She opened her eyes and addressed her sister very slowly. 'But Pa has, Daisy. He's believed every single one. And you know as well as I do that even he doesn't believe in this one. Why else would he have been going to take that cheque?' She blew her nose on the handkerchief Arthur Rose had given her at the bird's funeral. It was the end, and they had better get used to it. She got up, smoothed her skirt and made for the door.

Daisy got there before her. She would not let Rose leave the room. 'Pa's so full of brandy he doesn't know what

57

he believes,' she said. 'Please listen, Rose. Please. Today Hartslove helped us. When I told those people Garth was a ghost, they believed me because of the mist. If we can do that once, we can do it again.'

'It was just luck that Garth looked like a ghost,' Rose said, her impatience, never far beneath the surface, resurgent again. 'If it'd been spring, with the sun shining, he wouldn't have looked like a ghost at all and the cheque would already be in the bank.'

'It wasn't luck,' Daisy said, doggedly determined. 'It was a stopgap.'

'A what?' asked Clover and Columbine.

'A stopgap.'

'Is that a special type of ghost?'

'No,' said Daisy. 'A stopgap's something that holds things together until they can be properly fixed.'

'And when exactly will everything be properly fixed?' asked Rose. She tried not sound sarcastic, but it was hard.

'In one hundred and forty-eight days,' Daisy said.

'One hundred and forty-eight days?'

'That's how long it is until The One's Derby.'

A long pause followed this announcement. Rose did not know what to say. Eventually Clover, or perhaps Columbine, broke in. 'One hundred and forty-eight days is forever. If we've no money, we'll never survive that long. We shall starve. We shall freeze. We shall die.' There had been an article about such a family in the copy of the *Guardian* they were currently digesting. Clover and Columbine began to imagine their own obituaries.

'Be quiet!' Rose barked. She looked at Daisy. 'You've actually worked it out? To the day?' she asked, almost incredulous.

'It's one hundred and forty-eight days to the race, including the day of the Derby itself. I looked it up in Pa's racing book,' Daisy explained. Nobody contradicted her, so she continued. 'I'm thinking, you see, that though we can't stop people coming to look round, we could put them off, just as happened today. I mean, one hundred and forty-eight days isn't that many, really, and some days nobody will come at all. Obviously we can't rely on mist, and we don't want Garth to . . . to . . .' she swallowed. 'What I mean is that we could do our own hauntings, inside.'

Clover and Columbine were agog. 'We could dress up as dead de Granvilles, you mean?'

'That kind of thing,' said Daisy.

'Stopgap ghosts!' The twins' eyes sparkled. 'It would be fun. Perhaps one of the visitors will have a heart attack and die and we could write their death notice and get published.' The prospect was glorious.

Daisy ignored this. 'What do you think, Rose?' she asked tentatively. Rose's support was crucial. 'The One will win, Rose, he will.'

Rose hit her forehead with the palm of her hand. 'For

the love of God, Daisy! Just stop it with that when I'm trying to think what Ma would do!'

'That's easy, Rose,' said Lily, in an intervention none of them expected. In the firelight, her face, even paler than usual, shone. 'Ma would do nothing. She'd just drift, like the Dead Girl.' She smiled a wan smile. 'Ma's a ghost here already.'

The fire crackled and the door handle twisted. A sudden draught blew the door open. They all jumped. Nobody came in. Then they heard the rattle of teacups on a tray. 'Mrs Snips,' said Rose faintly.

'That's right, dearie,' said Mrs Snipper. 'Who On Earth were you Expecting?'

5

In the library, Charles sipped his tea as best he could. He was still twitching, wretchedly panicked by the recurring vision of Garth slowly cartwheeling to his doom. Eventually he dropped his teacup and pulled the bottle out of his pocket. Gryffed observed him, unblinking. 'What are you looking at?' Charles asked, uncorking the bottle. But though he took gulp after gulp, his hand still shook and the liquor was bitter in his throat.

He leaned against the chimney piece and thought of himself at Garth's age. How often, in those days, had he lain face down on the stone at the Resting Place? He was going to be a crusader then, just like his ancestors, and he was going to have a horse so famous that it would also merit a stone and an inscription. He slumped down. Hartslove had been his whole life. But when had he last seen the Dead Girl, with whom he had played as a child? When had he last felt the castle breathing? Once, he had been so rooted here that his bones ached when the castle was lashed with rain. Once, he had known just which candles would be snuffed at supper and which left alight. Once, he had felt hugged by the castle walls. How had he become as detached from Hartslove as he was from his wife and his children? His fingers closed over the bottle and raised it up. He stared at it as though he had never seen a bottle before. With a strangled cry, he tipped the remaining contents into the cold ash and watched them dribble away.

Gryffed sniffed the ash. Charles called him. Gryffed obeyed. Charles forced himself to march through the great hall, past the kitchen and down the steps to the cellar. Without pausing, he rolled up his sleeves and carried all the cases so recently carried down back up again. He did not think about anything else. It was all he could do to concentrate on the task in hand. Within two hours he had harnessed up the vegetable cart, returned the cases to the wine merchant and was standing next to the Furious Boy full of cash and good intentions.

At dinner that evening, during which, unaccountably, the candles all remained alight, he drank water. Garth had reappeared and was sitting in his usual place. Nobody mentioned the intruders or the cheque. Like his sisters, Garth gaped when he saw what was in his father's glass. It was left to Lily to ask if Charles was unwell. 'No, I'm quite well, Lily,' Charles said, though his skin was clammy and his body dry as dust. He lifted his tumbler with a trembling hand and licked flaky lips. 'I have a toast to make,' he said.

'A toast?' repeated Rose nervously.

'Yes, a toast. To Hartslove and The One,' Charles said. Garth looked at his plate. The girls looked at Rose. She sighed very deeply. Her face was bleak. Daisy's heart sank. It seemed an age before, with a small, resigned toss of her head, Rose picked up her glass. For a moment, Daisy thought she would smash it, but instead she raised it. 'To Hartslove and The One, Pa,' Rose said, though she looked at Daisy.

'Hartslove and The One,' Lily murmured.

'Hartslove and The One,' Daisy said joyfully.

'Hartslove and The One,' the twins echoed.

Garth alone said nothing. 'Garth?' Charles asked. 'Will you drink with us?'

'Not that toast,' Garth said, and ground his glass into the table. Charles set his own tumbler down without tasting a drop. The rest of dinner was eaten in silence.

When their father and Gryffed had left the dining room, Rose turned on Garth. 'Why couldn't you join in, Garth? Pa was trying. He was actually trying. Why couldn't you just have joined in? I mean, when did he last drink water?'

'He must be sick,' Clover or Columbine said fearfully.

'No, he's not, stupid,' the other contradicted. 'He's trying to be good.'

Garth shoved his chair out. 'I won't drink to The One,'

he said. 'The horse'll be the end of Hartslove, not the saving of it.'

'Never mind that stupid horse. You could have just done it for Pa!' Rose gripped her seat to stop herself leaping up and walloping Garth. 'I managed.'

'Pa!' Garth spat on to the floor.

'How dare you do that?!' shouted Rose. 'What's wrong with you?'

'What's wrong with *me*? What's wrong with *you*?' Garth shouted back. 'You should have seen Pa counting out the money for that horse. Piles of it. Just piles. Right underneath the "for sale" sign.' He felt his heart might burst. 'I hate him!' He sprang up, sending the firedogs clattering noisily into the hearth, and ran out of the door, slamming it behind him.

He did not stop in the hall. He ran right outside. It was windy and snow had started to fall again. He took no notice. He was going to do something even better than smashing the bottles. He headed for the stables, shoved open the yard gate and let it swing. Skelton's house was dark. Garth found a lamp and matches. He went to The One's box. The horse was lying flat out, almost asleep. Garth climbed on to the stable door. He barely felt the wind scouring his face. He looked only at the horse. This was what was wrong. This horse. This big, ugly, silly, money-eating horse. It did not belong here. It should not be here. He climbed down, pulled open the top bolt, kicked up the bottom bolt and opened the door. A flurry of snow blew in. The horse raised his head and slowly lurched to his feet. Outside did not look inviting. 'Do what you should have done the day you arrived,' Garth said loudly. 'Get out of here.' The horse did not move. Garth hurried to the back of the stable, set down the lamp and smacked the horse's rump. 'What's the matter with you? Go on! You're free.'

The horse blinked. 'I'm ordering you to get out!' Garth flung his arms in the air. 'Get out!' The wind chose that moment to gust and the door banged shut. The horse jerked not forwards, but backwards, straight into the lamp. It tipped over. In half a second, the straw was smoking; in three-quarters, small flames licked. Garth lurched for the door, but the lower bolt, which he had not secured, had dropped back into its socket. Garth was on top of the door in an instant, but for one absolutely clear-headed moment he did not jump down, kick the bolt up and release the horse; He decided to leave him to burn. That would be a truly symbolic end to everything. He could see his father's horrified face. He could hear 'Yankee Doodle' cut off midstream. He sat on the door, almost smiling.

The horse could smell the smoke. His eyes were like saucers. He nudged Garth's leg.

Garth felt nothing. His smile was fixed. He was suspended in time. A flame shot up and subsided. The horse uttered no sound, only trembled. Still Garth sat. The horse shifted. His tail swished against the flames and the air filled with the smell of singeing hair. The smoke prickled Garth's nose. Fire, the great cleanser, he thought. He felt a surge of something. This was how it would end. A huge great bonfire. During several long seconds, the smoke increased. The prickle moved from Garth's nose into his brain. The picture in his mind altered. He no longer saw a glorious bonfire and his father's horrified face; he saw the dreadful image of the horse alight. He saw the horse's mouth open. He heard the horse screaming.

With an awful groan Garth dropped down and opened the door. At once, the horse shot into the snow and Garth rushed to tip the contents of the water bucket over the lamp and burning bedding. The flames resisted only momentarily, and when they were doused Garth ran into the yard, snowflakes biting the tops of his ears. The One, confused, had not gone to the gate. He was pressed against the wall, his rug askew. Garth caught him and led him back to the stable. The One was not keen to enter. Garth let go, grabbed a fork and sifted out the charred straw, praying that the kerfuffle had not alerted Skelton. When he had buried the remains in the midden, he grabbed the horse again and this time the horse reluctantly followed him in. Garth refilled the water bucket and adjusted the rugs. Apart from the lingering smell and The One's look of alarm, it was almost as if nothing had happened.

Except something *had* happened. As Garth closed the door and leaned against it, he realised the full wickedness of which he was capable. It was a horrible realisation. The snow hardened into hail and he raised his face to its whipping. He leaned over the door. The horse jerked back. Garth looked him full in the eye. 'I'm sorry,' he said abruptly. 'It's not your fault.'

The horse's ears flicked. He had no idea what the boy was saying. He only knew that the fire was out, that it was warm in the stable and that there was hay. Nevertheless, though he settled quite quickly, he did not lie down again that night.

6

Garth returned to the castle. He would sit with Daisy for a bit, though he would not tell her what he had almost done. He would never tell anybody that. As he passed through the hall he touched the Furious Boy's sculpted arm and wished him alive. He would understand. He made his way slowly to where Daisy slept at the top end of the south-east wing and had pushed her door open before he realised she was not alone. Clover and Columbine were nestled together on the window seat like two little birds. Rose was sitting on an old rocking chair with a blanket over her knees. Lily was on the bed, curled around her birdcage, and Daisy was bundled into an armchair whose springs had long since given out. He would have retreated, but five faces were already turned towards him and Daisy was making room for him to huddle up beside her.

He squashed himself in. She leaned on his arm. Garth

found that he wanted to make his peace with them all. 'Is that a new dove, Lily?' he asked.

'Yes,' Lily said. 'It's my fourth. I found it in my room.'

'It's very pretty.' The dove's cooing comforted.

'We're discussing the best way to do our hauntings.' Daisy told him, glancing nervously at Rose, who was looking out over the moat and down towards the Resting Place. 'It was wonderful, the way you frightened those people off today, Garth, but I don't think our hauntings need always be so spectacular. All we've really got to do is Create An Atmosphere, as Mrs Snips might say.'

'Aren't we going to dress up?' Columbine or Clover asked. 'Isn't that what you said?'

Rose turned away from the Resting Place. 'In what? We've no dressing-up stuff,' she said.

'We could use some of Ma's clothes,' said Daisy.

Rose stopped rocking.

Lily uncurled very slowly. 'You mean, we'd go into Ma's room and take clothes from her closet?'

'Yes,' said Daisy.

'We couldn't,' said Rose.

'Why not?' Clover or Columbine asked. 'After all, she's not using them.'

The moon was emerging, and its pearly light stole into the room. Without saying a word, they all found themselves looking at the cobweb in the corner. It glittered. The dove cooed and cooed.

Garth coughed. 'I don't think Ma would mind. After all, clothes are just clothes and we can put them away after . . . after . . . after we've used them.' He wanted to say, '*after The One has won the Derby,*' but could not quite form those words. He no longer wanted to hurt the horse, but that did not mean he believed in it, and even for Daisy's sake he could not pretend otherwise. He picked up the lamp. 'Shall we?'

Rose tensed. 'Now?'

'Why not?' He turned. 'Come on!' he said, and strode purposefully out.

Rose felt obliged to follow him. Lily put down her birdcage and followed Rose. The others followed her. Down the passage they trooped, past Rose's room, and Lily's, past the room Clover and Columbine shared, past the old nursery, past the room that had once been their nanny's, past rooms unused for sixty years, past Garth's room set into the tower. In single file they skirted the spiral staircase that circled dizzily down from the top of the castle to the bottom and swung right-handed into a wider, grander passage, with ill-fitting mullioned windows through which small draughts constantly disturbed the de Granville battle-standards hanging from the beams. This was their father's passage. They tiptoed quickly past the Cannibal and past the Earl's Room, where their father slept. They could hear Charles moving about and none of them wanted him to ask where they were going.

At the end of this passage, again turning right-handed, the castle softened into their mother's domain. This passage was narrow, matching the south-east wing, and between long lancet windows overlooking the courtyard closely hung watercolours of flowers made a painted garden. It smelled like a garden too, for though everything was covered in a glazy film of dust, Mrs Snipper still hung bags of lavender and rose petals behind the curtain pelmets.

At their mother's door, Garth stood back for Rose. 'I can't,' she said. Lily shook her head. In the end, it was Clover or Columbine who pushed the door open. Garth held up the lamp. The furniture was sheeted, the room icy and as dismally tidy as the room of a dead person whose personal effects nobody quite likes to move. It was at that moment Rose realised she had been hoping that their mother might actually be there; that somehow she would have materialised from Daisy's cobweb and be sitting at her dressing table, putting up her hair. She knew her disappointment to be ridiculous but felt it keenly nonetheless.

Daisy slid past and hobbled straight towards the big dressing room on the far side, in which, though they had never actually been in it, they understood all their mother's clothes had hung. The door was unlatched. Slowly, Daisy pulled it open, dreading to find it empty. That would certainly mean their mother was never coming back. For a second, there was only darkness; then, as though waking from a spell, the silks and satins began to rustle and shimmer. 'Come in,' they seemed to whisper. 'We've been waiting.' Daisy found Garth behind her. 'Everything's here,' she said. 'Listen! Look!' They listened and looked together.

It took only three lamps and the pulling off of the sheets from the furniture for the bedroom to look more as they remembered it. Even the chill seemed to lift. Far from taking everything, their mother seemed to have taken nothing with her at all: not the china vase filled with hairpins; not the tiny muslin nightcap that always rested on a small cushion like a crown; not her silver-backed brushes. A bottle of cologne, half used, sat where it had been left, with a little heart-shaped cambric bag next to it embroidered with 'CdeG'. Rose picked the bag up. 'Clara de Granville,' she said. 'I stitched this.' She opened it and started when out of it fluttered what seemed to be dead moths. Lily caught them as they fell. They were not moths. 'A rose petal, a lily petal, a daisy, a columbine spur, a clover flower and a chestnut leaf,' Lily said, gazing into her cupped hands. She smiled a little sadly. 'We're in the bag.'

'Why didn't she take us with her?' asked Clover or Columbine. They had been barely four when their mother had left, and only now, in her empty room, did she seem real to them. Garth took the chestnut leaf and balanced it in his palm. Colourless and gossamer thin, only the tiny tracery of veins stood between it and a puff of powder. He hardly dared to breathe. That his mother thought of him as a chestnut leaf seemed entirely right. Had he been asked to choose something himself, it was what he would have chosen – a chestnut leaf from the chestnut tree at the Resting Place. He let the leaf float on to the dressing table. Rose opened a drawer. 'Let's put them in here,' she said. They obeyed. Rose shut the drawer and turned the tiny key.

Daisy went back into the closet and opened her arms. Soft muslins, scratchy brocades, ticklish furs and a faint smell of damp enveloped her. Some clothes slid off their hangers; others brought their hangers with them. Stumbling under a multicoloured billow, Daisy collapsed on to the bed. Rose caught the nearest dress, a pale green evening gown of fine silk embroidered all over with tiny lilac flowers. She held it against herself. The bodice, drawing to a tiny waist, was boned and lined; the skirt, without the crinoline to support the dome of the cut, hung in a shining waterfall. Lily caught another dress, this one grey and sprigged with aquamarine feathers. 'Put them on!' urged Clover and Columbine. Clover went to Lily and Columbine to Rose and, though the older girls never expressly gave their permission, began to unhook the coarse cotton dresses that Mrs Snipper had run up for them.

Before they had finished with the hooks, Daisy was bringing out soft chemisettes, gauze fichus and pantalettes of lawn cotton and lace, all spotless white and more delicate than the snowflakes still falling outside. Lily exclaimed with delight. Daisy disappeared again, and this time emerged draped in doeskin gloves, swansdown tippets and three woollen shawls still smelling of spices.

'Pa brought these home from the war!' Rose exclaimed. 'Don't you remember, Lily? He spread them in the drawing room and told us that they should slide through a wedding ring.' She picked up one of the shawls and held it against her. Green and gold thread glistened. She gathered the shawl, made a ring from her thumb and index finger and drew the shawl through. 'Ma folded one over her head and covered her mouth. Pa said she looked like a Turkish princess. You must remember.'

Lily nodded. They shared a smile.

Daisy was busy shaking out three high-waisted dresses of creamy muslin, each dress spun transparent as a butterfly's wings. Rose gazed at the dresses in amazement. 'These must have been our grandmother's, or even great-grandmother's,' she said. 'Nobody would dare wear such things now. They're completely see-through!'

'Put them on! Put them on!' chanted Clover or Columbine. Rose and Lily demurred, then, unable to resist and with the twins as willing helpers, they were slipping the gossamer dresses over their heads. Their cotton shifts protruded. 'Use these,' said Daisy, and handed over specially made matching underclothes of tissue and lace.

'You can't!' Garth was scandalised.

Rose and Lily disappeared into the closet and minutes

later wafted back, barefoot and shaking out their hair. Clover and Columbine gasped.

'You've turned into fairies!' Daisy breathed. 'Real fairies.'

Clover vanished, then edged out of the closet caged in a circular crinoline, its whalebones clicking. On her head, she had squashed a wide-brimmed hat, and round her ankles flapped a pair of long drawers. She flashed a feathered fan, then promptly tripped. The whalebones rose above her head like a heap of petrified snakes. Despite herself, Rose began to laugh in a very unfairylike manner, and Columbine, not to be outdone, ran into the closet and leaped into a huge black silk taffeta, all flounces and bounces.

'You look like a giant spider,' Garth said.

Whipping out a voluminous cambric undersleeve, Columbine plonked it on Garth's head and curtsied deeply. 'Garth, King of the Closet,' she said.

Garth whisked up a shawl and wrapped it round himself. 'No King of the Closet, me,' he said. 'I'm the Emperor of Siam. May I have the pleasure?' He whirled Columbine round until her skirt, heaving like the sea, knocked them both over. Helplessly, Columbine began to giggle, and Garth, head poking out from beneath the flurry, felt a burst of laughter bubble up from a place he thought had withered away.

Then, quite forgetting why they had come here, they began pulling everything on in ridiculous combinations. Garth found a pair of frilled drawers and a half-crinoline, which he tied round his waist. Attaching a plume to his head, he pretended to be an impatient coach-horse, neighing and scraping his feet. Clover and Columbine, their faces veiled like Persian sultanas, announced they were off to the opera. Rose pulled on a ballgown with matching high-heeled shoes. Only Daisy tried nothing on, though she longingly stroked a pair of Polish boots with leather tassles. In the end, pressed by Clover or Columbine, she wore a brown velvet nightcap with thick earmuffs which, after some disputation, they agreed must have belonged to an old man whose wife snored.

In the end, Lily outdid them all. As the laughing, arguing, jostling and jangling rose to a pitch, she appeared framed against the closet in the candlelight. The dress she wore was of blue-white satin warmed by a filmy froth of lace tumbling layer upon layer from wrist and neck. The skirt flowed from her waist like milk, and under its shadow peeped two narrow, pointed shoes sewn with pearls. She had pinned up her dark hair and set a silver comb above it. From the comb drifted a veil of wide-spun net, fragile as Garth's chestnut leaf.

'Oh!' whispered Daisy, but nothing more, for at that very moment the bedroom door was thrust open and first Gryffed, then Charles appeared. Charles's hair was rough, his shirt only half tucked into his trousers. His boots were unlaced and he was holding a pistol, raised and cocked. He stopped dead when he saw his children. 'You!' he exclaimed, stunned. 'Thieves! I thought thieves –' Then he spied Lily. For one moment he stood transfixed, then he dropped the pistol. It went off with a loud retort. Daisy gasped. Charles did not seem to notice. His face lost all its colour. 'Clara?' he whispered. 'Clara?'

There was nothing but petrified silence. Rose went to him. He jumped when she touched him, but he never took his eyes from Lily. 'It's Lily, Pa,' Rose said. She could feel her father's muscles tight as springs.

'Clara?' her father repeated, then suddenly his face purpled and Rose was hurled across the room. 'How dare you!' Charles cried. 'HOW DARE YOU!' He rushed at Lily. 'Your mother's wedding dress. Take it off! Take it off this instant!'

Lily tried to reverse through the closet door, but her crinoline was too stiff, and she found herself splayed against the frame like a moth against a window. Charles raised his hand. Garth catapulted forward. 'Don't, Pa! Don't you dare lay a finger on her!'

Charles hit Garth and in the same movement seized the comb from Lily's hair and tossed it aside, snagging the net veil on his jacket buttons. He pulled the veil off, then caught at the collar of the dress and tore it from top to bottom. The ruins fell about Lily's feet with a small sigh and she was left marooned. Aghast, with Clover and Columbine crying loudly, Charles fled back to his room.

For what seemed like an age, nobody moved. Eventually

Clover and Columbine's sobs quietened. Rose picked up a discarded glove. 'We shouldn't have come in here,' she said, livid with herself. 'We've done a terrible thing. We can't ever come in here again.' She began to blow out the lamps.

There was a small sound from somewhere near the door. Gryffed was sinking. The slug from the pistol had gone straight through his heart.

7

The dog was quite dead. Only habit had kept him upright this long. Now he lay peacefully, as accepting of death as he had been unquestioning of life. They all crouched beside him, calling his name. Garth and Daisy cradled his head. Rose and Lily frantically searched for a pulse. Clover and Columbine desperately stroked his back. Daisy got up first and, after kissing both Gryffed's ears, went very slowly to find Mrs Snipper. The old woman, roused from sleep and with her nightcap askew, took a moment to understand. 'Oh My Dear God!' she said, and followed Daisy up the stairs.

It was Mrs Snipper who eventually chivvied them out of their mother's room. 'But Gryffed can't stay here,' Rose said. She kept looking behind her. 'He can't, Mrs Snips.' She was trying not to cry.

'No, dearie,' Mrs Snipper said. 'You leave the Dear Dog to me.'

'He must be buried at the Resting Place,' Garth said. He knew that his sisters expected him to rant and rave against their father. They did not know what the early evening had taught him about himself.

'Who's going to tell Pa?' whispered Lily.

Daisy's face was gaunt with shock. 'I'll tell him,' she said. 'It was my fault. If I'd never suggested using Ma's clothes, this would never have happened.'

Mrs Snipper bristled to the fullness of her tiny height. 'We'll have none of that,' she said. 'You hear me, Miss Daisy? None Of That. Things happen. That's what. Sometimes there's blame. Sometimes there isn't. Gryffed Had His Life and now It's Over. Your Pa had a life and it's Gone Wrong. You're trying to make it Right Again. What's wrong with that?'

'Gryffed shouldn't have died,' Daisy said. She was beyond tears.

'And your Pa shouldn't drink,' Mrs Snipper reminded her, 'and this place shouldn't be for sale.' They reached their father's room, paused and walked on. The Dead Girl was standing under one of the standards. She raised one hand. They walked straight through her. Only when they were back in Daisy's room did Mrs Snipper leave them. When she got to her kitchen, Snipe was already waiting. She did not need to tell him what had to be done.

'It's the end, isn't it?' said Clover or Columbine, huddling into Daisy's bed and trying to make herself as small as possible. 'We'll have to move. We can't go on now.'

The twins expected Rose or Daisy to answer, but Garth knew it was his voice Daisy needed to hear. He swallowed. 'It's not the end. We can go on,' he heard himself say. 'It's terrible about Gryffed, but we're de Granvilles. Going on is what we do.' He knew it was not much to offer, but he could think of nothing else. They heard the front door bang and presumed it was Mrs Snipper. 'How would we manage without her?' Daisy whispered. They tried not to imagine what she was doing.

But it was not Mrs Snipper who slammed the door, it was Charles, and just like Garth earlier, he was heading for the stables, only he did not go near The One. Instead, he rattled Skelton's door. It opened a crack. Shoeless and in a gentleman's velvet dressing-gown, Skelton had been combing his whiskers.

'I need a drink,' Charles said abruptly.

Skelton was startled at first. 'It's very late.'

'I need a drink,' Charles repeated, and pushed his way in.

Skelton closed his door and his mind began to work. *Well, well,* he thought. *Now here's something.* 'You're giving up the drink.' He made a face like the parson.

'Just give me a drink.' Charles was pacing about.

'I'm really not supposed—' said Skelton sanctimoniously.

'For the love of Christ, man,' Charles roared in a torment of need. 'Don't I still give the orders round here?'

'Oh, indeed, sir,' said Skelton, with mock deference. 'Of course, sir.' Without further ado, he gestured to a chair and furnished Charles with a nearly empty bottle. Charles drank the contents in one. He exhaled and wiped his mouth. 'I've had a fright,' he said, half defiant, half apologetic.

'Indeed,' said Skelton.

'Is there more?'

Skelton demurred just enough to see the need rise like a tide in Charles's eyes. 'Wait,' he said, and with a broad, secret smile went to retrieve the first bottle from his stash.

In the dawn, Daisy heard Charles return. He was clearly listing heavily, crashing against the statues in the hall and ordering Gryffed, whose absence he was too drunk to notice, to be quiet. She wanted to tell him at once of the tragedy. She pulled on her dressing gown as he climbed the stairs. When she got along his passage, the door of his room was open and she called to him in a low voice. There was no answer so she peered in. Charles was lying face down on the bed, melting snow trickling down his neck. Daisy gazed at him, in all his wreckage. She wanted to hate him. She could not. She wanted to love him. She could not do that either. She put down her candle and with some difficulty drew the bedcovers over him. A small miniature of their mother had fallen out of his pocket. Daisy wiped it dry and placed it on the pillow.

She did not go back to bed. Instead, she went to their mother's room and found Garth outside the door. Neither seemed surprised to see the other. They went in together. Gryffed was gone. Everything else was just as they had left it: the pistol on the floor, clothes strewn like fallen leaves, the milky wedding dress spilled all over. Wordlessly, they folded and tidied as best they could. Sometimes they both started, imagining their father's footfall, but only the Dead Girl came. When everything was tidy, the three of them stood very quietly, Garth and Daisy breathing the last of their mother's scent. Daisy felt the Dead Girl touch her shoulder. The touch reassured. Garth was right. They were de Granvilles and de Granvilles did go on.

Garth stooped and picked up the pistol.

'What will you do with it?' Daisy asked fearfully.

'I'll throw it in the moat,' he answered.

'You promise?'

He hesitated. The pistol felt good in his hand. 'I promise,' he said quickly. With a last, lingering look, they left their mother's room and closed the door behind them.

They all heard their father tramping down the stairs at breakfast time, calling Gryffed's name. They stood up as he opened the dining-room door. Charles remembered something of the night but not everything, though he had a faint notion that he should be angry. Something to do with clothes. Something to do with their mother. Something, something . . . He eyed his children nervously. They seemed expectant. Daisy was speaking. Her words made no sense.

'Gryffed?' he said. 'He's here, isn't he? What do you mean, he's under the chestnut tree?'

Daisy repeated herself more slowly.

'Dead?' said Charles, and another, less faint recollection hit him. He heard the pistol's retort. It resounded again and again in his head. 'Oh God,' he said. 'Oh my God.' He reversed out of the dining room, running through the castle. 'Gryffed!' he shouted. 'Gryffed! Gryffed!'

Rose made to go after him. 'Let him be,' advised Mrs Snipper. 'That's best.'

After a breakfast that went entirely uneaten, the children pulled on coats and walked slowly to the Resting Place. A grave had been dug and Gryffed's body was carefully shrouded in a blanket. Garth and Rose lowered the body into the ground, and they all folded the earth around it. Charles appeared just as they finished. They moved aside to let him through. There was nothing to say.

8

Until the very end of January, the castle hung under an icy pall and no buyers came. Charles was locked in his library. Rose and Lily, Clover and Columbine drifted about. Garth juggled constantly with the set of knucklebones he kept in an old skull in his room.

Daisy alone went out, and she only went to the stables to visit the horse. When she was with him, sitting in his stable as he mooched about, or watching Skelton walk him round the yard, the ground being too hard for anything else, she could still believe in her dream. She could tell The One about Gryffed and cry as much as she liked. She could also confide her worries about Garth. Indeed, she could speak about anything at all, and when he was not staring into the middle distance the horse liked to listen to her. He began to look forward to her visits. Soon he preferred her to the middle distance. 'Some people might give you a pet name,' she told him when he sneezed all over her hair, 'but I'm always going to call you The One. That way you'll not forget who you are, and that's very important.' Though she mourned Gryffed deeply, Daisy could not give up on the future. In the still reaches of the night, she fretted that if Charles did not soon give Skelton instructions about training, the Derby might yet slip away.

At the beginning of February, when the ice was turning slushy, she found Arthur Rose in the yard, his cob tethered to the mounting block. Skelton had swept a clear path and was trotting The One smartly up and down, occasionally flicking a long whip. The young vet was deep in thought, two slender fingers on his chin. Daisy leaned her crutches against the wall, her heart quailing. Arthur Rose should not be here. 'What's wrong?' she asked.

Arthur removed his fingers, unable to keep his eyes from flicking behind Daisy, hoping for Rose. 'Nothing, nothing at all,' he said, pushing back two thick strands of blond hair escaped from a bow a century out of fashion. 'Your father asked me to come to make sure the horse is quite sound.'

Daisy knew this could not be true.

'Trot him again, please, Mr Skelton,' Arthur called.

The One was in frisky mood. He did not need Skelton's whip, but Skelton applied it anyway. At its sting, the colt bucked and shimmied. 'He's stocky,' said Arthur. 'Not like your father's usual purchases.'

Daisy looked at Arthur. 'He's The One,' she said.

Arthur returned her look. 'The One?'

'The One who's going to win the Derby.'

'Oh, I see,' said Arthur. He fiddled with his collar.

'Mr Snaffler sent you for money, didn't he,' Daisy said in the end.

'That'll do, Mr Skelton.' Arthur waited until Skelton was back in the stable before he nodded. 'I'm sorry.'

'Sorry or not, we can't pay,' Daisy said flatly. 'Or at least we can't pay until the thirtieth of May.' The vet looked puzzled. 'The day after the Derby,' explained Daisy. 'We can pay you then.'

'Is that because you'll be gone by then?' Arthur asked. A furrow appeared on his forehead.

Daisy drew herself up, every inch a de Granville. 'No. But even if we were to go, we'd still pay our debts.'

'Of course – yes – no!' Arthur kicked himself. 'I didn't mean . . . I meant . . .'

'Oh, I see,' said Daisy. 'You mean that Rose will have gone.'

He bit his lip. 'It's Mr Snaffler,' he said. 'He told me to come and settle up. Your father's bill is – well, Snaffler's forbidden me to treat any animal here unless the outstanding accounts are settled. Gryffed's hunting wound—'

'Gryffed's dead,' said Daisy.

Arthur blenched. 'Dead? Oh, Miss Daisy, I'm so sorry.' An awful thought struck him. 'Did he need me? I'd have come. Surely you know that. You know I'd have come, money or not.'

His anguish was so genuine that it made Daisy's lip tremble. 'He didn't need you, Mr Rose.'

'Poor Gryffed. What happened?'

'He just died,' said Daisy shortly.

'Your father must be very upset.'

Daisy did not answer. Instead she walked towards The One's stable. 'You never said if The One was sound or not,' she said, trying to make her voice normal.

Arthur gave her a moment to compose herself. 'The horse is sound as a bell,' he said, standing beside her.

'We'll have to start training very soon. The Derby's not far off, and we'll only get this one shot. Runners have to be three years old, don't they, and next year The One will be four.' She could not hide her anxiety.

Arthur pushed his hair back again. He felt a duty. 'It's a risky business, having a racehorse, Miss Daisy. Not all three-year-olds make it to the Derby.'

'I know that.'

Arthur still felt a duty. 'And you know that if the horse is to have a chance, you can't just turn up at Epsom. You need to run him in a Derby trial before running him in the Derby itself.'

'I know that too,' Daisy said, though her sudden pallor showed that this had never occurred to her.

'And there are entry fees and travel costs.' He had to say

88

it. She was silent. Arthur untied his cob. 'I'll tell Mr Snaffler that nobody was at home,' he said.

'Tell him to go to hell!' cried Daisy vehemently.

Arthur swung himself into the saddle and smiled sadly down at her. 'He'll get there in the end without our wishes.' He clicked his tongue and the cob moved off obediently. Daisy waited behind, then grabbed her crutches and swung herself after him. He slowed his cob when he heard her call his name. 'I wish you could marry Rose,' Daisy said.

Arthur blushed to the roots of his hair. 'I wish you could keep Hartslove,' he replied. He watched her swing herself towards the Resting Place. The wind got up and his eye was caught by the de Granville standard, the blood-red horse visible then invisible in the cross-currents. The cob walked on, unmoved by the 'for sale' sign that clanged against its post so hard that half of it became unhooked. Arthur could have leaned down to hang it up again. Instead, he left it hanging on a solitary chain, one corner dragging in the dirt.

Back in the yard, Skelton was busy. The let-up in the weather meant it was time for the saddle again. The groom tried his hardest, but as soon as the colt sensed the saddle anywhere near, he bucked and twisted, legs and hooves flying. For fully twenty minutes Skelton cursed and swore and took swipes. At last, red in the face, he threw the saddle down. 'I'll twitch you,' he said. 'See how you like that.' The colt, sweating and kicking out, eyed him balefully.

Skelton returned with a rounded handle of wood just over a foot long, a circle of cord threaded through a hole at one end. He shook it at The One, who tried to bite it, giving Skelton just the opportunity he needed. Seizing the horse's top lip, he slid the small noose over it and began to turn the handle. The noose tightened round the tender flesh. When The One tried to back away, the cord bit deep. When he half-reared, it bit deeper still. When he twisted, it bit deepest of all. In the end, realising that the pain intensified when he moved, the colt was completely still. Now Skelton himself was stuck. He couldn't hold the twitch and grab the saddle at the same time. He swore again at his own stupidity. When Daisy swung back into the yard, he tilted his head. 'You'll have to help me.'

Daisy stood as still as the colt. 'What on earth are you doing?'

'Come and hold this.'

'I won't,' she said. The One's eyes were set in a dreadful stare.

Skelton was unapologetic. 'Now look here, missy. Do you think the horse can win the Derby without a saddle on? He's three years old. This should have been done long ago. We've no more time to waste.'

Daisy shook her head.

Annoyed, Skelton twisted the handle further. The horse's eyes widened. His lip, bulging through the cord, turned a blueish shade.

Daisy's eyes fixed on the lip. 'Take that thing off,' she said.

'Look, you can either help me or go away,' Skelton said through his teeth. 'He's got to have a saddle on and you know it.'

'But not like this,' Daisy said. 'Take it off.'

'And who are you to order me about?' Skelton barked. 'Your father wants this horse entered in the Derby. That means he's got to be saddled.'

'Take it off! Take it off!'

To Skelton's utter fury that's exactly what he had to do. When the cord slackened, the One stretched his lip into the air in a way that would have been comical but for the pained and betrayed look in his eye. Skelton swore again, stamped across the yard and slammed the door into his house, leaving The One tied up and the saddle dumped on the mounting block.

Daisy tried to approach The One. The horse backed away until he could back no further and stood, ridiculously, with rope taut and his neck stretched out. Daisy stood quite still and repeated in a low, crooning voice, 'It's me, The One, it's me.' It was an age before he eased forward, a further age before he did not wince when she touched him. She longed to rub his lip but he would not let her do that. 'You know,' she told him, 'you *will* have to wear a saddle, just as I have to wear a dress.' She slowly raised her hands. He threw up his head. 'It's not nice, I agree,' said Daisy, 'but if we can solve it in our way, Skelton won't have to solve it in his.' The One sighed.

Daisy untied him and led him loosely behind her. When she picked up the saddle the horse baulked and flattened his ears. With the whites of his eyes always showing, he could look very fierce. But Daisy, crooning again, did not place the saddle on his back. Instead she walked with it to the harness room, now sadly bare. There was a fire in here since Skelton had been working on Tinker's traces. It seemed to Daisy that the solution to the saddle was quite obvious: The One did not like the feel of the cold leather after his warm rug. She wound the lead-rope loosely round a hook, went into the harness room, found a thick cloth and warmed it in front of the fire. She could not reach over The One's back from the ground so she took the cloth and the saddle to the mounting block and returned for the horse. He was curious now, rather than frightened, and followed Daisy quite willingly. The cloth smelled of dust and spiders, and when it touched his neck he liked the warmth. Still crooning, Daisy climbed up the mounting block and gently slung the cloth over his withers. His ears flicked back, but now he was sniffing her callipers, whose mix of steel and wood was even more interesting than the cloth. Daisy could feel his whiskers tickling her knees. She waited until he had quite finished before she picked up the saddle itself. It was important that he knew what she was doing. He regarded it with misgiving and moved away. It took Daisy an hour to get it on, an hour in which she never raised her voice, and when The One backed off, simply waited for him to return to her. She never put the saddle down, so in the end, it became part of her and The One barely noticed when she slid it on to the cloth. She did not attempt to do up the girth, but climbed down from the mounting block and wandered out of the yard. The One wandered after her. She meandered back to the Resting Place and sat on the flat stone. The earth on Gryffed's grave was still raw and Daisy wished she had something to sprinkle over it. The horse, meanwhile, lost interest in both her and the saddle. He began to pull up strands of dead grass to grind between his teeth. After a bit, Daisy pulled the saddle off and balanced it on her knee. The horse raised his head, then lowered it again. When he had finished with the grass, he came to her and sniffed the saddle. He stuck out his tongue. The leather tasted deliciously of salt and oil. Daisy allowed him to lick it all over, then lifted it on to his withers and slid it on to the cloth. The One blinked. He had already forgotten what the fuss was about.

Daisy walked the horse back to the stables. 'You really are a funny creature,' she said conversationally. 'Your bottom's higher than your withers and your head really is a little big. As for your mane and tail – was your father a blackberry bush?' The One flapped his ears. His mane and forelock flapped in sympathy. For the first time since Gryffed's death, Daisy laughed.

She stayed with the horse long into the dark, taking the saddle on and off, smoothing his rug, petting him and making his bed comfortable. Skelton appeared only to give The One his corn and fill the hay-rack. He made no comment about the saddle. The horse ate the corn with gusto and pulled systematically at the hay. The rhythmic chomping was so soothing that Daisy could hardly bear to tear herself away. In this warm loose-box, everything seemed so simple. But she had to go. The others would worry. She hugged The One, which made him snort, and kissed his velvet nose, which made him sneeze. 'See you tomorrow,' she said.

As she left the yard, she called his name. He would be too busy eating to look over his door. But as she turned away, his dark outline appeared and she stopped short. 'Oh!' she breathed. In the light of the yard lamp, he glowed as red as the horse on the de Granville standard. When she crossed the drawbridge, shaking the hayseeds out of her hair, she would have skipped had she been able.

That night, Daisy dreamed of The One, with herself in racing silks crouched on his back. She dreamed of the winner's enclosure and the astonishment of all when she whisked off her cap and revealed that she was no ordinary jockey, but the beautiful daughter of Sir Charles de Granville, with perfect legs. Then the dream got muddled, as she found herself not in jockeys silks but in her mother's wedding dress. She had done it up with The One's girth, and her father was shouting at her while her mother, shaking her head, was being swallowed up in the crowd though Daisy was calling and calling for her to wait.

At the stables, Skelton was not dreaming. He was staring down at Charles, whom he had found slumped over two sacks of oats, his mouth open and an empty bottle by his side. Skelton, who had supplied the bottle, poked him with the toe of his boot. Charles grunted but did not move. 'You and your fancy family,' Skelton said softly. 'You think you own this place, but let me tell you, I've served my time here. I'm owed, Charlie-boy.' Charles snored. Skelton smiled sourly. 'And what I'm owed, I'm going to get.' He contemplated leaving Charles where he was, but it was cold and Charles would be even more useless dead than he was alive so in the end the groom hoisted his employer over his shoulder, stamped over to the castle and dumped him under the Furious Boy.

9

The let-up in the weather brought another potential buyer, this time a widowed lady, still in mourning, and her agent. Charles went out to meet them. He was relieved to do so. Since the death of Gryffed, he could not face his children and they could not face him. The intruders would at least save them from each other.

The lady came in, raised her black lace veil and removed black kidskin gloves to reveal very white hands. She stood in front of one of the hall fires warming her feet and fluttering carefully darkened and thickened eyelashes. 'An unusual welcoming party,' she observed, gesturing at the statues. 'I like them.' She offered Charles her arm. 'You must show me round.' With an awkward smile, Charles took the arm, and he and the lady crossed the hall and went through to the drawing room, leaving her agent under the silent scrutiny of Rose, Lily, Daisy, Garth, Columbine and Clover. The man viewed the blank-eyed statues with distaste, brushed his hat and pointed a stubby finger at Rose. 'You can take me round,' he said.

Rose was too dispirited to object. 'What do you want to see?'

'Everything.'

Rose shrugged helplessly. She made her way down the stairs to the kitchen. After a moment's pause, Daisy beckoned to the others and they all followed, almost treading on the agent's heels. Irritated, he turned round. The children bundled to a halt. When he walked again, there they were, right on top of him. Daisy actually trod on the back of his shoe with her callipers. 'For the love of God!' the agent exclaimed to Rose. 'Are these your siblings?' He bent to rub his ankle. 'Tell them to get lost. I only need one guide.'

Rose nearly did as he asked. What did anything matter any more. But as she turned to obey, she saw the Dead Girl gazing at her from the top of the steps, a diamond teardrop in the corner of each eye. It was the first time Rose had ever seen the Dead Girl out of their father's passage. Rose breathed in, then out. She turned to the agent. 'What siblings?' she asked sweetly. Lily, Garth, Daisy, Columbine and Clover were immediately alert as hounds. The agent threw back an arm. 'These creatures – aren't they your sisters and brother?'

'What creatures?' Rose asked, more sweetly still. Angry now, the man seized Columbine. With perfect timing she became a rag doll in his arms and when he let go, sank to the floor, then rose again without a sound. 'Stop this!' the man expostulated. Clover nearly giggled. Rose opened the kitchen door. 'This is the kitchen,' she said. Mrs Snipper was banging pots about. Rose put a finger to her lips.

The agent was relieved to see a plump, ordinary looking creature, with a mobcap and an apron. He coughed and took a notebook from the pocket of his chequered jacket. 'What's the capacity of the range?' he asked. Mrs Snipper said nothing. 'Capacity, woman, capacity!' he repeated. Still nothing.

'I don't know the capacity,' said Rose.

'I wasn't asking you,' said the agent. 'I was asking the cook.'

'What cook?' asked Rose. Mrs Snipper's cheeks twitched and she banged the pots even harder.

The agent looked at Rose in a fury. 'Are you simple-minded or is this a silly game?' he barked.

'I don't know what you mean,' said Rose, turning the full force of her cornflower eyes on to him. 'Are you saying you can see a cook?'

'There *is* a cook.'

'If we could afford a cook, we'd hardly be selling the castle,' Rose responded gravely.

The agent ran to Mrs Snipper, but as he made to seize her, a cloud of ash gusted from the range and he caught a glimpse of a flame-coloured coxcomb. In seconds, Snipe had retreated, though the clouds of ash remained. The agent gasped and choked, seized Rose by the elbow and hurried her out of the kitchen, back up the steps and into the hall, the others following hard on his heels. Thoroughly disconcerted, the man gazed wildly about, trying to fix on something reassuring. But there was nothing to reassure, for surely, when he last looked, the Furious Boy had not had a pair of crutches stuck under his arms? In the doorway, Garth turned himself right over so that his head stuck out between his legs. 'Oh! Horrible!' the agent cried.

At once, Rose was all consternation. 'You look terrible! You should sit down!'

The man swivelled round and round. The children, the cook, the ash – it was a monstrous trick. He knew it, and yet still his neck prickled. 'Sit down?' he cried. 'Of course I don't want to sit down. How do I know the chairs are real?'

Rose laughed. 'Oh, the chairs are quite real.' She pulled one to the fire and pushed him into it. When the agent next looked, Rose was perched on the fender, and they seemed to be alone. 'I shouldn't really say this,' Rose said confidentially, 'but you probably did see other children. I never see the walking dead myself, but others apparently do.' She contemplated him. 'It's usually a bad omen, I'm afraid.' The man gasped.

'Oh, don't worry!' Rose was all soft concern. 'I'm sure whatever happens to you won't be painful, at least not very. Or perhaps it'll happen to your mistress.' She leaned forward. 'You've both probably got until the next full moon.'

'The full moon?' said the agent faintly.

Rose patted his knee. 'Don't worry. Your mistress need never know until she's parted with her money. No need for you to say anything. Would you like a cup of tea?'

The man clutched his hat so hard he broke the rim and, when his mistress arrived, shot up as though the chair had bitten him. The lady was laughing, her arm more closely folded into Charles's. Charles himself looked dazed. He could not look at Gryffed's empty basket. He would not meet Rose's eye. 'You really are so charming,' the lady said. Charles grimaced. The agent ran over and pulled his mistress away. 'We must leave,' he said.

'Leave? What nonsense,' the lady said haughtily, 'I like this place.' She tossed her head, hoping that Charles was as conscious of her pretty hair as she was.

The agent tried to regain some composure. 'The place is unsuitable,' he declared.

His mistress glared. 'I like it, I tell you.'

'It's not – I saw –'

'I'm afraid he saw the rats,' Rose said smoothly.

'Rats?' The lady looked sharply at Charles. 'In the castle itself? You never said.'

'Rats? I don't think so,' mumbled Charles.

'Not rats!' cried the agent, losing the battle with his composure. 'Ghosts, ghouls, quantities of dead children.'

Charles smiled quite gently. 'Not quantities of dead children, possibly one Dead Girl—'

Rose interrupted. 'No ghosts at all,' she said, and patted Charles's arm in an exaggerated show of support. He was surprised into silence. 'Absolutely not a one.' Rose made her smile as wide as it was false. Now the widow got a prickle up her neck.

'Look here,' the agent said. He did not like being shown up as a coward. 'Do you have other children?'

'Other than Rose?' asked Charles. 'Yes, I do.'

'That's right. You tell him, Pa,' Rose said. 'And don't forget to tell him we also have a cook.'

'We don't really have a cook,' Charles said. 'We only—'

'No need to go into all that, Pa,' said Rose, with a meaningful glance at the agent. 'You can tell them everything once the money's on the table.'

The agent took his mistress's arm and chivvied her out of the door. She objected. He whispered in her ear. Once in the courtyard, she laughed. 'What a lot of nonsense,' she began to say. A raven flew from the top of the keep and landed on the ground right in front of her.

'Good Lord!' cried Charles.

Rose curtsied deeply and pulled the widow down too. 'You must curtsey. You see, there's a myth – just a myth, I'm sure –' The widow ended up on her knees. She looked in vain to Charles to help her up. Charles was transfixed by the raven. 'I've never seen a raven here before,' he said.

'Raven, raven, no safe haven,' intoned Rose. 'And the person it touches will not last very, er, very muches.' She winced at the rhyme.

The raven squawked and hopped over to the widow. The widow, loudly declaring that she was not superstitious, nevertheless hopped away. The raven rose and tried to land on her shoulder. She shrieked and scrambled back into the trap. It was really very easy to frighten people, Rose realised with some surprise as the agent whipped their horses into a smart trot. Rose herself thought nothing of the appearance of the raven – or only that Daisy was right: Hartslove really did know how to help when help was needed.

High above, Snipe hoisted a cage over his shoulder, crossed the roof and slithered down the back ivy. He would have smiled if smiling had been in his nature.

Once the carriage had gone, Rose and Charles stood awkwardly together. Rose spoke first. 'We should never have gone into Ma's room,' she said. 'I'm so sorry, and about Gryffed –' She could not go on.

Charles shuffled his narrow feet. He wished the slug that had killed Gryffed had lodged in his own heart. He felt it there anyway. Every time he closed his eyes, he saw the pistol slowly revolving, killing each of his children. Brandy was the only thing that dulled the pain. Rose took his arm and walked him back up the steps. He knew she was trying to comfort him, but though Rose could not know it, she actually made him feel worse than Garth, worse than Daisy with her crippled legs, worse even than Lily, who, to him, looked even more like his wife than Rose did. It was not that Rose said hurtful things; Garth said far more hurtful things than Rose. Rose hurt him without words. She hurt him without even meaning to. She hurt him by being dressed in brown serge and in love with Arthur Rose when she should have been dressed in silk and in love with a curly-headed duke. She hurt him when she sat at dinner and tried to make everything normal. When he was with Rose, Charles needed a drink most of all.

Rose was aware that her father wanted to get away from her, but now she had started to speak she would finish. 'Pa,' she said, her heart hammering, for she had never before spoken to her father as though they were equals, 'we can't undo what's done, but couldn't we make a new start?'

'Rose,' he said. 'Rose, Rose, Rose.' For a moment, he allowed himself to see this new start. He saw the 'for sale' sign torn down. He sensed the bustle of happy servants. He heard his wife's gentle voice calling him in for lunch. But even as he saw and sensed and heard, the hole in his heart broadened and widened and darkened. It was too late, much too late. 'All over,' he said, and turned away.

His tone frightened Rose. It was the tone of a dead man, and for all his shortcomings, she – they – needed their father alive. She seized his arm more firmly. 'Not while we have The One,' she insisted. 'We drank a toast. Don't you remember?' Charles shook his head. Rose could not bear it.

'Don't shake your head,' she cried. 'Don't you dare. Daisy believes in the horse, even if you don't any more. Please, Pa. Can't you pretend? After all, that's what the rest of us are doing.' Charles scuffed the toes of his boots. Rose pulled his arm more gently. 'Come,' she coaxed. 'Come with me to the stables. Come. Come.' He did not have the strength to resist her.

They heard the row before they arrived. The One was tied up. Daisy had put the saddle on but Skelton dangled the girth. 'The saddle's one thing but doing up the girth's a different matter. The horse is ticklish. He'll kick out, and with all due respect, Miss Daisy,' Skelton was saying with offensive care, 'you're hardly going to be able to nip out of the way.'

The One glared sullenly from behind his forelock. Skelton buckled the girth to the saddle and let it drop, then moved to the other side of the horse, picked up the girth and tried to fasten it. A twist, a grunt, a curse: the saddle hit the cobbles with a resounding thump. Daisy's lips were so tightly compressed they almost vanished, her face so anguished that Charles was at last jolted out of his stupor. He wrenched himself away from Rose. 'Let her do it, Skelton.'

'I'm telling you—'

'Let her do it.'

Skelton held on to the girth. 'Sir Charles, she'll never be able to get out of the way.'

'Let her.'

'If the horse kills her, I'll not share responsibility.'

'Of course he won't kill me.' Daisy snatched at the saddle.

Skelton knew better than to tussle for it. He crossed his arms. 'Go on then,' he said. 'Show us how it's done.'

Rose stood by her father as Daisy moved closer to the horse and began to croon. 'Rose,' Charles said. 'I can't –'

'Just watch, Pa. Just watch.'

Daisy hardly saw her father. She was concentrating only on The One. 'Shall we show them?' she asked the horse. 'Shall we?'

The One's eyes flicked back and forth from Daisy to the saddle to Skelton, but Daisy knew he could hear her. She untied him and moved to the mounting block. Dropping the rope, she climbed on to the block, slid the saddle on to his back, then climbed down. She spoke to the horse with her hands, stroking his ears, then his neck, then his withers, and finally running her palms over the saddle flaps to his stomach. Skelton was right: the horse was ticklish. Nevertheless, very slowly and with complete confidence, Daisy took the girth and fastened the buckle loosely. The One's skin puckered at the feel of the leather and he curved his neck to see what she was doing. He shifted, but the saddle was secure. Prodded by Rose, Charles approached the horse and rubbed his nose. 'That was something, wasn't it, Skelton?' he said.

'It was, Sir Charles,' Skelton said. His expression was unfathomable.

'And the horse didn't try to kill her.'

'No, Sir Charles, but then he's standing still. It may be different once he moves.'

Daisy threw Skelton a look and began to walk around the yard. The One walked quite calmly beside her until they passed the barn door. A sharp breeze rattled it and a tile clattered down, smashing on the cobbles. Even an old horse would have taken fright, and The One was so young. Throwing up his head, he whipped the rope out of Daisy's hands and set off at a canter. At once, the stirrups, which Daisy had not thought to secure, slid down their leathers and punched him in the ribs. The One's ears flew back at this unexpected belting and he crashed round the yard and out of the gate towards the Resting Place, the rope dangling. In vain, Daisy called for him to stop. Charles and Skelton ran out after him.

With the saddle on his back and the grass beneath his feet, The One galloped round the Resting Place until, shaking his head against the slapping of the rope, he set sail for the river. At the start of the trees, he hesitated, skidded round and galloped along the fence. The straight line invited; the stirrups clanged; and when he heard the distant whistle of a train, he opened his shoulders and galloped. It took about a minute for Charles, Skelton and Daisy to stop their pursuit and to stand, their jaws dropping. The One was no longer galloping the thundering mad gallop of fear; he seemed to have forgotten about that. Instead he had made a discovery: that if he allowed his hindquarters to thrust and his legs to skim, he could gallop faster than the wind. He stretched out. He was enjoying himself. 'My God!' breathed Charles. The One had no intention of stopping and took no notice of the wicked rope snaking round those fragile front legs. Yet, inevitably, as the ground rose, the rope caught under one flashing front hoof and The One's flight came to an ungainly and violent halt as he catapulted right over. Charles howled. Skelton yelled. Daisy's teeth clamped her tongue.

Charles ran down as the horse rose. The One was gasping, the breath knocked out of him, but there was no white bone sticking through the skin and no blood. When the horse had stopped gasping, Charles asked him to walk. He walked. He asked him to trot. He trotted. The horse was not happy but he seemed unhurt. 'No harm, none at all,' Charles said, 'and did you see the speed? My God, this animal's a miracle. I've seldom seen anything like that, and he's not even trained yet!'

Daisy unclamped her tongue. 'Is he really all right?'

'Right as rain.'

'Thank God!' whispered Daisy.

Rose was pleased about the horse, but better still, Charles no longer looked like a dead man. A glimmer of a sparkle had returned. Even if The One did not win the Derby, he was to be thanked for that.

'What do you think, Skelton?' Charles was excited.

'A good horse, certainly,' Skelton said. He was breathing almost as quickly as The One. 'A very good horse indeed.'

They returned to the yard, Skelton deferring to Daisy in a way Daisy found both unsettling and gratifying. The One had certainly lifted everybody's mood. She fussed over the horse for the rest of the afternoon, and Skelton left them quite alone. Only after Daisy had gone back to the castle did he pull on his boots and slip into the stable. The One was lying down. 'No need to rise, laddie,' Skelton said. The horse rose anyway. Skelton made no move towards him, just stood for a while, making his calculations. The horse shook himself. Skelton stepped to the side, then, without warning, he rocked forward, then back, then forward, then back again, and when he was ready, he kicked The One's offside knee with vicious, carefully controlled force. The horse grunted and his leg shuddered. Skelton waited until the leg had stopped quivering before inspecting his footwork. The knee was unmarked but already beginning to swell. 'Perfectly judged, Mr Skelton,' the groom said to himself. He closed the stable door behind him. The horse's ears were flat back. Skelton laughed softly. 'It must be rotten being a horse,' he said, with no sympathy at all.

10

Breakfast had barely begun when Skelton appeared, sorry to inform Charles and his children that – such a pity, *such* a pity – though all seemed to have been well, it was now clear that the horse had damaged himself during the previous day's escapade. 'I didn't like to say anything with Miss Daisy being such a genius with horses,' Skelton said, manufacturing just the right amount of regret, 'and she couldn't have been expected to hold on when he shied in the yard, her being a girl, and, well, you know –' he gestured at her crutches – 'but a dangling rope's the most dangerous thing in the world, particularly for a racehorse. If only – oh well, that doesn't matter now. What's done's done, but I thought I'd better tell you at once.' He shook his head in the ghastly silence. 'I've had the hosepipe on the knee already, but I think it'll take more than cold water. As I say, such a pity, when we had such high hopes.'

Knives and forks, suspended in mid-air, dropped on to

plates. Charles was white. 'But he's The One,' he said. 'We saw him.'

'He *was* The One, sir,' Skelton corrected.

Daisy was on her feet. 'It's not true,' she cried. 'It can't be true. He was fine all afternoon. He was fine when I left him.'

Skelton bowed his head. 'I'm sorry, miss.'

'He was fine, I tell you.'

'He *looked* fine, miss,' Skelton said, 'but you see, when you've been around horses as long as I have, you'll know that injuries don't always show up at once.'

Daisy wracked her brains, trying to remember. She could see The One galloping; she saw the rope dangling; she saw him trip. The back of her neck froze. 'Oh God,' she said. 'What have I done?'

'It's not your fault, Daisy,' Rose said quickly. 'Accidents happen with horses.' Her lips were set.

'I'm going to have a look,' Daisy said, searching in vain for her crutches.

In the event, they all went to look. Skelton had left The One tied up in the yard. The rope was unnecessary since by now the horse could hardly move. He seemed puzzled by the fat bulge on his once shapely leg and sniffed it with pained amazement. It was, he knew, in some way associated with Skelton and he jibbed hard every time the groom approached him. 'He doesn't like me because I've had the hosepipe on him,' Skelton said, patting the horse on the neck. 'But without cold water, believe me, it would be worse for him.' There were puddles everywhere. The hosepipe lay coiled under the tap.

Daisy was completely dazed. There was the knee. There was no mistaking the injury. She, who had set herself up as The One's friend, The One's trainer even, had caused his racing life to end before it had even begun. 'It's a pity the ice house has fallen into disrepair,' she heard Skelton tell Rose. 'We could do with ice now.' Rose, standing with Lily, with Garth hovering and Clover and Columbine standing mute together, could only nod.

Charles, like Daisy, was too stunned to speak. To have fate conspire against him like this – again – just when he really had resolved to turn his own and his children's lives around! It was intolerable! It was iniquitous! Why was he so punished? He lurched round and staggered into Skelton's house. He would have a glass. He would have a bottle. He would drink a case. Truly, drink was the only security left to him.

Rose and Lily moved closer to the horse's head. His long ears flopped. His eyes were mournful. 'Can't something be done?' Lily had never really thought of the race except as a kind of dream. It was the horse's pain she was unable to bear.

'He needs more than Skelton's hosepipe. He needs a vet,' Garth said, bending down.

'We can't pay a vet,' said Daisy flatly. She did not know

what to do with herself. 'I'd sell myself if I was worth anything.'

'Arthur Rose would come if Rose asked,' said Clover or Columbine, trying to be helpful.

'It would be quite wrong to ask,' Rose countered sharply. 'It would be taking complete advantage.'

'But you could,' Clover or Columbine persisted. 'I mean, surely if The One was dying, if he was lying on the ground groaning, if he had a gaping wound and his blood was gushing . . .'

Daisy gave a hiccupping sob.

'Stop it! Stop it!' cried Lily, the white canary that had lately joined her doves fluttering in her hands. 'Don't say such things!'

The twins looked at each other. Nothing they suggested was ever right.

'Skelton said cold water was the best cure,' said Rose, scowling at them. 'Come on, Daisy. We'll help you. Turn on the hosepipe.' Rose felt it important that Daisy should be doing something, not just staring. She pulled her up and gave her a push. Daisy was dumb as she limped to the tap, and it was Rose who held the pipe against The One's leg as the colt first tried to back away from the gush, and then, hobbled by his lameness and appreciating the coolness of the water, stood miserably still. 'That's good, isn't it?' Rose said to him, trying not to mind that her feet were soaking. 'Look, Daisy. This really does help.'

Daisy took the hosepipe from her. She still could not speak. Eventually, Rose turned off the tap. 'I think that's enough for now. Let's get him back into his stable,' she said. Moving The One was a struggle. He did not want to put any weight on his leg, and huffed and puffed his dismay. Afterwards, Daisy, having silently tidied the straw and touched the horse's nose in mute apology, stumbled in tears to the Resting Place. Ignoring the cold, she lay face down on the flat stone. Rose, lingering on the drawbridge, watched her sister's shaking shoulders for a while, then spun on her heel, went inside and fetched her bonnet.

Inside Skelton's house, Charles was slumped at the kitchen table. He had thrown off his coat and his legs were spread, the soles of his boots flapping where they had worn through. Skelton flicked a speck of dust from his own boots, then brought out a bottle and a glass. 'Here,' he said.

Charles watched him tip out a generous measure. 'Every time I try to stop with this stuff, something makes it impossible,' he complained, half to Skelton and half to himself. 'It's as if there's a conspiracy against me. There *is* a conspiracy against me.' He downed the tot and held out the glass. Skelton poured another and one for himself at the same time. 'A restorative,' he said. Charles downed the second glass before Skelton had taken so much as a sip. 'I can't drink all your brandy,' Charles said, drinking a third glass a little more slowly.

'Don't you worry about me,' Skelton said silkily. Then he simply waited. After the fourth tot, Charles began to talk. He tried to speak of Gryffed; he failed. He tried to speak of Hartslove; he failed. After a fifth tot, he gave up trying to speak of home. Instead, he spoke of the war in the Crimea; of the maggot-ridden wounded and the worm-ridden dead; of the stench of fear and the foolishness of bravery. 'Why was I not killed, Skelton?' he asked again and again. 'So many others were – better men than me.' Skelton lost count of the number of times Charles reached for the bottle. 'A man in my regiment had his head blown off and I came through with barely a scratch. How, Skelton? Was I a coward? Did I always keep myself out of danger? Do you know what I dream every night?' Skelton shook his head. 'I dream that I'm running away whilst my men are being mown down like poppies.' He leaned unsteadily forward. 'Did I run away?' He seemed to think that Skelton might know the answer. When no answer came, he supplied one himself. 'If I didn't, how come they died and I'm back here? Tell me that.' He picked up the bottle. Nearly empty.

Skelton swirled his brandy around. 'Who knows why anything turns out as it does,' he said, and, getting up, he produced another bottle, uncorked it and threw the cork away. He pushed the bottle towards Charles, who filled his glass almost to the top. Skelton pretended to top up his own glass also. 'The war must have been terrible,' he said, leaving his glass on the table. 'Tell me more.'

Words tumbled out, at first surprisingly clearly, but half an hour later less so, and half an hour later still Charles's speech was slurred to a continuous mumble and his eyes were so red and bleary he could hardly see through them.

Watching every tiny change, Skelton finally raised his glass. Now was the time. 'To dashed hopes,' he said.

'Dashed hopes?'

'The One,' Skelton said. 'He could have made everything better.'

'Oh yes. The One.' Charles slopped his brandy. 'Poor Daisy. Poor, poor The One.'

'And poor you, sir.'

'Not poor me. Everything my fault. Suppose hopes entirely dashed?'

'I'm afraid they are with this The One,' Skelton said.

Charles suddenly banged his glass down and spilled the lot. 'Bruise,' he said. 'Just bruise – surely – go down – good as new – Daisy – not fair – Garth – young – not fair – not *right*.'

'I agree! I agree!' Skelton gave an understanding smile. 'But even if it was just a bruise, I'm afraid everything's too late now. I mean, the horse is already behind – not even a jockey on yet and no race as a two-year-old.' He shook his head. 'It's a great shame.'

'No hope?'

Skelton shrugged regretfully.

Charles put his head in his hands. 'No hope at all.'

After a long while, he made a giant effort to raise his head, though it felt far too heavy to lift. 'If there's really no hope – horse – go. Can't afford, see? Can't afford. Rose – clothes – husband – awful mess.'

Skelton licked his lips. His mouth was suddenly dry. He picked at his words as a cat picks at the innards of a mouse. 'A pity if he were to go, Sir Charles. Last horse here and all that.'

'Yes – pity – but we're ruined. Him – last horse. Me – last de Granville at Hartslove. Thrown everything away, see. Everything.'

'Don't say that, Sir Charles.'

'Why not? It's the truth. Wife tried to tell me. Horses and bottle . . .' He stared balefully at his reflection in the brandy.

Skelton shifted. He did not want Charles to be reminded of what Lady de Granville had said about the bottle. 'I have a little money . . .' he began.

'Silly Skelton,' interrupted Charles. 'Couldn't have enough.'

'As I say, Sir Charles,' Skelton continued, smooth as the amber liquid in his glass, 'I have a little money put by. Enough to keep the castle and the horse going until' – he paused – 'until Derby Day.'

Charles's shoulders were shaking, and at first Skelton thought he was crying. He was wrong. Charles was laughing the pitiless, sick laugh of the drunk. 'Derby Day!'

He downed another shot. 'You've enough to keep us going until Derby Day though we're not going to the Derby now. *You*'d give *me* money!'

Skelton grinned. '*Seems* silly, I know.' He sighed. 'But I'm serious. I have got money put by, and I don't like to think of the old place in strange hands. I'm very fond of it, see. Don't forget I've lived here man and boy.'

'Course you have, Skelton, course you have.' Charles fumbled at Skelton's forearm. Skelton did not object. 'You'll be out of a job. Reference. Least I can do.'

'I don't want a reference, I want to help,' Skelton said, pretending to take another drink.

'Can't take help from you. Servant and all that.'

Skelton tapped his head as though an idea had just come to him. 'Here's a notion, Sir Charles. What happens if rather than just taking my money, we strike a bargain? Would that make you feel better?'

'Bargain? Bargain?' said Charles. Skelton's voice was undulating like the sea. 'Water,' Charles said.

Skelton brought a jug. 'Thing is, Sir Charles, I'd happily give you the money, but if you're too proud to take it, you could give me something in return.'

Charles slurped the water straight from the jug. 'Nothing to give. Bailiffs want the lot.'

'Well,' said Skelton, 'let me see.' He waited, then slapped his palm on the table. Charles jerked. 'I've got it, Sir Charles.'

'Got it?'

Skelton removed the brandy. Charles must not collapse. Not yet. 'I'll give you my savings, and if The One wins the Derby, you give me the horse, the winnings and Hartslove.' Just as Skelton had hoped, Charles laughed as though this were the funniest thing he had ever heard. Skelton laughed too. 'Shall we do that, Sir Charles? Shall we?'

'Oh, Skelton! The One win the Derby? Why, the horse couldn't walk from the back of his stable to the front, let alone gallop first past a winning post! You'd be signing away your savings for nothing.'

'Of course I would! But it would be a good joke, eh?' Skelton got up and walked round and round the table.

'A good joke?' Charles was trying to follow Skelton. His head was beginning to spin.

'Aye! A good joke! Shall we have a final good joke, Sir Charles? You and me? Master and servant?'

'I don't know –'

'See here!' Skelton whisked out a piece of paper. 'You could even write our contract down! Nonsense, of course, but all part of the jape.'

Charles tried, and failed, to stand up. Skelton caught him. 'You need looking after, Sir Charles,' Skelton said, adding cleverly, 'and Miss Daisy loves that horse. Let old Skelton help, and make yourself feel better about it by allowing me my little joke.'

Charles was eyeing the brandy again. Skelton held the bottle just out of reach. 'What do you say, Sir Charles?'

'Joke,' Charles said faintly.

'Aye, cheer yourself up with a good joke!' Skelton flourished the paper. 'You write our little contract down here, and then you sign it and I'll sign it, and nobody else need know.' He shook the bottle so that a tiny drop of brandy trickled from the neck right down the side and dripped on to the table.

Charles was mesmerised. 'But I'd have to leave the "for sale" sign up, you know. Bailiffs come else. And this – just a joke. Horse can't sprint. Can't walk.'

'The "for sale" sign stays.' Skelton had seen the state of the departing buyers. He had no worries on that score. With a theatrical flourish, he produced a pen. 'Now, Sir Charles, you can write out the contract just as you like.'

Charles took the pen and in a dazed fashion began to write, his lips moving though no sound came out. He did not finish so much as just stop, and when it was clear he was not going to write any more Skelton seized the paper and read it. The contract rambled a bit. However, it was clear enough, and Skelton's main worry – that Charles's writing would show just how drunk he was – turned out to be needless. The writing was surprisingly steady and firm. The contract would stand up in court. There was just one thing left. 'We'll both need to sign it, Sir Charles.'

'Oh yes. But mustn't sign without reading. Lawyer man once told me.'

'Quite right, Sir Charles, quite right. But you needn't read it again. You wrote it!'

'So I did.'

Skelton signed and handed the pen back to Charles. Charles hesitated. 'I don't – I don't – horse can't walk – last past finishing post, not first –'

Skelton knew better than to press too hard. He put the pen down and held up the bottle. Charles looked at the pen. He looked at the paper. He looked at the bottle. Skelton poured another glass. The nectar glinted. Charles picked up the pen and signed. At once, Skelton took the paper and gave Charles the glass. Furtively slipping the contract into his pocket, the groom poured another glass for himself, and this time, after he had clinked his own glass against Charles's, he downed the whole thing in one.

11

Rose walked into the town. She had never done so before. It only struck her now that she had, in fact, seldom been into the town at all. The journey took her nearly three hours. She was never frightened amidst the wilderness of the moors, but the town frightened her. As she climbed out of the Hartslove valley and dropped into the murky depths of its nearest neighbour, it seemed quite different from the town she thought she remembered. She was certain that when she last came it had been a town of few carriages, with one main square and one or two streets of shops that her mother would have called 'respectable' and Mrs Snipper would have called 'Respectful'. There was not much 'respectful' about the place now. From a mile out, the sides of the road were a spit of hovels from which shoeless children played in the dead air hanging above the sulky canal. Along the towpath, thick-necked horses pulled heavy barges, their drivers idly cursing. On the edge of the town, a factory as big as Hartslove had been constructed entirely of smoke-blackened bricks, and from its roof three slim chimneys thrust themselves into the sky like dirty fingers. Rust clung to the factory's spiked iron railings and narrow, grimy windows offered no view either in or out. Rose knew the factory must make cotton since cotton fibres whitened the gutter, but you would never have guessed that a cloth so pretty could come out of a building so grim.

Men in khaki overalls passed her. They grinned and winked, their clogs clacking on the pavement. After them came a dozen or so navvies, muscles bulging and picks over their shoulders, heading for the site of the new railway station. They whistled. Rose hurried, wishing she had brought a shawl as well as a bonnet. She worried that her shoes were so filthy and her skin so tainted with smoke that she was bound to fail in her mission. She passed another factory just as the bell rang for the dinner break. Small doors in the red brick flew open, and in a great thunderclap of noise a gaggle of girls her own age rushed towards the gate. Their numbers forced Rose to stop and she was glad to give way. To work in such a place must be a miserable servitude from which the bell signalled temporary escape. Only the girls did not look either in servitude or miserable as they jostled and bantered and joked, swinging brightly coloured skirts and tossing off scarves to shake out curled hair. Rose could not understand it at first. Then it struck her. Why should these girls be miserable? They had no fear of the future: they *were* the future, and if you *are* the future, you are also filled with the sheer joy of the present. Instead of pitying them, she began to envy their boisterous independence. Their futures might involve the factory, but they did not rely on hauntings and horses. She pushed through them, both glad and humiliated that her unfashionable, unflattering clothes meant they did not even notice her.

Having asked directions, in a better part of town she found Mr Snaffler's black-painted door with its chiselled bronze plate. She rang the bell at once, praying that Mr Snaffler would answer the door himself, though she knew this was unlikely. Snaffler would not stoop to that. He was in, though. The veterinary cart, its plate matching the door, was outside. She braced herself to speak to a servant who would look her up and down and despise her. In the event, nobody answered the door. Instead Arthur Rose came up behind her and was mortified when he made her jump. 'I'm so very sorry,' he said, jumping himself. 'I coughed but you mustn't have heard me.' He was suspended so uncomfortably between his pleasure at seeing her and his concern at the peculiarity of her coming to call that he forgot to remove his hat. 'Is it Mr Snaffler you want?' He could hardly believe that, but then it was just as impossible that she would want to see him.

Though Rose had rehearsed a dozen times what she was

going to say, she was now completely off balance. 'It's The One,' she garbled, then stopped.

'Go on,' Arthur said.

'He's hurt his knee and—'

'I'm so sorry,' Arthur interrupted.

'You don't need to be sorry about that too,' Rose said, looking straight at him for the first time. 'It wasn't your fault.'

'No,' said Arthur, 'I mean I'm sorry to have kept you on the doorstep. I think you've walked here?' She gave a tiny nod. 'You need to sit. You need tea. You need to dry your shoes.' He opened the door. 'Won't you come in?'

Rose swallowed. 'Mr Snaffler . . .

'Is out,' Arthur said.

'But the cart?'

'*He* goes in a carriage.' Now Arthur smiled and his heart sang when Rose smiled back.

The hallway was filled with creatures, pinned and skinned or stuffed, including three small terriers, their mouths open in an eternal, silent yap. In the corner was propped a ruined stag's head, waiting to be thrown out. 'Oh,' said Rose, feeling slightly sick. 'What a strange advertisement for a vet. Like a doctor filling his hall with corpses.'

Arthur hurried her through. He hated the hall almost as much as he hated Mr Snaffler. He settled Rose in the parlour, then disappeared to bring tea, ignoring Rose's protests that she did not need any. Only when he had lit the fire although it was really very warm, and brought a footstool although her feet were not sore, did she manage to convince him that she needed nothing more. Still, it took some time before he managed to perch on the edge of a chair. 'Now,' he said, picking up his own tea then putting it down then picking it up again, 'The One. You say he's hurt his knee.'

Rose held on to her teacup. 'He tripped on his rope,' she said. 'His knee's swollen. He can't walk. Lily's crying because he's in pain. Daisy's – well, Daisy's collapsed on the stone at the Resting Place.'

'The Resting Place?'

Rose did not feel this was the time to explain. 'I know he's not really The One, but Daisy thinks he is, and Pa does too, although he doesn't know what he thinks at the moment, and if The One's lame, it will make Pa . . .' She tailed off. It was disloyal to talk of her father's drinking. 'It will make Pa sad,' she said finally.

'You want Mr Snaffler to come and look?'

This was the moment Rose had dreaded all the way here. If Mr Snaffler himself was not here, she still needed to say what she came to say. 'Yes,' she said, her voice rigid, 'and though I can't pay with money I can pay in other ways.'

'You mean exchange his services for a rabbit pie or something?' asked Arthur. 'I'm afraid Snaffler doesn't like that kind of thing. He's strictly a money man.'

'No,' said Rose, 'that's not what I mean. Mr Snaffler

once offered to marry me. I've come to tell him I'll do it.'

Arthur's head snapped as though a pistol had gone off. 'Miss Rose –'

'Rose.'

'Rose.' His breath was a rattle.

She spoke quickly. 'The thing is, Mr Snaffler likes me. Or at least he . . .' She had to collect herself. 'Well, anyway. Here I am. I'm making him an offer.'

Arthur sat so still that Rose grew frightened. 'Do you think he'll reject me?'

'Do you love him?'

'Love him?' She was taken aback by the absurdity of the question. 'Of course I don't love him. What's love got to do with it?'

'People marry for love,' said Arthur.

'Only in novels,' Rose replied with as much worldly wisdom as she could muster. Then, more quietly and rather sadly, she said, 'My parents loved each other. It didn't do them much good.' Before she could stop them, words catapulted out. 'Don't you see? I can't sew; I can't sing; I can't teach; I can't dance; I don't think even the factory manager would employ me because I don't know anything about factory work. The only things I know about are Hartslove and the Resting Place and the Dead Girl.' Arthur looked bemused; Rose carried on regardless. 'All I can do is marry, and the only person who's offered is Mr Snaffler, and now we need him because of The One, and though I don't really believe in The One, Daisy does, and it's so important to her, and I can't completely not believe either, because if I don't believe, what's left except Aunt Barbara, and Garth going into the army and coming back like Pa, and I should be able to stop it all, I should, but I can't because *I don't know how.*' She was standing up and panting.

Arthur got up too. 'You'd sell yourself to Snaffler for the price of a vet's visit?' He was shaking.

'It's not selling – it's not,' Rose's blood was up and now she was quite prepared to argue. 'It's a marriage transaction. Fathers make them every day. I'm just making my own. That's all.'

At last she stopped talking, and quite suddenly, without any thought as to the consequences, Arthur took her in his arms and kissed her full on the lips.

For Rose, the kiss was both the last thing and the only thing she needed. After so many months of trying to be brave, something cracked and a torrent of feelings rushed willy-nilly through a floodgate she knew would be better kept closed. However, just for a moment she allowed herself to be swept into the torrent because it was the loveliest thing, to be kissed by Arthur Rose, in whose arms she felt safe, not because he was solid and fatly prosperous like Mr Snaffler, but because with him she was not an older sister or an oldest daughter but just Rose, who was in love.

When Arthur raised his face from hers, he did not let go of her. 'I'll come,' he said.

For a last moment, Rose clung to him. He was her knight! He was her champion! He was going to sweep her up! He was going to save Hartslove! She wanted to fling her arms round his neck and kiss him again. She did not. 'No.' She stumbled over the words. 'We need somebody who can bring medicines.'

'I can get medicines,' Arthur said. He was clinging to the magic of the kiss. He would have promised anything, which was why Rose knew immediately that she must kill the magic completely.

'No, Arthur,' she said. 'You mustn't make promises too dangerous to keep. If Mr Snaffler found you'd been raiding his cupboards, you'd not just lose your job, he'd make sure that no vet within fifty miles would employ you.' She moved back further, hit the sofa and sat down with a bump.

Arthur coughed, then knelt and pretended to be busy with the fire 'There's nothing to stop me visiting The One in my own time,' he said almost as briskly as Rose. 'There's nothing to stop me using my own medicines. I'll be up tomorrow morning.' He put the poker down. 'I've to visit Mrs Pennyfeather's cow first thing. I'll leave home early and come to Hartslove on my way there.'

Rose was in a state of wonderment. From a first kiss to Mrs Pennyfeather's cow in under twenty seconds. She wanted to laugh, then cry. How kind Arthur was. But what advantage she had taken! There was an awkward pause. 'Home?' she ventured, to break it. 'Don't you live here?'

'No. I live in lodgings behind the factory, on Sacramenta Street,' Arthur said, standing up.

'What an odd name for a street,' Rose said.

'I don't know why it's called that.' Arthur fiddled with the poker. He would have kissed Rose again had she given him encouragement. She did not.

'I'd better go home,' she said at last.

'I suppose so,' Arthur agreed, though neither of them moved until they heard carriage wheels. Then both of them shot up. 'Mr Snaffler,' Arthur said quickly. He and Rose faced each other. Without any intention of doing so, Rose clasped Arthur's hands. Arthur clasped hers back. They breathed in unison. 'I don't want to see him,' Rose whispered.

'You never need see him,' Arthur declared with unexpected vehemence. 'I'm going to help you.'

'I don't know why—'

'I'm so glad you came.'

'But you could lose—'

'I can look after myself.' He clasped her hands tighter. They heard Snaffler walking up the path, and with their hands still clasped, Arthur hurried Rose out of the parlour, through the dreadful hall and down the back stairs to the servants' entrance. At the door, he still had her hands. 'Rose?'

'Yes?'

'Rose . . .' he faltered.

'Yes?'

'ROSE?' A roar came from behind.

Rose jumped.

'It's not you he's calling, it's me,' Arthur said quickly. 'Dear Rose, I wish I could take you back home. I don't like to think of you walking alone.'

'ROSE!' came the roar again.

Their hands slid apart. 'I'll be fine,' Rose whispered. 'Thank you.' She ran up the steps. He watched her, his hand still extended. She smiled at him over the railings. 'Arthur,' she said.

'Rose?'

'Until tomorrow.' The words, so ordinary in themselves, seemed to open a whole new world.

She was away only seconds before Snaffler appeared. He glanced suspiciously up the steps. 'What are you doing out here?'

'Coming back in,' said Arthur.

Snaffler grunted and shoved a sack of dead cats at him. 'Work to do.'

Arthur took the sack without comment. After he had laid out the last cat, he closed the door of the dissecting room and reached into the bookshelf. He brought down two books and slipped one inside the other. When Snaffler came to snoop, he found Arthur Rose apparently deep in a text describing uses for cat gut. Arthur worked very late that night. Snaffler thought him a fool, but since there was no payment for extra hours, he did not really care.

12

Rose did not stop to catch her breath until she was above the town, the factory fug a yellowing cloud below her. Then, for ten whole minutes, she stood amidst the crags and the curlews remembering not just Arthur's kiss, but his words and how he looked and how he still had his hand outstretched when they parted. She stretched out her own hand as though Arthur's arm was long enough to reach her here. She was sure that down in Snaffler's basement or in Sacramenta Street he was doing the same. The wind flapped her skirts against her legs and scoured her face. She pulled off her bonnet. How clean the wind was up here! How strong and happy! It was with some regret that she finally put her bonnet back on and half ran along the track worn by generations of packhorses over the long stretch of open moor until it eventually dropped down the gentler slope towards the road that ran in front of the Hartslove gates. She was not tired. It took until she saw the 'for sale' sign for her spirits to droop. She averted her eyes and hurried on. Daisy was no longer on the flat stone. Hugging her happiness to her like a guilty secret, Rose hurried across the drawbridge and courtyard. The Dead Girl had not gone back to their father's passage. She was watching from a window outside their mother's room. Rose waved.

It was late afternoon now and the light was fading. Garth and the others were still in the dining room, though lunch had finished hours before. Nobody had eaten anything and Mrs Snipper had long since collected the plates. Yet still they sat. Mrs Snipper greeted Rose in the hall. 'A right carry-on,' she observed tartly. 'The Master's nowhere to be seen; Miss Lily's been crying that you've Gone Off like her ladyship; Miss Daisy wouldn't even look at my pie because she says she's Ruined That Horse and Master Garth's spent the whole of luncheon with his head between his heels.'

Rose threw down her bonnet. 'I'm sorry,' she said. 'I've been to the town.'

Mrs Snipper gave her a sidelong look. 'Oh yes? Visiting?'

'I've been – I've been to the vet.'

'And the vet's going to come, is he?' Mrs Snipper did not ask which vet because she already knew very well, as Rose could tell. Mrs Snipper's beady eyes missed nothing.

'Yes,' Rose said. 'He's going to come, Mrs Snips. He wants to make The One better.' Two red dots appeared in her cheeks.

'Of course he does,' Mrs Snipper said, noting the dots.

'Let's thank Sweet Jesus and His Mother for that.' She scurried over to the lift, got in with the trolley, shut the door and cranked the handle to descend. 'Coming to make The One better indeed.' As the lift lurched down, she wiped her nose on her apron. In the kitchen, Snipe was perched on his stool. Mrs Snipper opened the lift door, bundled out and piled the plates into the sink before taking a big spoon and shovelling a great quantity of what looked like brown sludge but was in fact venison stew into a basin. She covered it and held it out to her son. 'Take this to that young veterinarian. It'll do for his supper.' Her nose twitched. 'And take him some rose-petal jelly. Yes, that's it. Rose-petal Jelly. They stock it at Pumphrey's grocers and they won't miss a jar. Don't get caught, mind. Old Pumphrey wouldn't think twice about sending you to Australia on a transport.'

Snipe made a careful exit through the range. Jelly. He'd never thought of that. If Pumphreys stocked a jelly of rose-petals, why not lily-petals? He'd take a jar of that as well.

Lily sprang up when she heard Rose's voice. 'Rose! Rose! We didn't know where you'd gone!'

Rose sat down under her mother's portrait. 'Arthur Rose is going to come to see The One,' she announced.

'Oh, thank goodness!' Lily's eyes brimmed over. 'Thank goodness.'

'Hurrah!' Clover and Columbine banged spoons on the table.

Garth lowered his feet to the floor and did three cartwheels for Daisy's sake.

Only Daisy seemed unmoved. 'How will we pay him?' Her voice was low and tired. 'What shall we sell?'

'Nothing,' said Rose, sweeping crumbs off the table.

Clover and Columbine swung wildly on their chairs. Rose was bossy and snarky and they did not always like her, but she was something solid in the shifting sea of their lives, and their relief at her return made them tease. 'We've been reading a book where the girl sells herself. How much do you suppose you get if you do that? The book never says. How much would you be worth, Rose?'

Rose blushed. 'You shouldn't read such rubbish.'

Clover and Columbine were astonished. They had expected a bigger eruption. Emboldened, they had a more genuine enquiry. 'What do you do if you sell yourself?'

'I've no idea,' Rose lied.

'You must know, Rose. You're almost grown up and you know everything.'

'Well, I don't know that,' Rose said mildly.

A thin thread of anxiety snaked through the twins' relief. If Rose was being nice, she must be ill.

Garth was spinning like a top, a trick he had learned from a troupe of travelling dancers one Christmas. Daisy usually loved it but now she did not notice. He stopped spinning. 'If you sell yourself, you do something unspeakable,' he said.

'How do you speak about something unspeakable?'

Even in their anxiety, Clover and Columbine were very amused.

'That's the thing,' Garth said darkly. 'When you do something unspeakable, you can't talk about it so it just rots you from top to bottom until you're a pile of stinking—'

'For goodness sake, Garth!' Rose gripped the table. 'I haven't done anything either speakable or unspeakable. I simply asked Arthur – I mean Mr Rose – if he would come, and he said he would.' To the twins' relief, her voice was more familiarly sharp, though she still looked as though she had found the first peach of summer.

The doorbell clanged. They all tensed. More prospective purchasers! Were they never to be safe again? They hurried to the hall, where they found two sisters-in-law with faces like frogs. 'How many bedrooms? We have fifteen small children between us,' was the ladies' opening remark.

'Fifteen children when you're so ugly? Now that's unspeakable,' Clover or Columbine whispered to the other.

It was not difficult to frighten these two creatures, for they were as thin as storks and nervy as hares. Their eyes popped when Mrs Snipper snapped down the lid of the teapot. Their hands quivered when a log shifted in the fire. Rose felt cruel as she provided the 'I don't see anyone' commentary whilst her sisters – all except Daisy, who was too dispirited to do anything – silently crowded round.

It was Garth who provided the spectacle that finally sent the two grasshoppers flying back to their carriage. Leaving the others, he went upstairs, wrapped the Cannibal's skin round himself, then slid, quite blind and at breakneck speed, right from the very top of the curling stairwell to the bottom, growling all the way. It was a new trick, and one he had been contemplating for some days. This was not like flipping over and over on the battlements. There, he could calculate and concentrate, in complete control of his body. On the curling banister, however, unable to see, unable to hear, unable to steer, he relied entirely on instinct to follow the twists. If he overbalanced, the drop on to the flags would not maim him: it would kill him. Without quite knowing why, Garth suddenly wanted – no, he really *needed* – to see if he could actually do it.

It had been hard to get properly balanced in the Cannibal; harder still to let go. The speed was ghastly, the blindness worse. His bowels were mush, his stomach liquid. He controlled his panic, though, and in the clammy, suffocating, rushing dark, with only a dead bear's skin between his warm, living body and the cold, hard flagstones, he kept his head.

The bear's monstrous and unexpected appearance – jaws agape, glass eyeballs winking – electrified them all. The skinny sisters, emitting gulping whistles, were out of the door before the bear roared over the final finial and crashed heavily on to the floor with an openly exultant Garth tumbling out.

His sisters stood for a second, hardly able to believe their eyes. Rose was first off the mark. 'Garth! You *idiot*!! *You absolute imbecilic idiotic idiot!* You could have been killed.' She seized him and shook him so hard he thought his head might come right off. 'Good God, Garth! Good God!' She felt quite sick. She did not know how she would ever stop shaking him.

'But I wasn't killed,' sang Garth as his head rocked back and forth. 'I did it!' His heart was beating like fury. He had not felt this good since drinking the brandy the day The One arrived.

Rose shook him even harder. 'Promise that you'll never, *ever* do that again. You *must* promise!'

Garth would promise nothing of the sort. 'I did it! I did it!' he sang. Clover and Columbine, now sitting on the Cannibal, echoed his song. 'Well done, Garth! Well done, Garth!' Their brother was the bravest person they knew. He was a hero!

'Shut up, you two!' shouted Rose, pushing Garth away for fear of doing him damage. The bear sagged, vicious eyes still winking. Rose forced herself to be calm. 'I can't believe you! Carry the Cannibal back at once before Pa misses him, and I forbid you – any of you –' she glared at the twins – 'ever to touch that horrible thing again.'

'Pa won't miss him. He'll be drunk,' Garth said, swaggering round the hall, still sparkling with the adrenalin rush. He pretended to dance with the Furious Boy.

Rose stamped her foot. All she could see was Garth lying

bloodied and broken on the flagstones. The joy of Arthur was gone. She hated Garth for that. 'Put the Cannibal back right now,' she ordered again.

Lily was staring up at the top of the banister, curled high above. 'How did you dare?' she whispered, her cheeks ghost-white. 'You could have been smashed to smithereens.'

'I dared, and I did it,' Garth said, whirling Lily round. 'I didn't mean to scare you. I'm fine, Lily. Really.'

The clock chimed six. Daisy appeared. 'I'm going to the stables to hose The One's knee again,' she said, glancing at the Cannibal. 'What's happened?'

'Doesn't matter,' said Garth. 'Don't worry, Rose. I don't have to do it again.'

To his surprise, Rose was crying. 'Why did you have to do it at all?' she sobbed. 'If something happened to you, Garth, I couldn't bear it.'

Garth stopped dancing. It had never before struck him that Rose cared.

Daisy, still unsure exactly what had occurred, discovered her crutches under the Furious Boy's arms and was already out of the front door. Rose steadied herself and followed with the others. 'I'll put the Cannibal back,' Garth called after them. 'I'll catch you up.'

When they had gone, he dragged the heavy skin back up the stairs. It took a little time, and when he'd deposited it in the proper place, he sat for a moment on the bear's hairy back and relived the madness. He could feel the sweat growing clammy on his forehead. *Nothing could be more frightening than what I've just done*, he thought exultantly to himself. *Nothing*. Yet a little voice still nagged. *Nothing, of course, except riding a horse. You'd still not dare to do that.* 'Shut up! Shut up!' Garth cried. 'What does riding a horse matter when I've ridden the Cannibal?' He ran to the stables and the voice diminished, though however hard he tried to ignore it, it refused to vanish entirely.

13

Arthur Rose's cob was standing patiently in the Hartslove yard before seven o'clock the following morning. It was barely light, but already the young vet's nimble hands were soothing and flattening The One's knee with liniments and cooling lotions. Rose, Lily, Daisy, Clover and Columbine formed a silent audience. 'You're his nurse, Miss Daisy,' Arthur said. 'I know you'll do everything that's needed.' Daisy gave a wan smile as Arthur issued instructions and waited for Skelton, who hovered, to object. However, instead of blustering or skulking, the groom listened carefully. He seemed as anxious as Daisy that the horse should recover, and although The One clearly disliked Skelton, Daisy was grateful. She could not do everything alone.

Arthur fiddled with his cob's reins, preparing to leave. Finally, he screwed up his courage. 'Any buyers for the castle?'

The children exchanged glances. 'Not at the moment, and perhaps never. Perhaps The One'll recover and win his race. Then the "for sale" sign can go,' Rose said in determined tones.

'Don't be silly, Rose,' whispered Daisy.

'I'm not being silly,' Rose said. 'It's possible, isn't it, Arthur – I mean, Mr Rose?'

Arthur fiddled with his reins some more. 'It's possible,' he said, and tried to smile. In truth, the prospect, however unlikely, filled him with gloom. If the de Granville fortunes changed for whatever reason, Rose would go to London. She would have wealthy suitors. There would be a society wedding. Arthur might get an invitation, but he would not be the bridegroom. 'I hope everything works out for you,' he said in the more formal tones he used for other clients.

Rose, hearing nothing but the hopeful beating of her heart, gave him a brilliant smile, and Arthur captured it and treasured it as you treasure something that will not be yours for long.

Daisy, who could not stop apologising to The One for having been the cause of his misfortune, packed the lotions into a basket. 'I don't think Mr Snaffler knows that Mr Rose has been here,' she said to Skelton. Skelton tapped his nose conspiratorially.

The One himself was confused. His knee still hurt, but since it now smelt of liniment rather than of himself, he viewed his whole leg as an odd, rather inconvenient appendage. When he tried to walk, he was very surprised to find that it came with him. 'We'll put down extra straw,' Skelton said after Arthur had gone.

'How can we get extra?' Daisy burst out. She knew the straw merchant would not bring more without money.

'Don't you worry about that, missy,' Skelton said. 'Old Skelton will sort it out.'

And sort it out he did, as well as doing more than his share of tending, hosing and bandaging over the following fortnight. It was only when, after three weeks, the knee was still not right that he grew impatient, and one morning Daisy found him actually berating the horse for still being lame. Skelton jumped when he realised Daisy was listening. 'Just telling him to try harder,' he said with an oily smile. After that, he was more careful.

By Arthur's sixth or seventh visit the knee was still stiff. 'It's no good, is it?' Daisy said. 'He's ruined.' She was done crying. The One had forgiven her, but she would never forgive herself.

'He's not ruined,' Arthur said. 'I think he'll mend.'

A flash in Daisy's eyes. Then gloom again. She could not say that she did not believe Arthur without being rude, so she just said, 'Never in time, though.'

'When's his first race?' Arthur shook up a new lotion he had brought.

'We were going to run him first in the Two Thousand

Guineas at Newmarket. That would be his Derby trial. It's on May the eleventh,' Daisy said. 'That would have given him time to travel to Epsom and recover before the Derby itself on the twenty-ninth.'

Arthur straightened. 'And we're now at the end of February.' He stood back in contemplation. 'You know,' he said, with some puzzlement, 'in injury terms, The One's really been quite fortunate.'

'Fortunate?' Daisy was shocked.

'I don't mean fortunate to be injured,' said Arthur hastily, 'just that the injury itself is an almost textbook case of being bad enough to lame but not bad enough for any long-term harm. If he had to be injured, this one has been pretty well judged.' He felt the knee again. 'It is a puzzle as to how he did it.'

'I let him go.'

'Yes, but . . . ' He stopped. Conjecture was not helping. He gazed at Daisy quite straight. 'Miss Daisy, when I say that the horse could be fit, I'm not saying it to make you feel better. I know I'm still in the middle of my training, but that's my professional opinion.'

Had Daisy looked at Skelton at that moment, she would have seen his thick features shiver with relief, for although Charles's contract was watertight and safe, he had begun to wonder whether his blow to The One's knee had been as brilliantly calculated as he imagined. But Daisy was glued to Arthur's face. She was trying to believe him. And there was something else. 'It's not just a question of getting him fit,' she said slowly. 'It's a question of breaking him in. I know he's three, but nobody's ever ridden him. Even if we could ride him tomorrow, there's too little time.' She swallowed the lump in her throat and stroked The One's ears. 'So thank you for what you're doing, but I really think it's impossible.'

'Nothing's impossible,' came Garth's voice. He had been sitting on the stable roof, as he often did when Arthur came, watching Daisy's face. He could not bear to see her so low. He vaulted lightly down and landed on his hands. 'When do you think he'll be better?'

Arthur pursed his lips. 'Another fortnight?' he suggested. 'We'll know for certain by then.' Despite herself, hope sparked in Daisy's eyes. 'I'm not saying that he will be better,' Arthur said, suddenly nervous of his own judgement. 'I'm just saying that you shouldn't give up.'

Garth lowered his feet to the ground and wiped his hands on his shirt. 'If he was better in a fortnight, you'd still have time, Daisy,' he said.

'That's right,' said Arthur, bolstered by Garth's optimism. 'Are you going to ride him?' he asked Garth. Daisy bit her lip. She did not dare look at Garth. How could Arthur know about her brother's terrors?

Because he was looking at the horse, Arthur noticed nothing and pressed on. 'You're perfect, Master Garth! Light and agile, plus by Derby Day you'd know the horse inside out. There couldn't be a better jockey.' Garth curved backwards to hide his face. Arthur walked round The One with mounting excitement. 'Of course, it's not often done, a complete amateur riding in such important races as the Two Thousand Guineas and the Derby, but there's no reason why you shouldn't. No reason at all.'

He looked round. Garth had vanished. 'Oh!' Arthur frowned. 'Did I say something wrong, Miss Daisy? If I did, I'm so sorry.'

'It doesn't matter,' Daisy said.

Arthur gathered up his things. 'Don't give up hope.'

'I won't,' Daisy said. When Arthur had gone, she hoped Garth would come back but he did not. She straightened the horse's rug and rubbed her nose against his neck. She loved the smell of him. 'Shall we hope?' she asked him. 'Shall we really?' He snuffled softly. It could have been yes. It could have been no. She saw he had rubbed some of his tail hairs off on a splinter. She collected the hairs and made herself a bracelet. 'A red circle of hope,' she murmured. The One was more interested in his hay.

As soon as Daisy returned to the castle, she went to Garth's room. He would not answer her knock. Tentatively, she tried the door. It was locked. Daisy twisted her bracelet and called his name. She wanted to tell him – tell him what? That he need not even think of riding The One? How exactly would that help? She realised she was glad he had not answered. She went away.

Garth heard her go. He was slouched on the floor, the delight of the Cannibal ride stripped away. Arthur's words, so kindly meant, had set off the nagging voice again, and this time Garth could not silence it. The air-ballets amidst the ruins were nothing. The flipping over the battlements was nothing. The Cannibal ride was nothing, nothing, nothing. None of these things was worth anything if he could not conquer the one fear he could not face. He would never be able to ride a horse. He could hear his own voice in chorus with the nagging voice. *You coward. Coward. Coward. Coward. Coward.*

He felt under his bed until his fingers curled around something smooth and cool. Despite what he had told Daisy, he had not thrown his father's pistol into the moat. It had killed Gryffed, yet he had found he wanted to hold it, to keep it. He could not understand why. Perhaps it was because it was his father's. Perhaps it was the weapon itself: the weight; the cold barrel; the intricate mechanism that doled out death with a bang and a puff. He drew it out and balanced it in his hand. He knew there was a bullet left in it. He did not know whether the safety catch was on or off. He pressed the stock against his cheek. What if the horse did recover? If it did, he could neither ride it nor say he could not ride it. Both were impossible. He doubted even Daisy knew the full extent of his fear, and his acrobatics meant that the others, who never thought about it, actually reckoned him brave. They would despise him if it ever became clear that he could not do the one thing they really needed him to do, and for no other reason than he was scared to death. He stared unblinking at the gun. Only when he was sure that Daisy was not waiting in the passage did he slink out of his room. Furtively, he climbed the spiral stair and opened the door to the roof. He shivered and made his way to the ruins.

Snipe was mending the roof above Lily's room with lead he had stolen from a church guttering – not from Father Nameless's church, of course, but from a church in the town whose vicar set snares which Snipe regularly emptied. He froze when Garth appeared. Snipe did not wish to know others' business and did not wish others to know his. He could, however, sense something about Garth that made him leave his work and follow him.

Garth stood for a long time on the very edge of the ruins. He was quite calm. More than calm. He was pleased – happy even – because what he was about to do made the flipping and the Cannibal ride pale into insignificance, which was precisely the point. If he could do what he intended to do, then at last everything would be different. Even riding would seem easy. He breathed slowly and made himself go through all the stages. It was cheating to do things blind. First, he would focus on the Resting Place. Second, he would place the barrel of the gun against his forehead. Third, he would pull the trigger. If the bullet was in the firing chamber, a hole would be punched through his head. He would fall but he would not know it because he would be dead. If the bullet was not in the firing chamber, he would never be frightened of anything again.

He focused. He put the barrel to his forehead. He frowned just once. He pulled the trigger. He never saw Snipe springing forward as the gun went off. He did hear a crack. He did see smoke billow out. He never saw the bullet bury itself in the lead of the north-west wing. When Garth realised he was still standing, he dropped the gun. Then he dropped to his knees. He was not just shaking. He was not just dizzy. He was actually rattling: bones, teeth, brain, nails, even the hairs on his head. Not an atom of him was still, or perhaps everything was still and it was the world that was shaking. Whatever. He had done it. He had actually done it. He had held a primed gun to his own head and pulled the trigger. He did not ask himself what had happened after. All he knew was that he had held the gun steady and that the glow beginning to rise from his toes was a hundred times more powerful than the glow from flipping over the ruins, a thousand times more powerful than the glow from the bottle of his father's brandy, and a million times more powerful than the glow from the Cannibal. He really did feel ready for anything. He picked up the gun, held it to the sky, then hurled it as hard as he could into the bottom of the moat.

*

Daisy was unsure about many things, but as she hosed The One's knee the following day, of one thing she was absolutely certain: though she loved Garth dearly and never wanted to crush his dreams, in the unlikely event that The One did get better in time, Garth could not ride him. If The One made it to the racetrack, Garth could not spoil his chances. She concentrated hard on the hosing, not wanting anything to show in her face. Garth was walking round the yard in a crab, much to The One's amusement. 'I know what you're thinking,' he said, and Daisy blushed, 'but it'll be fine. I rode inside the Cannibal down the spiral stair. If I can do that, I can do anything.' He would never, ever tell her about the gun.

'That was different, Garth.'

'How different?'

'You know how different. The Cannibal's a dead bear, not a living horse,' said Daisy shortly. She turned the hose off, cleaned a bone comb and began to tidy up The One's mane. The One tossed his head as she teased out the long tangles.

'You weren't there, Daisy,' Garth said. 'Really, I rode the Cannibal to test myself, and I passed the test. Don't you believe me?'

'I believe you,' Daisy said, tugging at the ripples, 'but –'

She was all prepared for Garth to lose his temper. Instead he put his hands on her shoulders and made her face him. 'I can do this,' he said in a tone half grave, half pleading. 'I can.'

It was impossible to turn him down. And anyway, Daisy thought glumly, it probably didn't matter. The One would most likely never run, so Garth would never ride. It was not much comfort, but it was all she had.

Rose was also glum. She did want The One to get better – of course she did – but his recovery would be the end of her meeting Arthur at the Hartslove gates, as she had taken to doing, and walking with him along the track over the moor. When he had first found her waiting, Arthur tried to thank her for the food he regularly found on his kitchen table. Rose denied any knowledge, but she knew Arthur did not believe her. They made a curious couple, often walking without talking, as though they knew each other too well for words. Nor, when they parted, did Arthur kiss her. Rose was at first disappointed by this. Yet as she watched Arthur's cob's tail swing away, she felt that within the space left by Arthur's restraint, her love was growing stronger. When Arthur told her that it should be clear in another week whether or not The One was sound, her heart sank.

The week was filled with hosing and very gentle walking. Though Daisy tried to suppress her hopes – and refused to think about Garth – hope would spring up, particularly as The One's leg began to look normal again. Towards the end of the week, she even put on the saddle and did up the girth. The One stood like a rock. Daisy had taught him well.

Skelton was busy too. He showed Daisy how, through vigorous massaging of neck and haunch, she could begin to build the muscles The One would need if he was to run his fastest. At first Daisy was nervous, but The One seemed to enjoy her attentions, and when she finished, particularly if Skelton was nearby, the horse would edge so close to her that you could not fit a piece of paper between them. 'You're a very forgiving The One,' Daisy murmured to him, pressing her cheek to his. Skelton smiled secretly.

Garth came to the stables every day, half hoping for a relapse. Though he knew Daisy preferred to be on her own, she was welcoming. So much was unspoken between them that for the first time they were awkward with each other.

The weather turned. For two days there was no frost, and with all the grooming The One's winter coat loosened and his colour deepened into molten copper. Only when Daisy tried to thin his mane, forelock and tail did he object, thrusting his gawky head high and curling his top lip in disgust until Garth devised a tumbling and juggling routine that the horse followed, goggle-eyed, whilst Daisy tugged and pulled. At last his mane flowed down his neck in a smooth wave instead of sprouting like a wire brush, and his tail, always too long and full for elegance, no longer trailed after him like a hedge full of birds' nests, though he still did not look much like a racehorse.

To all this, Charles was a ghostly spectator, kept as such by Skelton who always made sure there was an uncorked bottle of brandy or wine beside his open window. If Charles could be kept completely drunk until Derby Day, he would barely remember the 'joke'. Skelton also made certain that it was he who reported to Charles on the horse's progress, and he was careful how he did it. 'Ah, Sir Charles,' he sighed, 'what special children you have. Though they know the horse is really finished, they still cluster round him. They want to make him feel wanted.' A strategic pause. 'I hope you don't mind, but I've made an arrangement with the young vet that he should tend to the horse, and perhaps even pronounce him recovered – just to allow the children a little hope, do you see? I mean, without hope, what has poor Miss Daisy got left in her life? Best allow the girl her dreams. Can't do any harm.' Charles nodded and took another drink. Skelton was a good man to be bothered about the children, and he was obviously paying the vet from his own pocket. 'Thank you, Skelton,' he said.

'It's a pleasure, Sir Charles,' Skelton replied.

On the first day of April, the waiting was over. 'Arthur's going to get The One to trot today,' said Daisy at breakfast. Nobody said, 'On April Fool's Day?' but everybody was thinking it.

'Pa should be there,' Daisy said. They all avoided each other's eyes. Somebody would have to tell him, because their father no longer came to meals, and when he did they wished he would not: they found him pitiful and they did not want to pity him. 'Who'll fetch him?'

'Pa's lost interest,' Rose said in the end.

'Pa's not well,' said Lily loyally.

'Pa's drunk from morning until night,' Garth said bluntly. 'I don't know where he gets the drink from. Does anybody?'

'The cellar?' said Rose

'The cellar's empty.'

The conversation stuttered to a halt. Nobody volunteered.

After breakfast, Daisy found her crutches waiting for her by the front door. She went straight to the stables. The One greeted her with a whinny. It was raining, so Daisy kept him inside. For about the hundred and fiftieth time, she put the saddle on and tightened the girth. The One took no notice. He was watching Garth, who was now perched on the top of the door. Daisy bent and touched The One's knee. 'Do you think he's really better? I just can't tell.'

Garth dropped into the stable. 'He seems fine to me.'

Skelton appeared. The One snorted and laid back his ears. 'Young vet been?'

'Not yet,' Daisy said.

'I'm quite sure the horse is better,' Skelton said crisply. 'It wasn't that much of a blow.'

'That's not what you said at the time,' Garth pointed out.

'I said what I thought,' Skelton replied without missing a beat.

'And you really think he's better?' Daisy asked.

Skelton shrugged. 'Got my fingers crossed, like you,' he said. He was not lying.

The day dragged. By the time Arthur came, Skelton was back in his house and the rain had settled to a steady downpour. Arthur was flustered. 'I'm sorry,' he said, vaulting off his cob, his hat brim dripping. 'Mr Snaffler kept me back to try to save a lady's canary. Shall we get The One out?'

Daisy nodded. She had been waiting all day, yet now that Arthur was here she suddenly wished he was not. She began to gabble. 'Was it the lady's favourite pet? It must be hard to make a canary better.'

Arthur gave an unusually waspish laugh. 'It's more that the owner's a favourite client,' he said. 'The bird can't be saved, but the lady's paying good money to find that out.' He was angry, Daisy could see. Her heart sank. She found it difficult to fasten the head-collar buckle. 'You should put your horse in the barn,' she said. 'He won't like getting wet.'

Arthur shook his head. 'I can't stay long. Mr Snaffler thinks I've gone to the apothecary for something.'

'Perhaps you'd like to come back another time?' Daisy suggested quickly.

Arthur came into the stable and took off his hat. 'No,' he said. 'I said I'd make my decision today and that's what I shall do. Let's see now.' He patted The One and bent over the knee.

Daisy moved away. Garth stood with her.

Skelton reappeared. 'So, what's what?' he barked.

Arthur ran his fingers very slowly from The One's shoulder, right over his knee and down to his fetlock. Lastly, he picked up the foot and flexed the knee joint, feeling and listening to everything his hands were telling him. He pulled the leg forward, making it stick out straight. 'Is he walking any better?'

'He's not limping,' Daisy said, 'though we haven't let him go far.'

Arthur put the foot down. 'Open the door,' he said to Skelton. Skelton opened it. Arthur began to strip off The One's rug. 'Goodness,' he said with some admiration. 'He looks a picture.' Daisy hardly heard. 'Now,' Arthur said, 'take him out and run to the far gate so that he has to trot beside you.'

'Trot straight away?' Daisy was disconcerted. 'I don't know.'

'He needs a proper test,' said Arthur gently.

'No – I mean yes – I mean –' Daisy gestured at her legs. 'I mean I can't trot.'

Arthur could have kicked himself. Garth took hold of the rope. 'I can.'

Passing Skelton, The One shied, then sauntered along shaking raindrops out of his forelock. Sauntering was no good. 'He needs to trot,' Arthur said.

'Get on!' came a great shout from Skelton. He could

not disguise his anxiety. 'Get on, horse, and show us what you're made of.' He cracked an old lash.

The One's head flew up. For a moment, Garth was off his feet, dangling on the end of the rope, then he was running and The One was trotting, though not properly, and they were at the far side of the yard. The rain streamed down. The cobbles were awash. The One whipped round and trotted back in a more orderly fashion.

Arthur, soaked through, had his hands on his hips. 'Go again,' he said.

Garth pushed The One round. The horse did not want to go again. He did not like the rain. He wanted Daisy and he wanted to be back inside his stable. 'Get on with you!' cried Skelton and cracked the lash.

The One baulked and set off at a hand canter. Garth was again swept off his feet. 'Slowly,' Arthur and Daisy cried together. 'Slowly!'

All Daisy could see was history repeating itself. 'Please, oh please, The One! Go slowly! Garth! Don't let go!'

The One returned. Arthur was not yet satisfied. 'Once more,' he said.

Garth set off again, and this time The One trotted, flinging his legs out as though he were a dancer. When he got to the gate, he turned smartly round and not even God could have prevented him from trotting, at speed, straight back into his stable. Arthur followed him in and closed the door. 'Well, I never,' he said.

'It's bad news, isn't it?' Daisy said. She sat down heavily. 'He's not right.'

'My dear Miss Daisy –' Arthur was beaming – 'he's sound! At least, so far as I can see.' He heard Daisy choke.

'You made him go three times.'

'I always make horses go three times,' Arthur said. 'That's the best way to be sure. Now, as you know, a mended knee is always weaker than a knee that's never been broken, but as I've said before, this injury was strange, so we can be very hopeful.'

'We can ride him?'

Arthur grinned at both Daisy and Garth. 'You can ride him.' He pulled his sodden hat back on. 'Build up the pace slowly, though, and don't gallop too soon. Now I must rush.' He was back on his cob before his smile became sadder. His work here was ended. He wondered if Rose would be waiting by the gate in this rain. He was halfway down the drive before he heard somebody calling. Daisy was swinging on her crutches, her skirt dragging. She caught his stirrup and he could see that her dream was thoroughly alive again. He almost said, 'Hope is one thing, but dreams are something else,' but she spoke first. 'When we're in the winners' enclosure, promise you'll be there too.'

'Miss Daisy—' Arthur began.

'Just say you'll be there.' She shook the rain off. She was laughing.

He had never heard her laugh before. 'If The One wins, you'll have important people to speak to.'

'Who could be more important than you?' Daisy's whole face was alight. 'You've made The One better!'

She was irresistible. 'I'll be there,' he said. She let go and swung back up the drive.

He found Rose half drowned. 'Well?' she asked, knotting her hands.

'It's my last visit,' he said.

'Oh.' She did not have to explain the guilty disappointment in her voice. They began to walk, and though the rain never ceased they walked slower and slower so that by the time Arthur returned to the surgery, the canary was dead and buried and Mr Snaffler was so angry he cut a shilling from Arthur's wages.

14

'I can't! I can't!'

It was four days later. The rain had stopped at last and Garth, Daisy and The One were at the Resting Place in the haze of a promising dawn. The One was saddled and bridled and attached to Daisy by a long rope. She had been teaching the horse to walk and trot at her command, and now, since Garth had made it impossible for Daisy to refuse him without a permanent breach between them, something Daisy knew she could not bear, not for anything, it was time for Garth to get on. For nearly an hour he had been perched on the top of one of the tombstones. It was impossible, it was intolerable, yet it was horribly, shamingly true that despite the acrobatics, despite the Cannibal, *despite the gun*, at the last moment before mounting, he found his mouth still filling with fear and, worse, his legs refusing to spring. He could not mount. His fear drained all his strength. Sweat ran down his back.

'I've got him,' urged Daisy. 'He can't go anywhere.' She was having a hard job holding The One. The horse was jittery and excited at no longer being cooped up in the yard. He could smell the wind. His legs itched to stretch. 'Just lean over the saddle so that he can feel your weight,' Daisy instructed. 'You don't have to put a leg over.'

Garth took a deep breath. 'OK. Bring him close again.'

Daisy brought The One close, murmuring all the time. 'You talk to him,' she said to Garth. 'He knows your voice.'

Garth tried to speak and failed. The horse he knew so well from the ground was a foreign beast from this higher angle. Garth's terrors taunted him. *You'll never conquer us, coward boy! Not even when you're dead!* His skin was grey as the dawn.

Daisy brought the horse closer. She saw how Garth was. Soothing the horse, she walked him away again. 'Calm, The One,' she said, 'just be calm.' He still nudged and jogged, unable to understand what Daisy wanted of him. She let him out on the long rein and allowed him to put his head down. The sight of him grazing might be reassuring to Garth, but The One did not want to graze; he longed to be moving and Daisy found herself dragged about.

Garth set his face. 'I'll try again.'

Daisy nodded. 'Just a quick slither over his back, then off again. That'll be enough for today.' It would not be enough. Both she and Garth knew that. They had thirty-eight days to prepare the horse for something that normally took at least a year's steady work. She gathered the rope and walked The One back to the tombstone. 'Now,' she said. Garth took a breath and prepared. He was going to do it. He really was. He bunched up, ready to spring. The One shook himself. Garth's mouth filled again and his stomach turned. The horse was huge. Should he choose to misbehave, he was uncontrollable. Garth would fall off and break his back and be even more crippled than Daisy. *Silly! Silly!* Garth shouted silently. Millions of people rode every day without harm. Most of them were not brave at all. And he was brave. He was braver than most. He could do it. He would do it. He got halfway across the saddle, then The One jinxed at something in the chestnut tree and Garth crashed on to the grass. *You see! Uncontrollable!* Garth knew then that he was lost. He longed to explain to Daisy – *My fear's like a pit! Don't you see? I keep thinking I've leaped over it, but I never make it to the other side.* He said nothing.

Daisy kept all expression out of her voice. 'You'll manage tomorrow.' They walked back to the stables.

'Success?' asked Skelton. He knew the answer because he had been watching. He was desperate to interfere but Daisy did not want him anywhere near and he could not risk her complaining to Charles. Charles must be kept away from the horse, lest even in his drunken state he smelled a rat. Only if Daisy herself asked could Skelton help. Surely, surely she would have to soon?

'Success,' lied Daisy, though she knew perfectly well

that Skelton had seen everything. She was surprised when he did not contradict her. Perhaps Skelton was learning to be nicer. It was not impossible.

The next day Garth still did not manage, and after three failed attempts ran back to the castle, sick with humiliation and self-loathing. Daisy started after him, dragging The One behind her. 'Go away!' Garth's cry was half strangled. 'Go away!'

With tears of pity and frustration rolling down her cheeks, Daisy took The One back to the Resting Place. Why did Garth feel he must ride? She did not care if he did or he didn't. She only cared that he was so unhappy and that time was ticking away. She leaned against the chestnut tree. The One fidgeted, grew bored and began to pull at the newly forming buds. After a while, Daisy moved to one of the tombstones. Thirty-seven days until the Two Thousand Guineas. If The One did not run in that, he could not run in the Derby. During this thirty-seven days, then, not only must the horse be ridden and his pace worked up to a gallop, they also had to get him to Newmarket, where the Two Thousand Guineas would take place. That was nearly two hundred miles. If they walked The One twenty miles a day, the journey would take ten days not including any rest along the way. That left twenty-seven days of preparation. She faced the inevitable with a sinking heart: she would have to ask Skelton for help.

She whispered The One's name. He blew on her hair.

The stirrups were down, the saddle empty. Daisy gazed at it. She gazed and gazed. She had not been on a horse since her accident. Everybody said it was too dangerous. It was also completely impractical. Yet the saddle was so empty, so inviting. No. Stupid. They could not afford another accident. Yet, yet. The saddle glinted. She hauled herself on to the tombstone. The One stood like a rock. She would just lean over the saddle. Where was the harm in that? Even from the height of the tombstone, the horse's back was too high for her. To lean across she would have to jump, and that she could not do. She was going to climb down. But there was the stirrup, gleaming. She only had to put her foot in it and she would have a step. She touched it with her toe. The One remained still. *Perhaps my foot won't fit into the stirrup*, Daisy thought. *After all, callipers are broader than a boot.* Her foot slid in. All she had to do was push up and she would be able to lean over the saddle. Just a little push. But if she pushed off from the tombstone, she would be suspended in the air with nothing solid to lean on except the horse. She slid her foot out. She took a jagged breath. The One shifted. 'If you move even one inch I shall fall,' she said. The One flicked his ears. He was standing four square. Daisy's foot crept back into the stirrup. Without allowing herself to think any more, she pushed. Now she was stranded, so there was nothing else to do but bend over the saddle, stomach hard against the slippery leather. She felt like a sack of potatoes, face down, her head dangling somewhere near the offside stirrup, her hair all flopped over and tickling her nose. Unused to the weight, The One braced and remained still only because he saw something interesting in the chestnut tree's branches. From above, Snipe was a silent observer.

Daisy had no hold of the reins. She was not well balanced. There was nothing to stop The One from galloping or even jumping the fence at the bottom of the park if he chose. She did not know whether to breathe or not. The One walked off. The stirrup began to bang against her head. It hurt, and her foolishness hit her as hard as the steel. She scrunched her eyes shut so that she could not see the ground. She had no idea how she would stay on. Was it better to fall on to her crippled legs or her head? Her heart thumped in her ears. Soon The One would trot. Worse than anything else, she had let go of the rope. He was going to stand on it and lame himself again. She wished, uselessly and frantically, that she was back on the tombstone.

The One carried on walking, and through the thumping in her ears Daisy heard a whispering. At first she thought it was The One's hooves on the grass. Then there was a word. 'Steady,' the whisperer repeated, just that one word again and again in a sing-song. 'Steady.'

Daisy nearly opened her eyes but in a sudden flash chose to believe that the ghostly crusaders were taking charge. That was it. They were helping her. She scrunched her eyes more tightly shut to believe harder.

The One swung his shoulders. The weight on his back was odd, yet so long as the whisperer was by his side and he could walk freely, he did not feel inclined to buck or jib. Daisy felt pressure on her right leg. Somebody was shifting it. Now her leg was over the saddle. She was astride, though still bent over. The One began to jog. Daisy's leg was held firm. She shook her hair back but never peeped. 'Don't leave me,' she silently implored the whisperer.

They would have made a strange sight, had anybody been watching: Daisy, hunched in the saddle; The One, ears half back and half forward; a thin, foxy figure, almost invisible, whispering. Nobody was watching though. Garth was searching for the pistol in the moat; Skelton was spring whitewashing the stables; Daisy's sisters were helping Mrs Snipper; Charles was lying, mouth open, on his bed.

When they had traversed the Resting Place four or five times, Snipe hooked the long rein over the stone and Daisy felt herself lifted down. She leaned against the tombstone, very shaky, her hair sticking to her cheeks and the insides of the tops of her legs stung raw from the unaccustomed friction. Only when the whispering stopped did she open her eyes. Her crutches were resting on the flat stone. The One was grazing again. There were no ghosts in sight.

Daisy gazed at the saddle. She could hardly believe she had sat in it. She buried her head in The One's shoulder. After a while, she took the rope and picked up her crutches. Underneath them was a jar marked Lilypetal Jelly. She opened it, smelled it and showed it to The One. He wanted to eat it. She shook her head. 'It's not for you,' she said. 'It's another present for Lily.' She put the lid back on. 'It must have been the ghost who loves her that's just helped me.' She would not doubt it for a second. 'Thank you!' she whispered. Carrying the jar carefully back up the field, she hid it under the lip of the drawbridge.

At the stables, she found Skelton up a ladder. 'Master Garth manage this time, did he, then, missy?' Skelton asked. He was certain of another failed day. Now Daisy would beg for his help, and he had his answer all prepared.

'The One's been ridden,' Daisy said without a smile.

Skelton drew a sharp breath and narrowed his eyes. 'What do you mean?'

'I mean, he's backed.'

'But I saw Master Garth going up to the castle,' Skelton burst out. 'I saw him.' Daisy took the horse into the stable. Skelton came down the ladder and followed her in. Daisy must be lying. He could not let this go on any longer. His whole future depended on that horse. It was getting harder to be cautious. He gripped his hands together. 'So Master Garth'll gallop him this week? Time's not on our side.' He could not stop his voice rising slightly.

'I know that,' Daisy agreed. She had no idea how she and The One would gallop, but she would not discuss it with Skelton. She took up the curry comb.

Angry, the groom pressed her more. She did not answer.

Eventually he went up to the loft and began forking the hay. In his mind's eye, he could still see the horse galloping along the fence the day he had escaped. The speed! It was extraordinary! The horse had a chance, a real chance. He stabbed his pitchfork deep. And every day, because of these stupid, stubborn children, the chance was diminishing. Yet they would not thwart him. He stabbed his pitchfork deeper. This time next year he *would have* his own horses in these stables, his own carriage in the empty coach-house and somebody else to do the whitewashing. He threw the pitchfork down and clamped his pipe between his teeth. He knew he must be calm. 'Remember,' he told himself sternly, 'the girl wants the horse to win as much as you do.' He stamped on a spider. 'She'll come for help in the end. Of course she will. She'll have no choice.' He kicked at the hay. Yes, she would come to him. He must just be patient. He put his pipe away, picked up the pitchfork and glanced out of the loft door. From up here, he could see the Hartslove pennant gently slapping the flagpole. He began to imagine what pennant he would fly when he was lord of this manor. A brilliant idea struck him. He would appropriate the de Granville flag and fly it as his own. Sir Charles would not like that. None of them would. He ran his eye over the castle's silhouette. Actually, once he owned the place, perhaps he would not live in it. Perhaps he would sell it as an institution. He spat. Perhaps he would sell it as a school for bad boys, the kind of school in which he had grown up and whose scars he still bore on the backs of his legs. It would be sweet revenge to be the benefactor, enthroned in the big chair on speech days with the boys forced to bow and thank him for their torture. He'd be The One then. Oh yes. He'd be The One, and he would never let anybody forget it.

15

Lily received the lily-petal jelly with a gentle exclamation of delight. 'Why, thank you,' she said to Daisy. 'Did Mrs Snips make it?'

'No,' Daisy said. 'I found it on the flat stone. It's another present from – well, you know, whoever.' She said nothing about riding The One. The very thought would have frightened Lily into a fit.

She left Lily still exclaiming and went to the tower bedroom to find Garth. He had not found the gun, which was unsurprising since it had been removed from the moat and was now tucked safely under the chestnut tree wrapped in Snipe's spare smock. Garth's door was not locked. He was sitting on his bed not juggling, not doing acrobatics, not even staring at a book. Daisy had never seen Garth doing nothing before. She faltered. She did not know how to say what she had to say without hurting him, but she steeled herself to do it. She had to. The whispering crusader might not come again tomorrow and she could not manage alone.

'I've been on him,' she blurted out.

If Garth had been still before, he was stiller now. Daisy ran her hobbling run over to him and took his hands. 'Oh, Garth!' she exclaimed, and she could not stop her joy spilling out. 'It was strange to be up there again. I was so frightened that I kept my eyes shut the whole time. I just so wanted to do it. I –' His face closed tighter and tighter. 'Garth,' she implored. 'Garth, listen. It doesn't matter if you don't want to ride. I can do the riding whilst we're here, and we'll find a jockey for the race. There'll be plenty looking for a ride. But you need to help me. You've *got* to help me. I can't do it by myself again. I can't manage without you.'

Garth removed his hands. Daisy, crippled Daisy, despite her callipers, was telling him that she had, without any help, ridden an unbroken three-year-old racehorse, *and enjoyed it*. It never occurred to him to disbelieve her. The feat seemed impossible, yet Daisy never lied. He spoke in a voice both distant and dismal. 'If you've managed perfectly well by yourself today, you'll manage tomorrow. Or ask Skelton.'

'I wasn't by myself today,' Daisy said. 'The crusaders helped me.'

He frowned. 'They'll help you tomorrow.'

'They might not come back tomorrow and I don't want to ask Skelton. I want you.'

Garth hunched against her.

Daisy saw how things were and refused to accept them. She climbed on to the bed and for the first time in her life forced Garth to be close to her and forced him to listen. When he pushed her away, she pulled him back; when he tried to stop his ears, she forced his arms down, and all the while she kept talking, talking, talking, telling him how it had been to move without crutches and to lose the weight of her callipers. She avoided mentioning The One by name, knowing that would only make Garth feel worse, if feeling worse were possible. She spoke only of herself and her feelings. 'I was high up, Garth, high up. And I was free, like you're free on the ruins. I could feel the wind! Don't pull away. Don't block your ears. I know you understand. I know you do.' It was impossible for Garth to ignore her without physically throwing her out. Some of The One's hair was stuck to her callipers. The sight of it made him want to hit something. And still Daisy talked as though she would never stop. 'I was so light and I'm usually so heavy. I could go anywhere.' She never let up, not for a minute, describing the amazement, the wonder and the sheer, heart-stopping exhilaration of being her full self again. It was harder and harder for Garth to remain aloof. This was Daisy talking: Daisy, who had never scoffed at him; Daisy, who bore her lameness without complaining; Daisy, who had come to him because she needed him.

Finally, she ran out of words. 'So will you help me?' she asked. Everything hung on his answer, yet still Garth did not speak. Slowly, she moved away from him. Nothing. Slowly, she levered herself off the bed. Nothing. She stopped by the door. Nothing. She stopped in the passage. Nothing. Nothing. She made her way to her own room.

Garth did not appear in the dining room that evening. He did not appear at breakfast. It was not until Daisy took The One to the Resting Place that she got her answer: Garth was waiting. The look on Daisy's face stayed with him until the day he died.

The One was in frisky mood, and Garth, nervous for his sister, quickly grew irritated. 'Stand, *stand*!' He wondered, briefly, if Daisy had dreamed what she said had happened yesterday. 'Just stand. *Stand!*' he ordered again and again through gritted teeth. Despite his hard-won determination to help, it was still humiliating watching Daisy perched precariously on the tombstone and trying to hook her toe into the stirrup. She, however, although her face was red and her hair sticking up, was unfussed. 'Shhhh! Shhhh!' she said, trying to soothe both Garth and The One. 'This stupid skirt! If only I could wear proper breeches.'

'Perhaps you shouldn't try again today.' Garth wanted this to be over. 'Stand! Why can't you STAND?!' He held the reins more tightly. The One was too big. He was too strong. What was Daisy thinking? What was he thinking?

'Bring him round again.'

Reluctantly, he obeyed and with a scuffle and some mumbled cursing Daisy was at last slumped over the saddle, her leg hitched over, scrambling about untangling her skirts and settling herself. The One did not wait for these niceties. He began to swing away. Garth, jogging to keep up, was almost as terrified for Daisy as he would have been for himself. This was madness! If she was thrown, it would be his fault. He should never have agreed to help. 'Isn't this enough?' he said after a minute. He wanted her off the horse.

The One jinked. Daisy gave a small gasp and seized a big chunk of mane. It would have been utterly intolerable for Garth had Daisy's eyes not been alight with wonder. He could not resent that. He could not destroy it. 'It's so extraordinary, Garth. I'm walking faster than you!' The One's neck was a thick red line in front of her. 'Let the rope out,' she said.

'But—'

'No, really, Garth. I'll be all right. Let the rope out.'

Most unwillingly, Garth began to pay out the rope. The One walked faster until he came to the end of the tether. He jerked to a halt. Tentatively, Daisy picked up the reins. An ear flicked back. She knew she should do something with her legs, but they were not used to being held at this angle and she could not move them. She could, though, tense a muscle. That would have to be enough; that and her voice. 'Walk on,' she said. The One walked, though whether in answer to her instruction or because he felt like it she could not tell. She tensed her muscles again. Perhaps she could trot. The horse shot forward. Daisy banged down hard on his back. He baulked, grunted and shot forward again. Daisy was pitched on to The One's neck, then almost out of the saddle.

'Woah! Woah!' cried Garth, still hanging on to the rope. The One fought the rope and trotted faster. Daisy bumped faster. The horse's hooves jarred. Daisy's bones jarred. The horse gathered himself together. 'He's going to buck,' cried Garth. 'Oh God! Daisy!' She would fall now, and he could do nothing to help her.

The One did not buck. He broke into a canter so long and free that the rough sea became a perfect swell. The horse's hooves no longer jarred. Daisy's bones settled. She scarcely left the saddle at all. With Garth still hanging on to the end of the rope, The One described three perfect circles around him before bringing himself to a very respectable halt.

Garth quickly approached. 'Get off now,' he begged. 'It's enough for now. More than enough.'

'I want to ride by myself, Garth.' Daisy was beaming.

'I can't let you,' Garth said. 'It's too dangerous. You know it is. It's years since you rode by yourself. You'll have forgotten how.'

'Who taught you to tumble?' Daisy asked. 'Who taught you to juggle? Who taught you to balance in the Cannibal down those wicked stairs?'

'It's not the same.'

'Why not?'

'I don't have . . . I don't have –'

'You don't have callipers?' Daisy was no longer beaming. She spoke quite directly. 'Is that what you were going to say?' She did not seem like Daisy any more. She seemed, he thought, like a crusader herself. 'Undo the rope, Garth. I can manage.'

He swallowed. He undid the rope.

Daisy did not gallop off. She made The One circle, start and stop, trot for a moment or two, then walk again. And Garth saw what Daisy meant. Though she sat awkwardly and her legs did not touch his sides, she and The One flowed into each other in a way Garth never had with any horse, not even before he was frightened. Whatever the horse chose, Daisy chose too. They trusted each other. Garth waited for a wash of resentment or self-pity to engulf him. Neither did. As he watched Daisy, to his relief and surprise, he was instead overcome by a great sense of pride.

At the top of the field, Skelton's eyes were on stalks as his fists clenched. It was not right. The cripple! What was she thinking? Yet as he watched, he could not deny that the horse was moving well. He unclenched his fists. The girl could not do any harm. In fact, she might even do some good. He went back to the stables, whistling.

Daisy worked on The One for the next fortnight, with Garth helping to get her on and off. The horse never threw Daisy – that never seemed to cross his mind. However, not everything went smoothly. Although the horse occasionally cantered when instructed, pulled up on command and sometimes turned in the right direction, mostly he did as he pleased. Since, in the main, what The One wanted to do Daisy wanted to do, this lack of discipline did not worry Daisy unduly. Sitting astride, the stretching shoulders in front, the powerhouse of muscle behind, the red mane and tail billowing in the spring gusts, she felt like a queen. The only thing she would not allow was a full gallop. This was partly because she was still nervous of the injured leg and partly because although her confidence grew every day, she knew she would not be able to rise and balance in the stirrups as a full gallop required. The horse seemed to recognise this. He never took off, although sorely tempted.

For a while Daisy wondered if, after seeing her ride without mishap, Garth might volunteer to try again and this time succeed. She knew she should welcome this, encourage it even. Yet she dreaded it. She loved her new role. In the event, she need not have worried. Garth never volunteered, and when he suggested that they should leave the Resting Place and go on to the moor, this was not because he wanted to try to ride again without Skelton seeing, it was because he could no longer bear Skelton seeing her ride instead of himself.

Skelton's relief at the horse being ridden did not last long. Daisy was neither galloping the horse nor teaching him how to start under orders, and the horse could not win without doing both. He came to the moor and tried to ingratiate himself, but his help was always refused. What could he do? Only what he was doing already: watching, cursing, grinding his teeth and keeping Charles well topped up with brandy.

16

With slightly better weather came more prospective buyers. Twice, The One's training was interrupted by three hauntings in one day. The hauntings could not be abandoned, however, because in his hopeless state the children knew their father would accept any offer at all. Ingenuity was stretched past breaking point and the strengthening sun did not help, casting the castle in a lovely glow and bathing the hall statues in gold. Even the Furious Boy seemed to lose his venom as he basked in the warmth. Still, Mrs Snipper visibly and Snipe invisibly did all they could to spook and terrify. Once, Snipe let dozens of white ferrets loose. Another time, he unleashed a tide of human skulls down the Dead Girl's passage. Yet these feats took some organisation and could not keep being repeated. The sisters got fed up with the silent ghost trick, and Rose, deprived of the company of Arthur, did not always play her part to perfection.

One day, late in the afternoon, a large carriage turned in. The wistful prettiness of Lily, wandering over the grass, along with the grand rustiness of the gates and the gaping potholes encouraged the father. He did not see the lurking Snipe.

Over the years, Jonas Entwhistle had made something of a study of drive gates and wistful daughters, and the combination at Hartslove set his antennae humming. Here, undoubtedly, was a household in deep financial distress. The fine house he was hoping to find at the end of the potholed drive would be cheap. He insisted on giving Lily a lift, and when she refused manhandled her into the carriage. You could learn a lot from wistful girls, even on a short journey up a drive.

Snipe was outraged. Those creatures! To lay their hands on Miss Lily! The lice on his head prickled. His secret fingers itched to punish.

The intruders were in raptures when they saw the castle, less for its melancholy beauty than because of the envy that a castle, a drawbridge and a moat would evoke amongst their acquaintance. The father swelled visibly as his horses swept under the archway, whilst his wife, squat as a chicken in her fringes and tassles, was already imagining invitations reading 'Mrs Jonas Entwhistle, At Home, Hartslove Castle'. When the carriage drew to a halt, the Entwhistle children – two girls and a boy – descended in a squabblesome gaggle that their father observed with pride. His brood! Lily, pale as a moonbeam, descended last. Snipe never took his eyes from her.

Not bothering with the door pull, the intruders piled into the hall and exclaimed loudly at the statues. The cacophony brought all the children and Mrs Snipper, running. 'Ah!' declared Jonas Entwhistle, slapping a naked nymph appreciatively on her marble behind and hanging his hat on the Furious Boy's arm. 'We've seen the notice. You're for sale, righty righty?' He addressed the nymph, laughing at his own comedy and thrust a ham-hand at Charles, who had shuffled into the hall, his hair rough and his shirt open. 'Jonas Entwhistle's the name. Wife's Mrs Entwhistle; girls are Lilith and Merle. Son's Robert but we call him Robin.' He slapped his generous thigh. 'Robin Hood, see! Just the castle for him.' He roared with laughter. 'We'll take ourselves round.' He barged through the hall and up the stairs. His family delayed only to scoff at the statues before following him, voices blaring and jangling.

In the face of this blundering invasion, it was impossible to conduct a haunting. The intruders crashed carelessly into their mother's room and barged into Garth's. Worse, they bounced on Daisy's bed, making the cobweb quiver to breaking point. It was less a house viewing than a medieval bombardment. Garth longed for the pistol, most especially when Robin, grinning, stamped back into the hall pretending to fire a musket and, in his clumsiness, knocked over the Furious Boy, who bounced and rolled until, with a loud crack, the marble arm on which Mr Entwhistle had rudely hung his hat broke off. Garth felt a personal stab of pain. He picked the arm up. 'You moron!' he spat through gritted teeth. 'You fat, stupid moron!'

'What? Eh? You've a damned cheek, calling my boy names.' Mr Entwhistle bustled in and retrieved his hat. He tried to seize the broken arm. Garth clung to it. Mr Entwhistle left the arm. He was not getting involved in a tug of war. He inspected the Italian plasterwork on the hall ceiling. 'Very fancy,' he commented in disparaging tones. 'What's the point of it?'

Charles did not hear. He was faintly protesting at Merle and Lilith who, finding Daisy's crutches leaning against the bottom of the banister, were pretending to be lame themselves. Garth kicked the crutches away. He wanted to kill somebody – not the intruders: they were not worth the bother. He wanted to kill his father. It was Charles's fault that these appalling people were here. It was his fault that Hartslove was for sale. It was his fault that Gryffed was dead. At this moment, Garth could think of nothing that was not his father's fault. Head down, he cannoned out of the hall, up the stairs and locked the door of his desecrated room behind him.

Mrs Entwhistle brushed down her skirts. 'What do you think, Jonas?' she asked.

Charles blinked at the broken Furious Boy and recaptured enough of himself to make a decision. Whether they bought the place or not, these people must leave. 'You'll want to be home before nightfall,' he said, 'so you'll need to be off.'

'Righty right,' said Mr Entwhistle. 'Gather yourselves together, children.' He seized Charles's hand and shook it vigorously. 'I'd a feeling, you know, when I saw the "for sale" sign, that this old place would be for us. Near enough the town to oversee my mills and far enough to keep the children's lungs healthy. My lawyer'll be here tomorrow to negotiate a price. Promise not to sell it to anybody else in the meantime?' Charles nodded and removed his hand. Anything to get these people out.

Jonas Entwhistle twinkled at his daughters, now fighting over the crutches. 'Girls! Girls! I can't hear myself think!' He dug Charles in the ribs. 'Children! Aren't they a joy?'

'Remember what you said!' shouted the boy.

'Oh yes,' said his father. 'When you move out, Robin wants you to leave that dreadful old bear you've got lying around in the big passage. He'll have a great time with it.'

'I'm going to shoot at it,' Robin declared. 'Bang, bang!' He aimed his make-believe gun first at his sisters, then at Lily and Rose, then at his father.

Jonas Entwhistle chuckled. 'Come, Entwhistles all! Homey-home we go. Time for our dinner, righty right.'

In the courtyard, there was an inconvenience. The Entwhistle coachman was scratching his head. A wheel had dropped out of alignment; the carriage was unusable.

'It's the potholes in your drive,' said Mr Entwhistle, visibly annoyed. 'You'll have to lend us your carriage.' This made him less annoyed. The de Granville carriage would make the neighbours gape.

'We don't have a carriage,' said Rose.

There was a rumble, and Tinker appeared pulling the vegetable cart. 'Premium White Boars' had been crudely painted on the side. Clover or Columbine was driving. Both jumped down. 'We saw your carriage and thought this might be of use,' they said. 'It's the pigs' market cart, as you can see, but it'll get you home safely.'

Merle and Lilith were aghast. 'We're not going through the town in that.'

'Of course not,' their mother agreed. 'Jonas, send James for our *other* carriage.' She seldom had the opportunity to say this and relished it now. She did not like the de Granvilles. Twitching, shuffling Charles was ridiculous; his children as cold as the statues in the hall. The castle deserved a family with a bit of life to it and she would make sure it got it.

Jonas was inspecting the damage. 'James'll never make it to town and back tonight, my dear. We can send him off with the carriage horses, but it'll be tomorrow before he can return.'

Daisy was aghast. These people could not stay. 'You'll have to get home somehow. There's nowhere for you to sleep,' she said. 'We haven't had guests for years.'

Mrs Entwhistle's tassles rippled. 'Don't you worry. You

won't have guests tonight. What are you thinking, Jonas? Just get us home. The place is filthy.'

'I'm sorry, my songbird, but home's only possible if we use this pig cart or walk – or, of course, if you ride one of the carriage horses,' Jonas said, not unreasonably.

At once, his daughters set up a clamour. 'Don't be so stupid, Father. We're not walking or riding a carriage horse and we definitely aren't going in that cart.' The painted letters stood out even more brightly in the gathering gloom.

'Shut up, cretins!' interrupted Robin. 'Dirt or no dirt, why shouldn't we stay here? The castle's practically ours.'

His sisters brightened a little. 'He's right, Mother. And dirt's better than people seeing us in a pig cart,' they shrilled. 'Besides, we've never stayed in a castle before.'

'We've no dressing maids or night attire,' Mrs Entwhistle said as though that clinched the matter, but her voice was not as certain as her words. Darkness was falling fast, and no matter how loudly she complained, her husband could do nothing about that.

Clover and Columbine tapped her on the arm. 'We can give you night attire,' they said, solemn-faced. 'The curtains in the billiard room will be perfect.' Mrs Entwhistle glared at them. They all returned to the drawing room.

A highly awkward hour followed as a tight-lipped Mrs Snipper, rejecting all assistance, rustled up some dinner. Rose and Daisy sat mute. Daisy had persuaded Garth to come down and he stood by the door, glowering. Into the silence Clover and Columbine read out the details of a Manchester murder from the newspaper. '"The policemen have arrested nobody yet and have warned householders to check that no elderly neighbours have disappeared. Nobody in the district should buy meat from disreputable butchers." Whatever can that mean?'

Charles drank four glasses of brandy without water.

When Mrs Snipper called them into the dining room, Jonas Entwhistle seized a sconce and peered at the pictures. 'I'll make you an offer for a few of these,' he said. He paused for quite a time at the Landseer. 'That your ma?'

'Wife,' Charles said.

'Dead?'

Charles shook his head.

'I see,' said Jonas. 'A bolter, righty right?' His eyes glinted. This was the business.

'No,' said Garth, his voice low and dangerous. 'Not righty right. My mother's not for sale.'

Jonas Entwhistle took off his glasses and shook his double chins. 'I think you'll find even mothers are for sale, for the righty-right price.' Now that they were stuck here, he seemed determined to find everything amusing again.

Mrs Snipper pushed in the trolley. 'I hope you're hungry.'

'Starving,' Robin said. 'I could eat a horse.'

'Well, isn't that a Lucky Coincidence,' Mrs Snipper said, smiling glassily, and with great delicacy spooned out great domes of something mousse-like. Heaped plates were presented to all the intruders. It took them a minute or two to realise they were eating alone, observed like laboratory rats by the silent de Granvilles.

'No scoff for you?' Jonas paused, mouth open. 'Some religious fasting thing, righty right? We're more chapel people ourselves. Keep God in his place.' His only answer was the chatter of Lily's birds from the sideboard.

'What *was* that?' asked Mrs Entwhistle. She could feel the mousse slightly grainy on her tongue.

Mrs Snipper made a show of wiping down a mousetrap. 'Waste not, want not,' she said. Mrs Entwhistle gulped.

The second course arrived with covers on. Again, the plates were set only in front of the intruders. Charles, holding on to his decanter, noticed nothing. Clover and Columbine, whispering, turned very slowly and gazed at Lily's birdcage. 'Only three left,' they said in unison, and turned back to stare at the plate covers. 'What a shame.' The Entwhistles' hands, hovering over the covers, dropped to their sides.

After a suitable gap, Mrs Snipper returned. 'Enjoy that, dearies?' she said. She lifted one of the covers. Three lamb cutlets glistened. 'I'm sorry you don't like cutlets,' she said. 'I served them specially.'

Jonas's stomach rumbled. He was starving. 'Lamb? Oh, for goodness sake. We thought –' He glared at the birdcage, then at the twins.

A cake with cream and stewed fruit arrived. This was

187

served to everybody except Charles, who waved it away. The intruders sighed with relief when they saw the Granville children pick up forks and spoons. When they had all finished, the candles snuffed themselves out.

'Irritating things, candles,' said Jonas. 'We'll soon put gas in here, righty right.' He relit the candles. 'Not keen on fruit?' Jonas asked, noticing that Garth had pushed his to one side. He picked it up with his fingers. 'Waste not, want not, as your old servant says.'

Garth watched him chew and swallow. 'Bats aren't fruit,' he said.

Jonas choked. His wife screamed. His children shrieked. 'Don't be so silly!' Jonas shouted. 'Look here, nobody makes a mousse out of mouse. Nobody stews bats. It's a joke, righty right. A joke. It's the sort of joke snooty people like to play. It's why the French revolted.' He itched to wallop Garth.

Back in the drawing room, his wife and children subdued, Jonas decided to be frank. He sat down next to Rose. 'You people kill these old castles, you know. You and the dirt.' He brushed down his trousers. 'We'll be doing you a favour, getting you out of here. You're a pretty girl, you know. You should be out in the world, righty right. As for her –' he nodded confidentially at Daisy – 'she should be in a place for cripples, not a burden to you all. They do say that being crippled's the wages of sin, and although it seems harsh, what other explanation is there? You pretty ones need to get away from this –' he gestured around – 'and her. And, indeed, from your housekeeper. Mrs Snapper, isn't it? She's fit for an asylum.'

'Snipper,' Rose said.

'Snip, Snap, whatever.' He patted Rose's knees with sweaty hands. 'Your father's a sad case too, righty right. Drink's going to kill him.'

'Don't you dare say that! Don't you dare!' cried Clover or Columbine.

Jonas Entwhistle clicked his tongue. 'Look,' he said, quite kindly, 'it's a crying shame that you're all stuck in another century, and it's not the last century or even the one before that. Do you want to be left behind?' It was terrible to Rose to hear her own thoughts in this man's horrible mouth. Jonas could see that something had hit home. He leaned back. 'Your family've had a go here. It's our time now.' He winked at his son. 'There'll be generations of Entwhistles at Hartslove, eh, Robin? Girls'll be queuing up when you're of an age to marry.' He hooked his thumbs into his waistcoat. He was genuinely sorry for Rose. She looked so stricken. 'You can always come back and visit, you know. Lilith and Merle'll welcome you, won't you, girls?' He heard Garth growl. 'Oh, I hear you, young man. But can you read and write and keep an account book?' Garth slowly bent both legs over until they were resting on his head. 'Very fancy,' said Jonas, quite unimpressed. 'Tell me, is that going to earn a crust for your sisters? You can't expect to be mollycoddled by women all your life, you know.'

Rose rose. 'Bed.'

They were halfway up the stairs when the bell in the church began to toll. Mrs Entwhistle jumped. 'That'll keep me awake.'

'Me too,' complained Robin.

'And we can't have that,' said Jonas heartily. 'Who's tolling that bell? It's not very neighbourly, not at this time of night.'

'A priest tolls it. He lives in the church,' Clover or Columbine said.

'Does he pay rent?'

'I think he prays for us.'

'I like a man who says his prayers.' Jonas listened, then shook his head. 'No. I really don't like a man who tolls a bell in the night. We'll have to find him something else to do.'

They reached the top of the stairs. The bell was still tolling.

'Bang, bang,' said Robin.

Rose opened the door of a long unoccupied room. 'Bang, bang,' she replied, her eyes hard as diamonds. 'Bang, bang, bang, bang, bang.'

17

The visitors were asleep. Robin, at his own insistence and to his father's amusement, was installed in the grandest room in the castle.

Charles lay collapsed on the drawing-room sofa. Garth kicked him.

'Don't kick him, Garth. He can't defend himself.' Lily carefully arranged their father's legs, wrapping one of Gryffed's old blankets round them.

Garth turned on Clover and Columbine. 'You should never have tampered with their carriage. You should never have painted that notice on to Tinker's cart. We should never have let them stay here. Never.'

'We didn't tamper with the carriage,' Clover or Columbine retorted. 'We don't know how that happened. But when we saw it, we just thought . . . we just thought . . .'

'You didn't really think at all,' shouted Garth. 'You never do.'

'That's not fair!' cried Clover and Columbine. 'We did think. We thought that at least if they were here, they couldn't be at the lawyer's drawing up papers and we could still put them off.'

Their father groaned.

'Stop shouting!' begged Daisy. 'You'll wake him.'

Garth chucked his knucklebones into the air.

'For God's sake, Garth!' Rose's nerves were strung tighter than a bow.

Garth threw the bones higher.

'Please, Garth,' implored Daisy. Garth stopped. 'Look,' Daisy said, 'Clover and Columbine are right. If the Entwhistles are here, we can still try to put them off. I mean, maybe we could wake them and force them to watch Garth being a ghostly tumbler on the roof. It worked before.'

Rose shook her head. 'It's too late. Too late for anything.'

'No,' insisted Daisy, 'it's not, though perhaps the Garth thing wouldn't work. The father's too hardboiled. He'd see Garth was missing and know at once what was what. We need something else.'

'You shouldn't have said anything about Father Nameless,' Garth snapped at Rose. 'We might have done something with the bell.' He began to juggle again.

'You think a tolling bell would be enough to scare a man like that?' Rose wanted to snatch the knucklebones.

'No, it wouldn't,' agreed Daisy, her voice rising. 'Why,

oh why did these people have to pass by today? The Derby's so close!'

'Sod's law,' said Garth.

'Who was Sod?' asked Clover or Columbine.

'Christ in Heaven, Clover! What does that matter?'

'I'm Columbine,' said Columbine.

Daisy peeled some crumbling plaster.

'Daisy! What are you doing?' Lily was on her feet.

'Nothing.' Daisy dropped the plaster. 'I was just thinking . . .' They looked at her expectantly. 'Why on earth are we bothering with the father?' she said slowly.

'Because he's the one who makes the decisions,' Garth said.

'Yes. But the children have got to live here too, and he can't really live here if they don't want to.'

There was a moment's pause.

'Daisy's right,' said Garth. 'If we're going to try to frighten anybody, it should be Robin. Let's do more than frighten him. Let's chop one of his fat arms off and –' Garth still ached for the Furious Boy.

'No,' said Daisy. 'Let's do something worse.'

They all gaped. 'Worse than cutting off someone's arm?' Lily felt faint.

'A missing arm's a missing arm,' said Daisy. 'It's what goes on in your head that kills.'

An hour later something very curious slipped into Robin's room. The boy was snoring. The figure began to cry loudly.

Robin stirred but did not wake. The figure stopped crying for a moment, shook dust from the hangings and began to cry again. This time Robin did wake and found, hovering by the bed, the Furious Boy, no longer a cold statue but a living creature, white as milk except for a bloodied stump where his arm had been. The Boy was holding his severed limb above the pillow. The limb was dripping blood. The walls of the castle dampened Robin's screams and he soon realised that nobody could hear. He cowered. 'Go away!' he whispered hoarsely.

The statue spoke in a curious, sing-song hiss. 'I want something.'

A drop of blood landed on Robin's nose. He did not dare wipe it off. 'What do you want?'

'Revenge.'

Robin began to mewl. 'I didn't mean to knock your arm off. Really, I didn't.' A tiny particle of courage returned. This must be a nightmare. In a moment, he would wake up. 'Bang, bang.'

The Furious Boy grimaced horribly and produced a long, curved knife. Robin felt a warm flow down his leg. 'Oh,' he shrieked. 'I'm murdered! I'm murdered! Oh sweet Jesus, save me.' He bit his fingers. He rocked. 'I can't be awake. I can't be.'

The Furious Boy indicated with the knife that Robin should get out of bed. 'How? I'm injured! I'm dying!' Robin pulled out his legs, only to find that the warm flow was not blood: he had wet himself. 'Mother! Father!' Nobody came. He crumpled on to the floor feeling the point of the knife where his pantaloons met his frilled shirt. He crawled to the door, shot up, flung it open and ran the whole length of the passage, through several other doors – some large, some small – some cobwebbed, some not – under portraits and old stags' heads and past three rusty suits of armour until, climbing some stairs, he eventually turned a corner where he found lamps burning. His family must be here. He shoved open the nearest door and saw his mother's shoes and his father's boots strewn about in the manner of people accustomed to servants. Their lumpy figures were humped in the bed. Peeping from below the pillow, for fear of burglars, was the necklace his mother had been wearing.

Robin breathed very quickly as he pulled back the covers, for a moment terrified of what he might find. But his parents were there, both fatly snoring. Robin dropped to his knees. He had often complained of his parents' snoring. Now it was as comforting as a lullaby. He started to shake them awake, then stopped. He did not want to be laughed at. He did not want them to know that he had wet himself. 'It was that horrible dinner,' he said loudly. 'It's upset my digestion. That's all.'

A rush of air; a tap on his shoulder. Gut-dissolving dread. This was not the Furious Boy: it was Daisy. She grabbed his arm and dragged him with her. 'Never mind your parents,' she panted. 'He's after you. Run!'

Blindly, his wet pantaloons clinging to his legs, Robin followed as Daisy hobbled round more corners, up more stairs, down more passages. Once he tried to look over his shoulder. 'DON'T!' Daisy smacked him sharply. 'Just hurry!' Robin did not look behind again. When they got to the hall, Daisy halted, though she was twitchy and constantly on the lookout. 'I think we've shaken him off,' she said.

Shafts of moonlight lay like lances across the floor. The Furious Boy was there, pale and one-armed, but with no soggy stump, no blood and no knife. Robin let out a long breath. 'I *was* dreaming,' he said. At once, he let go of Daisy's hand, furious that he had held it in the first place. Daisy went to sit on the fender, half in and half out of the dark.

'I had a nightmare,' Robin blustered, sounding just like his father. 'A stupid nightmare, righty right.' He hoped she had not noticed his wet pantaloons.

'Yes,' Daisy said, 'I know.'

'How do you know?'

She moved so that he could see her better and gave an enigmatic smile. 'I just know.'

No smile had ever made Robin more uneasy. 'We'll get rid of this horrible thing,' he said, pointing at the Furious Boy.

'Of course you will.' Again she gave that smile. She swung one leg gently, her callipers clanging against the ironwork. 'We got rid of a similar statue once.' She clanged her callipers again. 'Well, almost.'

'What do you mean? Almost?'

'It was a girl and I knocked her leg off, you see. She was a nymph, just like these.' She gestured at some of the other statues.

'So?'

'That's why I'm lame.'

'You mean its – her – leg landed on your leg?'

'Oh no,' said Daisy. 'Her leg landed on the floor.'

'You mean you fell over it?' He began to laugh hysterically.

Daisy carried on swinging her callipers. 'No. Nothing like that.' She paused.

'I suppose you did something really stupid.' Robin couldn't stop his laughter, even though he wanted to.

Daisy did not seem to notice. 'The night after I knocked the leg off, the statue came to me. She was crying. I'm not sure exactly what happened next.' Daisy hesitated nicely and stared at the floor. 'All I know is that a week or so later my right leg began to feel strange – you know, as if I'd been sitting on it for too long. Then, one morning, it just wouldn't work at all.' Robin stopped laughing. A light sweat covered his forehead. 'We called the doctor and he tried so many things. Everything, I think. Nothing helped. My leg just got weaker and weaker, and after my right leg collapsed, my left one started. In the end they both just withered away.' She looked up. 'If I take my stockings off, I could show you.'

He started. 'No! Don't you dare!'

'I don't blame you,' Daisy said. 'There's nothing worse than a withered limb – unless it's two withered limbs.' She left a tiny pause. 'Does your arm feel funny?'

'Of course it doesn't,' snarled Robin. But did it?

Daisy pressed on. 'I came to find you, to warn you.' Another pause. 'I thought I saw the Furious Boy with a knife.'

'*It was a dream*,' said Robin, his voice strangled. 'The Furious Boy with a knife was a dream. Look! He's been here all the time.'

Daisy shook her head. 'Don't you understand? That's what I thought about the nymph. She was still here, yet –' she gestured to her legs. 'Are you sure your arm doesn't feel funny?'

'NO! My arm's just fine. You can't be crippled by a statue.'

'Not in a normal house,' Daisy agreed, 'but you can if you live here. I should know. Let me look at your arms.'

Robin began to curse. This silly halfwit was really scaring him with her fibs. And they were fibs. He absolutely knew it. They were fibs, fibs, fibs. Weren't they? He punched both his arms up and down. 'My arms are just perfectly fine and dandy.' He lied. His arms were not fine and dandy. Surely one was throbbing? Surely the other was aching? Surely they were both *withering*. He was sure of it. Then he was unsure. Then he was sure again. 'Oh God, oh God!' he moaned.

'You're lucky,' Daisy said.

'Lucky?' He was pulling up his sleeves. He had to see. He had to know.

'You can still escape,' Daisy said. 'Perhaps if you leave here and never come back, the statue will forget.' Robin was gurgling as he frantically inspected each arm in turn. 'You know,' Daisy spoke dreamily, 'I once saw somebody with a withered arm. Everybody spoke to him as if he was the village idiot. It must have been so humiliating. Even more humiliating than wetting yourself.' Robin groaned. 'I don't know for sure what happened in the end,' Daisy said in the same dreamy voice. 'I think his parents had him locked away in an asylum for lunatics and left him there until he died. There's lots of asylums for cripples in Liverpool, you know. I expect your parents wouldn't want you quite so close, though. It's easier to forget about people if they're further away.'

There was a noise. Daisy's mouth flew open.

'What now?' Robin squeaked and whipped round. The Furious Boy had vanished and three of the nymph statues were rotating on their plinths pointing white and bony fingers in Robin's direction. He reversed into the fireplace and tried to hide behind the firedogs.

Daisy fought hard not to laugh. She would let Robin burble and blubber for a minute or two, then take him back up to his room where he would see the Furious Boy for a final, unforgettable time. She grinned at the three 'nymphs' doing their job so perfectly. Except not so perfectly, because whilst Daisy managed to swallow her laughter, the sight of Robin quivering behind the firedogs completely overwhelmed Clover and Columbine. They began to shiver and shake and, in most unnymphlike fashion, to bend, hold on to their stomachs, to cough, to sneeze, to silently implore, to wring their hands until they finally collapsed amid a babble of completely uncontrollable giggles.

So jangled were Robin's nerves that it took him a long moment to hear the giggles and an even longer moment to really look. Once he had looked, however, it took him no time at all to realise that he had been duped, utterly and comprehensively duped and hung out to dry like a prize idiot. At first he was speechless. Then he was howling, quite beside himself at being taken in. He lunged at Clover or Columbine with fists, elbows and teeth. 'You monsters! You filthy devils! I'll pay you back for this! I'll break your bones. I'll cut off your arms and legs. I'll stamp on your faces and feed your brains to the crows. Your lives are over, OVER! You're finished! You're dead! You'll never frighten us away from here! We'll turn you out tomorrow morning with nothing – *nothing, do you hear?*'

Daisy was on her feet. She could hardly believe it. The whole evening's work undone in a second! *How could they?* She banged her fists against the fender, so boiling with fury at Clover and Columbine that she could quite easily have added to Robin's hideous threats. But the twins were too far gone. Though they knew they had ruined everything, they just could not stop their giggles. Whenever one almost succeeded, the other would start again until, gasping and horrified but still helplessly hiccuping, they rushed past Daisy, down the stairs and into the kitchen. Robin pursued them. Daisy pursued Robin.

The twins whisked out through the far door and slammed it. Robin was still shouting. 'Tomorrow I'll be back with a gun and then there'll be *real* blood. Bang! Bang! Bang! BANG! You'll scream and beg for mercy, you see if you don't. But there won't be any mercy. I'll shoot you one by one.' He ran past the range. A crunch and a cloud of ash. A hooded, smoky black figure seized Robin, threw him over one shoulder and vanished. Now Daisy screamed and bumped slap bang into Mrs Snipper. 'Mrs Snips! Mrs Snips!' Daisy clung to her. 'We were just pretending – then the twins – then something . . .'

Mrs Snipper hurried Daisy up the stairs and back into the hall. 'Go to your bedroom,' she commanded. 'Go on.'

'But –'

Mrs Snipper shook her. 'Don't you know that Hartslove looks after its own, Miss Daisy?' She was a tiny, hedgehog figure in a voluminous nightcap and knitted shawl, but she carried the authority of the castle with her.

Daisy ran to her room, flung open the shutters and

threw herself on to the window seat. In the moonlight, she could see the outline of the chestnut tree. There was movement. She clapped one hand over her mouth. Part of the gnarled and knotted trunk had detached itself and taken on the blurred form of the ashy figure, Robin still over its shoulder. The boy was silent now – at least Daisy could hear nothing. She wondered, with dread, if he was actually dead. A little distance from the chestnut tree, a ghostly horse appeared. Daisy cried out. White from nose to tail, the horse appeared to float, hoofless, above the ground. The hooded figure pitched Robin on to its back and sprang up behind. At once, the horse launched into a hand gallop, careening in wild zigzags around the Resting Place until it melted into a cloud that seemed to spin towards the river. The cloud vanished, reappearing two long minutes later. For several seconds, the ghost horse towered over the moat, then it reared and pitched Robin off like a sack of dead rabbits.

Daisy was already hurtling downstairs, out of the front door, across the courtyard and on to the drawbridge. There was no sign of the ghost horse. She peered into the moat where, to her relief, she could hear Robin spluttering and puking. She crossed the drawbridge, lay down on the moat's edge and held out a hand. 'I'm here,' she called.

'Go away! Go away!'

'Come here! I'll help you.'

'Go away!'

'Do you want the ash man to come back?'

'No! No!'

'Give me your hand then.'

Robin still refused her hand but he did crawl out of the moat. Daisy dragged him back into the hall.

Dawn was beginning to render the lances across the floor of the hall fuzzy and indistinct. All the statues were back in their places, though whether the real statues or not Daisy could not tell and did not care. She propped Robin against a plinth. He was shrunken, like a balloon without air. Daisy had no idea what had just happened. That the horse was The One, she was pretty sure. And who else could the ash man be but Skelton? That could all come later. The important thing now was not to squander this illusion as Clover and Columbine had squandered the statue trick.

Robin clutched his arms round his knees and forced his voice through a crack in his throat. 'Who was that man?'

'Don't know,' Daisy said with nearly complete honesty, 'but then we don't know all the ghosts here.'

'He wasn't a ghost. He was real. He can't get in here, can he? The door's locked?'

'Ghosts can do anything,' Daisy said.

'For God's sake, you cretin.' Robin gripped her wrist. 'He wasn't a ghost. Is the door locked?'

Although Daisy knew that there was no lock, it being several hundred years since anybody had thought one necessary, she hobbled to the door. 'It's locked,' she said because that seemed easiest. She pressed her nose against the window. 'There's nobody there.' She returned to Robin and crouched down.

Robin wanted to curse and cry at the same time. He still wanted to kill Daisy, but he did not want to be alone. He wished they had never come here. 'You must know who he was! He stank of rotten things and said I'd no right to touch lilies.'

'Lilies? Are you sure?'

'Of course I'm sure.' Robin began to shiver. 'We'll block the fireplaces. We'll put cannon on the roof. We'll fill the moat with burning oil. He must never touch me again. Never.' He stared fearfully into the hearth. 'Oh God! He could get in down here!' He wanted to move. But where to go? 'We'll pull the place down and start all over again.'

Daisy drooped. Despite Skelton's last-minute effort, the night was a complete failure. Far from putting Robin off, they had simply made him vicious. The dark was thinning fast. 'Better go back to bed,' she said.

Robin jerked. 'I can't sleep on my own.'

'I don't suppose the ash man will be back tonight.'

'He said . . . he said . . . he said he'd bring me a present.'

'That's nice.'

He glowered at her. 'Can't we just stay here?'

'You stay here if you want to.' Daisy was so tired she wondered if she could actually drag herself upstairs. She hauled herself to her feet. 'You smell. You'll need to wash yourself. There's water in the kitchen and you'll find some of Garth's clothes airing near the range.'

'I don't want to go down there.'

'Then stay smelly,' she said. She hobbled up to her room and lay on the top of her bed. There was something under the cover. She put her hand in and drew out a small bag. Inside was a robin. It was very pretty, with its brown back and red breast. It was also stone dead.

18

The Entwhistles were gathered in the dining room when Daisy came down. Their carriage – their *second* carriage, as Mrs Entwhistle kept repeating – had already arrived. Mrs Entwhistle and her husband had slept well. They did not, however, wish to repeat the dinner experience. They would breakfast at home. Merle and Lilith appeared, yawning. Jonas Entwhistle, finding Charles just where he had been left the night before, had marched him into the dining room and was delivering a lecture on household management. It took Robin's appearance to silence him.

If his daughters were dishevelled without their maid and their hairbrushes, his son was a wreck. Robin had neither bathed nor changed his clothes. He smelled of unmentionable things. He was also hideously flushed and his eyes were hollow. He could not stand still. 'We've got to fix cannon on each corner,' he said without any preamble, 'and block up all the fireplaces. We'll need guard dogs, lots of them. Big ones with teeth.'

'What on earth are you talking about?' Mr Entwhistle blinked. 'What's happened to you?'

'Didn't you hear me?' Robin's voice was high and querulous.

'I heard you. Look at yourself! Have you . . . have you –' Jonas could not bring himself to identify his son's smell.

'Guard dogs and cannon, Father. Order them now.'

'Guard dogs? Cannon? This is 1861, righty right? Who do you think's going to invade?'

'It's for the girls' protection,' Robin said, 'and for Mother's. There was an intruder last night.' He glared at Garth and Rose. Clover and Columbine were lurking, shamefaced, behind them. 'A real intruder. Not some poxy girl dressed up as a statue.'

Mrs Entwhistle felt for her necklace. 'An intruder? Thank goodness this was under my pillow.'

Robin turned on her. 'Who cares about your necklace! He wasn't after that! He came for me!'

'For you?' Mrs Entwhistle's eyes were wide.

'Yes. And he was made of ash from the kitchen range!'

'An intruder made of ash? God in heaven, Mr Entwhistle! Our son's gone mad.'

'An intruder?' Charles caught the tail end of the conversation. 'Not possible. Gryffed would have –' he broke off. Why did he never remember?

'Gryffed?' said Mrs Entwhistle, thoroughly bemused. 'Who's he?'

'He's dead,' said Rose.

'Why is nobody listening? There was an intruder!' Robin stamped his foot and pointed to the doorway. Daisy had just appeared. 'Ask her.'

'I'm afraid he's right,' Daisy said. 'There was an intruder.'

Mrs Entwhistle felt for her necklace again. 'For the love of God! Is nowhere safe?'

'Now then, Mother,' Jonas said. He did not know what to make of any of this. He looked back at his son. 'If you disturbed a burglar, why didn't you wake me?'

'I couldn't, Father.' Robin's words tumbled out. 'He grabbed me and burrowed underground. We came out by a tree. I think he was part of the tree. Perhaps it's an ash tree. We galloped on a white horse. It was hideous and he said vile things but I wasn't at all frightened of course. Not at all. All the same, we need to protect ourselves. I mean, next time he might take one of the girls and God knows what he'd do to them.' Mrs Entwhistle and his sisters shrieked. 'Perhaps he wouldn't bring them back,' Robin added, to make his sisters shriek louder.

'Be quiet! All of you!' ordered Jonas. His son looked very strange, and Jonas did not like anything strange. He forced himself to smile. 'You had a nightmare, son. That's all. Pull yourself together.'

Robin stamped his foot. 'He threatened me, Father. I had to beat him off. He threw me in the moat.'

'Was that before or after he turned into a tree?' Jonas asked, his patience beginning to run out.

Robin turned furiously on Daisy. 'You tell him.'

Daisy felt the little bag in her pocket. 'I don't want to.'

'I don't care if you don't want to. Tell him.'

'Are you sure?'

'Of course I'm sure. Tell them now this minute.'

Daisy fiddled with her hands. 'I'm sorry, Mr and Mrs Entwhistle,' she said. 'It's just as Robin said.'

'There!' cried Robin. Mrs Entwhistle began to fan herself.

'Though actually,' Daisy continued, 'it's worse.'

'Worse?' Mrs Entwhistle sat down with a bump.

'Yes, worse,' Daisy repeated. 'You see, the intruder said he'd leave Robin a present. Isn't that right, Robin?'

Robin nodded.

Daisy brought out the little bag and opened it. 'I think this is it.'

Jonas seized the bag and tipped the contents on to the table. Robin's breath was a jagged high croak.

'For God's sake, boy! It's just a dead bird!' his father shouted.

'But, look at it! Don't you see what kind of a bird it is, Jonas?' his wife whispered.

'Birds are birds!'

Daisy whipped the little corpse out of the way as Jonas crashed his fist down. 'Be careful of the poor robin!' she cried. 'It must have died because its wings are withered and it couldn't fly.'

'A robin? What? A robin with withered wings? Oh, this is nonsense,' cried Jonas, glaring at Daisy, then Robin, whose croak had dissolved into a whimper. 'Don't be such a sissy, boy!'

Merle and Lilith were wailing. 'We want to go home.'

'Home? This is going to be your home!'

Daisy approached Robin. She was holding the broken bird out to him, and on his other side Garth was stroking the Furious Boy's arm. Robin took no notice of Garth, but there was something about the dead robin amid the breakfast crumbs that spooked him more than anything he had seen the night before – indeed, more than anything he had seen in his life. It was not that the robin looked tortured. It did not. But it did not look peaceful either. Its beak was open, as though death had crept up on it when least expected. In the milky glaze of its dead eyes, Robin's own reflection was distorted. And those wings. Those pathetic, helpless wings. Robin would have run outside and ground the bird into the dirt if his legs had agreed to carry him. That stuff with the statue had been a joke, right? He knew it. *He knew it.* Yet there were Daisy's withered legs, and she was looking so weird – almost as if she were sorry for him. He could not help running his hands up and down his arms. 'I hate you all and I hate this place,' he groaned. He glared at his father. 'Can't you see? This whole castle's ugly and deformed, and if we live here that's just what we'll become. I don't like it. I don't want it.'

'You'll want what I tell you to want!' shouted Mr Entwhistle.

'I won't,' Robin shouted back.

'Jonas! Jonas!' cried Mrs Entwhistle. 'The boy's not well.'

The girls backed away from their brother. 'We don't want to live here either. We don't want to end up mad like him.'

'But this is a castle! A castle!' Jonas argued angrily. 'It's fitting. It's our right.'

His wife drew her tassles around her and forced herself to touch her son. 'There, there.' She turned on her husband. 'There's other castles,' she snapped. 'I'm not asking the neighbours round to meet intruders and dead things.'

Mr Entwhistle thumped the table. 'We ARE going to live here.'

'We aren't,' said his wife. 'Robin's right. There *is* something rotten about this place, and if my boy's permanently damaged –' she shook her necklace at Charles as she pushed her children out – 'I shall hold you personally responsible.' Her husband was still thumping the table. 'The carriage, Jonas.'

Mr Entwhistle knew that tone. He carried on thumping even as he began to deflate. 'I simply don't understand what's happened here.' When he finally stopped thumping, he looked to each of the de Granvilles for an explanation. None was forthcoming. Mrs Snipper brought him his hat. 'Goodbye, dearie,' she said. Complaining, Jonas Entwhistle found himself chivvied out of the dining room. He was still complaining when the front door slammed behind him. As he got into his carriage, his complaints became more muffled until eventually they merged with the crunch of carriage wheels.

In the long pause that followed, Charles retreated to the library and Daisy found herself surrounded.

'How on earth did you manage that?'

'Yes, how *did* you do that?'

'Was there really a horse?'

'That poor robin.'

'Where did you find it?'

'On my bed,' said Daisy when she could get a word in.

'No, Rose meant before that,' said Garth.

'I didn't find it before that. It was in a bag on my bed.'

'Who put it there?'

Daisy shook her head. 'I've no idea. And there *was* a horse. It was The One.'

'Of course, but how did you make him white?'

'I didn't,' Daisy said. 'I really didn't have anything to do with it. Nothing at all. It must have been Skelton. I absolutely swear it wasn't me.' She turned on the twins. 'You two! How could you have giggled? You spoiled everything!

We should never have needed The One or the dead robin.' Her relief at getting rid of the intruders was quickly turning to concern. The One's first gallop! In the dark and with a great lump of a boy on top of him!

'We're so sorry!' cried the twins. 'We didn't mean to.' They were mortified and nervy. They could not imagine how they had giggled.

Daisy swallowed. What was the point of shouting at the twins now? 'I'm going to the stables. I've got to see if The One's all right,' she said. Her crutches were leaning against the door.

The twins hung back. The thought of The One being lame again was almost worse than the Entwhistles.

'You really think it was Skelton? It doesn't seem like him at all. What does he care about the place – I mean, really?' Garth was running with Daisy. Rose and Lily hurried close behind. The twins followed reluctantly.

'It must have been him,' Daisy said, swinging as fast as she could. 'Just because we don't like him doesn't mean he's completely bad. I mean, he was helpful when The One was lame, and I suppose he doesn't want to move from here either.'

The One's head was poking from his top door. Skelton came out of his house when he heard the chatter. 'Is he all right?' Daisy called as she unfastened the stable bolt.

Skelton was taken aback by Daisy's alarm. He was on his guard at once.

'We've really come to thank you,' said Lily quickly. She thought his feelings might be hurt by Daisy's question, which did, after all, imply some criticism. 'It was so clever of you to think of the whitewash. I mean, we thought of the statues, but a whole horse! We're so grateful. It must have taken a while to wash the stuff off.' She was beaming at him, and a beam from Lily was quite a beam.

Up in the loft, Snipe scratched his lice and watched. That Lily's beam was directed at Skelton did not bother him one bit. He knew it was his due, and took it as such.

Skelton, who had only seen Clover and Columbine taking Tinker to the castle the day before, began slowly to understood why The One had been curiously damp when he had fed him earlier. He had thought the stable roof must be leaking, though he was not aware there had been any rain. He had looked about a bit but had not gone into the shed where the whitewash was kept. Had he done so, he might have been surprised to find a number of things not as he left them. As it was, he returned Lily's beam and searched her face for more clues. 'It was a good idea,' he said in a tone that invited her to disclose a little more about what he was being thanked for doing.

'You looked different all in black,' Daisy said as she put The One's head-collar on. 'And how did you appear from the kitchen range and get The One painted and out at the front all at the same time? You must have had some help, and I can't believe it was Mrs Snips.'

Skelton, his face blank but his mind working furiously, tapped his nose. 'Old Skelton has friends, you know,' he said evasively.

'What friends?' Garth asked.

'Garth!' reproached Lily.

Garth and Skelton scrutinised each other. Skelton pointed in the vague direction of the church. 'Some friends are silent friends, if you get my meaning,' he said.

'Of course!' said Lily. 'Father Nameless.'

Skelton grinned at her. 'Let's say no more about it, eh?'

The One stepped daintily into the yard and shook himself. In the sunlight, a few dried whitewash spots were still visible. Daisy flicked them off and ran her hands down his legs. They were cool and smooth. She felt his knee last. It was flat and only naturally warm. No damage – at least none that was visible.

'I just can't see Father Nameless helping Skelton,' murmured Garth to Rose as they watched Clover or Columbine trot the horse across the yard, wanting to make up for their giggling.

'Why not?' said Rose. 'After all, he's going to lose his home too.'

Garth did a series of slow cartwheels. The dead robin fell out of his pocket. Lily picked it up. 'We must bury it with due honours,' she said. 'It died a hero's death.'

'It probably died of old age.' Garth took the bird from Lily. 'But let's give it a funeral anyway.'

The One stretched his legs. The night's excursion had not upset him. He liked the foxy-featured man who had come for him out of the shadows. He also liked the whitewash, which had been delicious to lick. He did not like the wobbling boy, but he had not lasted long. The One smelled Snipe in the loft and stiffened, ears pricked, hopeful of further excitements.

'He looks more like a racehorse today, missy,' Skelton said.

'He should rest, shouldn't he? He shouldn't work again so soon after his first gallop?' Daisy found it hard to believe that one mishap with a rope could result in devastation but a mad caper in the dark result in nothing at all. Clover or Columbine did a great deal of running before she allowed herself to believe that all was well.

'Quite right, missy,' Skelton agreed. He could not imagine who had used The One, and right under his nose too. He was not angry, however. Whoever it was had done Skelton a favour. He pressed his advantage. 'You know, I'd not have risked a gallop if I hadn't thought the leg would stand up to it. But I was sure it would, and I want to do my bit for this old place.' He coughed. 'Training begins again tomorrow? The horse needs more fast work.'

Daisy nodded. She did not feel she could do much else. She turned to Garth. 'Do you think we could take down the "for sale" sign? Last night was all very well, but The One must never be used like that again.'

'If you take the sign down, your father's creditors'll come running,' said Skelton, wanting to demonstrate just how helpful he could be. 'I'll just shift it. It'll be harder to see if a tree's in the way.' He winked at Lily.

'You've been so obliging,' Lily said.

'Always a pleasure, missy,' he replied. 'As I say, we've got to stick up for the place.'

By mid-morning, the sun was blazing properly for the first time that year and the valley almost purred. The children buried the robin and spent the rest of the day at the Resting Place. Clover and Columbine, still very repentant, read aloud funny bits from obituaries. The One idled beside them. Daisy held the horse at first, but as the sun grew hotter and he settled, eyes half shut, in the lumpy shade of the chestnut tree, she unclipped the rope and went to lie on the flat gravestone. Lily sat beside her, and Garth, who climbed into the chestnut tree, observed them both as he juggled. They talked amongst themselves about the night before, filling in each other's gaps. Clover and Columbine apologised again for laughing. A stranger might have thought them very relaxed, not being able to see how their ears were straining all the time for carriage wheels. The Entwhistles would most likely not return but on a lovely day like this other intruders were a distinct possibility.

By mid-afternoon, however, when nobody had come and Skelton had hidden the 'for sale' sign under the branches of an oak tree, the tension eased. After dinner that night, they all filed into Daisy's room and sat under the cobweb. 'All will be well,' Daisy said. 'All manner of things will be well.' Nobody replied. They did not disbelieve her; they did not believe her either.

19

With only two weeks left until the Two Thousand Guineas, Daisy no longer slept. All would not be well. Though she urged The One to gallop when loose in the field, she knew he needed to gallop with a proper jockey. She was also beginning to realise that the horse's arbitrary obedience, so charming to her, meant that he might not gallop the very second the starter shouted 'off', thus losing valuable seconds. When she spoke to him firmly he listened, but Daisy was not silly enough to believe that he actually understood. Yet what else could she do? Since the Entwhistle haunting, Daisy felt it should have been easier to consult Skelton. Rose and Lily certainly liked him better. Lily had even insisted that they invite him to tea to thank him properly. Yet The One still disliked the groom, and Daisy sided with the horse. She would not consult Skelton. She would just hope that the riderless gallops sufficed as preparation.

Garth had marked out a curving racetrack amid the bumps and tussocks of the moor. According to Charles's racing books, the Two Thousand Guineas course was straight whilst the Derby course ran left-handed. Daisy concentrated on the curve of the Derby course. The One must get used to galloping round left-handed corners. She did not want to admit that this was a waste of time since The One seldom ran true in any direction. Sometimes he ran to the left and sometimes to the right. Sometimes he ran straight. Occasionally, he turned right round and galloped back the way he had come. Daisy could not stop him and she doubted she would ever be able to.

To practise a racing start, Garth requisitioned one of the old Hartslove standards. Standing on a small heap of stones, he raised the flag and dropped it as he imagined the starter would do. Sometimes The One responded instantly because the flag gave him a fright. Other times he would watch the flag with interest and canter at a time that suited him better. There were even times when he did not bother to canter at all. None of this was any good.

Then there was the question of actually getting the horse to Newmarket for the Two Thousand Guineas, and from Newmarket to Epsom for the Derby. Even amidst her worries, Daisy would not admit that The One might fail in the Two Thousand Guineas and never qualify for the Derby at all. She concentrated only on the practicalities. In the rare moments when Charles was fit to speak, she tried to ask him about travel arrangements. He stood still. He murmured. Then he drifted away without answering. If she pursued him, he would stumble into a run. Finally, Daisy asked Rose to ask Arthur. Rose was shocked. 'I can't ask him. He's helped us already, Daisy. Besides, you know what'll happen if I do. He'll pay the travel expenses himself. You know he will.' Daisy did know. She did not really want Rose to ask Arthur. She was just putting off the inevitable.

Skelton had been waiting for this moment. 'The horse will go on the train,' he said at once. 'We'll rent space in a van. You've been galloping, I hope? You've got the horse to do a proper racing start? Not much point taking The One south if he's going to show you up now, is there? Shall I list Master Garth as jockey?' He fixed Daisy with a look from under a new cap.

Daisy did not pretend. What was the point? Skelton already knew the answers to his own questions. 'You know Garth's not riding. We'll need a jockey,' she said.

Skelton could not resist. 'Really, Miss Daisy? Never mind. I expect Master Garth's too brave for a flat race. He'll be waiting to jump those great big fences on a Grand National horse. I'm told that even men who've fought in wars quail when they see Becher's Brook, but I expect Master Garth, with all his acrobatics, would relish the challenge.'

Had Daisy had anybody else to turn to, she would have walked away. There was nobody. 'We'll need the entry fee as well as money to pay for the train,' she said.

Skelton took off his cap and scratched his head. 'You asking me to stump up for everything?'

Daisy bit her cheek. He was going to make her beg, and for The One's sake, and for Hartslove's, she was going to have to oblige him. 'Yes,' she said, 'I'm asking you for the money. We'll pay you back from the winnings.'

Skelton replaced his cap. 'I'm sure you will,' he said. 'I'm sure you will. You've left it very late, you know. Very late. I didn't like to interfere.' Daisy looked at her feet. 'Luckily for you,' Skelton continued, 'I've been a bit clever. I've already sent the entry – fifty sovereigns.' Daisy gasped. 'Yes,' said Skelton, 'fifty whole sovereigns. You see why I'm anxious. We'll just have to hope we'll get a place in a van. There's a lot of horses wanting transportation these days. I can only do my best. You remember, missy, that if we miss the race, it won't be my fault.' Daisy swallowed. How hopeless she was! She should have arranged all this weeks ago. And fifty sovereigns! She'd had no idea the entry would be so much.

Skelton was enjoying himself. 'Mind, even if we do manage the travel, the horse'll hardly have time to get over the journey before the race, and we'll be lucky to find a jockey down there who's actually willing to take the ride. But you leave that to me, Miss Daisy. I'll do what I can.' He waited.

'Thank you, Mr Skelton,' Daisy said.

It was worth fifty sovereigns to him to hear her say it so meekly, and what made it even more enjoyable was the fact that Skelton had already booked a place for The One on a train from Manchester and had already been in touch with a very particular jockey. Now he was properly in charge, things would go as he wanted them to.

When Daisy showed Rose and Lily her ticket, they were dismayed. 'Where will you stop the nights? How will you manage on your own?' they asked in turn. 'You should have asked Skelton if one of us could go with you. Will you come home between the Two Thousand Guineas and the Derby?'

'I couldn't ask Skelton to buy two tickets for us,' Daisy said, her stomach churning now that everything seemed to be speeding up. 'And no, I won't be back between the races because there's no time.'

'We want to be there,' said Lily.

'We *must* be there,' Rose corrected. She did not add 'to comfort you when it all goes wrong', though that was what she was thinking.

Garth seemed less dismayed than Rose. Indeed, he fingered the ticket with excitement. Daisy was glad. She did not want Garth to feel badly. Clover and Columbine, deeply immersed in one of their newspapers, wished her luck.

On the day of departure itself, the most upsetting goodbye was to Charles. He looked amazed. 'Where are you going?' he asked.

'To Newmarket, then to Epsom.'

'But why?'

'He's The One, Pa,' Daisy said. 'We're going to win the Derby.'

Through a brandy-filled fog, a small alarm sounded. Charles scuffed his feet. 'Where's Skelton?'

'In the courtyard. We're walking The One to Manchester. I'll go in the cart. Then we're going on a train.'

Charles put an unsteady hand on Daisy's shoulder. 'Coming out,' he said. They walked slowly together, Charles leaning heavily so that Daisy's limp was more pronounced than ever. 'Sorry,' Charles said.

'Doesn't matter, Pa.'

In the courtyard, Charles shuffled over to Skelton. 'What's all this?' He flapped one hand at Tinker and the cart, and the other at The One, who was being held by Garth. 'Useless. You said.'

Skelton took Charles's elbow and steered him out of hearing. 'Absolutely useless, Sir Charles,' he said, 'but we must humour the little lady. She's determined the horse should run, and I don't want to disappoint her.' He patted Charles's arm. 'I'm paying. Glad to. Anything to keep Miss Daisy happy.'

'But he won't win.'

'Win?' Skelton guffawed. 'Didn't I tell you what that vet said? The horse couldn't win an old crock's race! His leg's all to pieces.' He leaned in. 'The horse only canters now. It's all he can do. Miss Daisy thinks he's fast only because she's never seen a real racehorse.'

'It'll be awful for her. Awful.'

'Aye, it will. But worse not to go when she's set her heart on it.'

Charles gripped Skelton's hand. 'You'll take care of her, Skelton. Real care.'

'As if she were my own,' Skelton said.

Charles shuffled back to Daisy, put both hands on her shoulders, said her name, and then shook, tears rolling down his face. Daisy had to pull away so that she would not cry too.

Mrs Snipper came out. She was brisk. 'There now,' she said, setting a basket of provisions next to Daisy's crutches, which had been neatly tied together and already stowed in the cart. 'Now, On You Go and Take Care. You say the cart'll be back here by the End of the Week, Mr Skelton?'

'A friend's going to drive it back,' Skelton said.

'Skelton has many friends,' said Garth sarcastically.

'More friends than you've got guts,' Skelton remarked in a stage whisper that fortunately Daisy did not hear.

As Skelton, leading The One, and Daisy in the cart passed the Resting Place, they heard somebody shouting. Charles was pursuing them. For one moment, Daisy thought that he was going to insist on coming with them. She hated the way her heart sank. But Charles was holding out a small, carefully wrapped roll of cloth secured with a red ribbon. 'The jockey's silks,' he said. 'You'll need the jockey's silks.' Daisy took the roll, undid the ribbon and shook out a rich copper-coloured jacket with a silver H embroidered front and back, and a copper silver-quartered cap. 'Oh!' she whispered. She held the silks up. The breeze filled out the blouse.

'Our colours,' said Charles. 'Red. Forget why.'

'Because we've got a red horse,' said Daisy softly. The One, impatient, was already walking on, and Tinker fretted to follow. Daisy smiled tremulously, rolled the silks up and gave Tinker his head. Charles raised his hand. He wanted to say 'Hartslove luck.' He only managed 'Hartslove.'

20

The One enjoyed the walk until very late in the evening when they arrived on the outskirts of the city and he was assailed on all sides by clatter and stink. Now he bucketed and shied along the streets, splashing himself and everybody else with all manner of filth. Rolling his eyes and sweating profusely, he refused point-blank to go through the gate into the railway station, and Tinker, following his lead, refused likewise. Daisy had driven Tinker all the way. At her insistence, she and Skelton now swapped places. Skelton did not argue. He saddled The One and Daisy found a streetside mounting block to help her climb on. Hordes of beggar boys shouted rude remarks about her legs. She took no notice. Her familiar weight calmed the horse, although it was only after a good deal more fuss that he finally agreed to enter the concourse's great vault. Once inside, he was both astounded and calmed by the fact that despite the random blasts of steam, the engine's whistles and all the echoing racket of humanity in transit, the dozens of dray horses lined up inside were munching their nosebags with worldweary nonchalance.

Daisy was as astounded as The One, though not by the dray horses. She was astonished by the size of the place. Why, the inside of the railway station was almost as big as Hartslove. She was grateful that Skelton quickly found the stalls where The One would stay until he was loaded on to the train in the morning. Though humming with argumentative grooms and street urchins scrabbling for tips, at least they were quieter than the platforms. It was at the stalls that Skelton's friend found them, and when he drove Tinker away, despite The One, Daisy felt very alone.

Skelton offered a hostel. Daisy refused. It was unthinkable to leave The One unattended. She sat firmly on her trunk. Skelton left her, and Daisy found it not so unpleasant, for after the crowds had dispersed, the rhythmic clip of the railwaymen's hammers and the creak of the nightwatchmen's lanterns formed its own lullaby. She made herself comfortable and, with the silks tucked under her cheek, slept surprisingly soundly, not even stirring when somebody covered her with a cloak.

She awoke with a start as the porters arrived, joshing and joking. She was snug under the cloak and The One was amusing himself snatching at the ticket collectors' hats. Daisy got up, shook out the cloak and folded it up, looking around for its owner. She could see nobody likely, so she left it neatly in front of the stall. Skelton appeared soon after with a scoop of barley and dirty grass in a hessian sack. 'This'll have to do for the horse's breakfast,' he said. 'Hey! You!' He beckoned to a porter. 'Take all this.' He gestured to the luggage. The man threw everything on to a wooden trolley. 'Where to?'

'Newmarket train,' Skelton said. 'We've a runner in the Two Thousand Guineas.' The porter raised his eyebrows and, later, two fingers when Skelton did not offer a tip.

Once the engines' furnaces were lit, the night-time lullaby of the railway resumed its daytime rumble and roar. Skelton and Daisy, both holding on to The One, had to fight their way through to the horseboxes on the first of the three trains they had to catch. The One baulked and refused to walk up the ramp. Rough handlers with no time for hysterics simply lifted him bodily. Daisy was allowed into the van only to settle The One's rug, then was hurried away to sit in a carriage further up the train. She could hear whinnying as she left. 'I'm not abandoning you, The One,' she cried, but she felt as though she was.

When the train gave its great starting judder, she clutched Mrs Snipper's basket. 'We've just got to bear it,' she said, as though the horse could hear her.

Above The One, lying flat on the roof of the train, were Garth and Snipe. Neither spoke – Garth because he did not know who the man with the red coxcomb hair was, and Snipe because he never spoke to anybody if he could help it.

Garth had never had any intention of letting Daisy go alone. He said as much to Rose in the note he left. Snipe had been sent by his mother, for whom he had also conducted a bit of business in the town. When the train was well in motion, Garth let himself down into the van. Snipe sat tight.

The One was very glad to see Garth. Bemused and rattled, he could not properly find his feet and slithered and slipped as the train lurched and jolted, jerked and blew. Only when the train's haphazard convulsions steadied into a more regular rocking did the horse begin to relax and soon, like the other horses, he rocked and dozed, dozed and rocked as though he had lived on a train all his life. Garth was careful to climb back on to the roof before they had to change trains. Daisy did not need to know that he was here, and he did not want Skelton to see him.

Daisy remained with The One on the two remaining nights of the journey. In the morning, she always found herself covered with a different cloak. Railwaymen, she decided as she folded it neatly, imagining these to be her benefactors, were a very nice breed of people.

The two first trains were filled with normal traffic. Only on the final train to Newmarket were the horse vans packed with other racehorses, swaddled and bandaged like delicate china, their owners, grooms and jockeys, along with quantities of those underfed and hopeful boys without whom no racing entourage is complete, crammed into the carriages. The One, being neither famous nor important and with only Skelton and the crippled Daisy as support, was relegated to a squashed end stall, far from a window. To Daisy's great surprise, the horse loaded without protest and when, at last, they arrived in Newmarket, he was not only calm, he appeared to have had his white socks washed and his forelock brushed.

On the platform, Daisy regarded the other horses with dismay. Lofty and slim-legged, they were storks against The One's sturdier heron. Neither did they show any interest in people's hats, the scattered remains of porters' lunchboxes or any of the flotsam and jetsam to which The One was as irresistibly drawn as a browser in an old curiosity shop. Whilst these graceful creatures stood disdainfully as their rugs were adjusted, The One had a good scratch on a convenient pillar. When Daisy picked out his feet, he twisted his neck and took hold of her blouse. Skelton tutted. The other grooms smirked.

The Newmarket racecourse was not at all as Daisy expected. In the windblown open, with wooden stands in seemingly random places, it was noisier and seemed more chaotic than the railway station. Some people had raised tents and were camped like gypsies; others marked their territory with dirty blankets or made temporary homes in carts. Horses were everywhere, and not just racehorses, but trainers' hacks, dray horses, riding cobs, ladies' half-breds and endless scruffy ponies. 'Where do they race?' she asked one of the hundreds of officious-looking men with binoculars and top hats. He vaguely gestured to a patchily railed stretch of turf on which four families were sharing a hog roast. Grease and old embers stained the grass. Daisy was horrified.

The racehorses' stables instilled no further confidence. Tatty and leaky, The One's stall had a gaping hole in the panelling where a previous occupant had taken a dislike to his neighbour and tried to kick him. It was hardly the cosseted accommodation most of the runners were used to at home. Nevertheless, after Skelton had filled the water bucket, put food in the manger and placed the basket full of the One's brushes in the corner, it was home of a sort. Daisy also found her crutches, though she had no recollection of giving them to Skelton. 'The race here is just a trial,' she reminded The One. 'Don't forget that the really big day's not until we get to Epsom.' As she waited for Skelton to find a jockey, she hoped The One's stomach felt less knotted than her own.

Skelton appeared at last accompanied by a man resembling a leaf of creased paper. 'This is Grint,' Skelton said. 'He'll be doing the honours.' The jockey grunted. Skelton stripped off The One's rug. Grint ran an unenthusiastic eye over the horse. 'May not look much' said Skelton, 'but if you ride him properly he can win.'

'Dare say.' Grint was not unfriendly. He did not like to speak because an accident had deprived him of nearly all his teeth.

'He's very willing, Mr Grint.' Daisy felt she must say something. 'He's going to win the Derby.'

'Dare say.'

'Would you like to see our racing colours?'

'Dare say.'

Daisy got them out. The little man made no comment.

'The horse can recover from the journey today and we'll get him out in the morning for you to try out,' Skelton said. 'Seven do you?'

'Dare say.'

'I'll give you your instructions then.'

The man touched his forelock and left.

Once again, Daisy refused a hostel. She was fearful of horse-tampering and slept across the rope that constituted the makeshift door. At five o'clock, she could not pretend to be asleep any more so she got up and walked The One out on to the course, brought him back, petted him, sang to him and brushed him until he shone. By seven o'clock the horse was saddled and ready and, in her eyes anyway, despite his inelegant shape, the most handsome horse on the Newmarket heath. She told him so many times as she stroked his long face and dusted invisible specks from his blaze. He blew sweet draughts into her neck and danced at the rubbish blowing between his feet.

Many jockeys appeared, yawning, most getting their first glimpses of the mounts they hoped to ride to victory the following day. Like the rest, Grint was dressed in dirty trousers, his calves strapped into leather chaps, boots sticking out the bottom. He did not speak to the horse and with only marginal help from Skelton sprang into the saddle and took up the reins. The One skipped lightly. For the first time a grin split Grint's toothless face. Daisy liked the grin. It seemed to bode well.

'Now then,' said Skelton, fussing with the stirrups, girth and over-girth, 'the horse is green as a willow, I'll grant you that, and he's short of gallop work. But he can gallop, believe me. For a pipe-opener, take him steady for about four furlongs, then let him go. That's all he'll need this morning. Is that understood?'

'Dare say,' Grint said.

'We'll watch from the stand,' Skelton told him.

The jockey rode exactly as instructed. The One cantered, then galloped without very great distinction. Daisy bit her knuckles throughout. By the time The One drew up, he was panting. Grint, on the other hand, was barely warm.

'Well?' said Skelton. 'Will he do?'

'Dare say,' Grint said, leaping off.

Daisy was busy checking The One's knee. 'It seems to be all right.' She ran her hand obsessively over and over. 'But then, it seemed all right before when it wasn't.'

'Nothing wrong with the knee,' said Skelton.

The rest of the day dragged. In the evening, many grooms purged their horses with laxatives, then swaddled them up against the night air. Skelton brought a purge for

The One, but The One would not take it and eventually Skelton tipped it away. That night Daisy was convinced the knee was swelling and checked it every half-hour or so. The horse did not mind, for he, too, was restless in his draughty stall, wary of his left-hand neighbour, a big black colt who constantly bit his rope, and intrigued by the horse opposite, a grey who arrived late with a goat for a companion. Even at midnight the stables saw a procession of owners, trainers and stable lads moving in groups amongst the horses, inspecting, checking, adjusting, criticising, appraising. 'It's always like this, the night before a big race,' a boy said to Daisy as somebody kicked her for the twentieth time. 'If yer wants ter sleep, don't stay 'ere.'

Just after dawn, Skelton appeared with extra oats. He forbade Daisy to do any grooming in case the horse sensed something special was afoot and boiled up. Still, once she saw how the black colt's lad was braiding his charge's mane, Daisy could not resist copying. The lads might laugh at her – which they did – but The One would be turned out properly. Skelton hissed when he brought Grint to collect the silks. Daisy was unabashed. 'Doesn't he look fine, Mr Grint?'

'Dare say.' Grint took the silks and left.

When the saddling bell rang, Skelton tacked the horse up and together he and Daisy walked him to the paddock. They were the last in. Strung up to fever pitch, the quality of the other horses was even more pronounced. They stalked after their grooms, heads high, knowing their own worth. Daisy's hopes were shaken to their very foundations.

Grint appeared. In the Hartslove colours and with tight-fitting breeches, there was almost nothing of him. He was also carrying a whip. 'You won't need that,' Daisy said at once.

'Dare say,' came the inevitable response. He sprang into the saddle. Skelton tightened the girth and over-girth. Daisy put her arms round The One's neck. She did not care who saw her. 'Do your very best,' she told him. 'You're The One. So long as you don't forget that, all will be well.' She touched The One's snip. 'This is only your first race,' she said, 'so just do your very best. And, Mr Grint?' The jockey looked down. 'Try to make sure he sees the starter's flag drop, and say go when you want him to go.' Grint touched his cap. Skelton led the horse out before Daisy got a chance to insist on doing that herself.

She struggled to the stand, past the bookmakers, the swindlers and the fortune-tellers. Skelton joined her when he had sent The One on his way. His face was like iron as they climbed to the top of the stand. The One must qualify for the Derby. He must. Daisy was impressed. Skelton really did care. 'I'm sure he'll run as well as he needs to, Mr Skelton,' she said, noting how tightly the groom's fists were clenched.

'Damn right he will,' was the response.

The horses milled about at the far end of what was called

the Rowley Mile. The coloured silks glinted and clashed, green against purple, orange against pink. The starter called the horses into a rough line. Daisy could see the red and silver quite clearly. She could also see that The One had his head stuck in the air. He was not looking at the starter. Nor, Daisy could tell, was he listening to Grint. He was staring at something in the middle distance, and occasionally he whinnied, perhaps for her, perhaps not, Daisy could not tell.

The crowd held its breath as the horses inched together. There was a second of complete silence as the starter raised his flag. The moment he dropped it, the horses shot off and the crowd surged.

In seconds, the race took shape: two horses streaked ahead at an unsustainable pace; ten bunched up behind, saving themselves for a final sprint; a few, disconcerted by the pace, already straggled. There was no red and silver arrow amongst any of the groups. The One was still at the starting post, having not yet decided to take part. Daisy went stiff all over. Skelton punched his left fist into his right palm. 'Now, I tell you, NOW!' he roared.

Skelton's voice could not have carried. Nevertheless, Daisy saw Grint pick up his whip. 'But I said –' she cried out. Grint cracked the whip across The One's flank. Startled, the horse rocketed forward. Grint whipped him again. The One whirled a full circle. It was at the third whipping that, ears flat back, he finally began to gallop, and only with luck in the right direction. It was not enough for Skelton. 'Again!' he bawled, and as if in answer, the whip kept cracking. The One was galloping in earnest now, not racing but fleeing the sting raining down from on high. He was quite unaware of overtaking the back markers. He was quite unaware of overtaking the middle bunch at the half-mile stage. Three furlongs out he overtook the second bunch. Only one front-runner was left, and still Grint was waving the whip. Daisy did not know she was screaming. She did not know that she had her palms flat against her head. All she knew was that wicked whip and The One being punished for galloping as he had never galloped before.

Though the race lasted for under two minutes, to Daisy it was a nightmare without end. As the crowd cheered the winner home, she was stumbling down the stand. As The One thundered past into second place, she was leaning hard on crutches that somebody thrust at her. As the winning jockey punched his fist in the air, she was hobbling back to the paddock. Everywhere, punters held aloft winning betting slips or ground their failures underfoot. But Daisy was intent only on getting to The One. She had no idea how he would greet her. She had no idea what she would tell him. It did not matter that Skelton had hired the jockey. It did not matter that Skelton had issued the riding instructions. Daisy had brought The One here. Daisy had wanted him to win. She had told Grint as much. She was responsible. And she knew something else, something dreadful: The One could not run in the Derby. He could not, because never, ever again could he be given over to a jockey and be at the mercy of that whip. Better to lose everything than that.

She forced her way through gaggles of trainers, lads and ordinary racegoers. Though many had lost money, they were loudly applauding. 'Well done to you, girl!' 'Second in the Two Thousand Guineas, no less!' 'Good lord, child, what do you give him to eat?' 'Who'd have thought it!' 'All set for the Derby now!'

The black horse's lad passed her. His charge had come nowhere. 'Congratulations! Never thought I'd see the day when an ugly brute like yours would best my beauty.'

Punch-drunk, Daisy could see people trying to jostle The One. The horse himself was in a wild panic and would not allow anybody near. Indeed, Grint had to leap to dismount, neatly flicking the reins over the horse's head. Daisy had not seen Skelton overtake her, but he was at The One's side, already attempting to fling a rug over the horse's back so that nobody should see those whip marks and spoil the moment by complaining. And The One was helping, because it was impossible to see anything when he would not be still even for a second.

At last, Daisy reached him. The horse did not even notice her. She stood a little to one side, tears streaming down her face. She would not speak to Grint, who was busy pulling the saddle off. She dropped her crutches and waited until she could grab The One's reins. 'He's too strong for you, missy,' somebody advised. 'Let the man hold him.'

'Go away!' cried Daisy. 'Leave us be.'

Fortunately, the winner of the race appeared and the crowd changed its focus. As soon as there was space, Daisy led The One out on to the open heath.

It was two hours before the horse understood that the whip was not going to fall again; three before he was even vaguely calm. All that time, Daisy walked at his side, never scolding when he buffeted and bruised her, never forcing him to go where he did not want to go. She did not offer an apology. What could she say that was apology enough? She walked to the wilder bit of the heath. Her legs ached with all her exertions. That Skelton would have accepted the applause meant for her and The One meant nothing to her. That he would also have collected the prize money meant even less. Neither applause nor money could make up for what The One had endured.

When The One calmed enough, she undid one of the buckles attaching the reins to the bit and used the rein as a long loose rope. She found a sluggish stream and hoped the horse would drink. The One pawed at the stream. He wanted to drink but was still beset by tremors. Daisy's legs felt so weak now that she had to sit down. She rocked, her arms clasped about herself. She could hear vague noises in the direction of the road. Racing was over. People were going home. 'The One!' she whispered. 'The One!' It was all she could do to say his name. She carried on rocking until the tiny tinkle of the stream gradually soothed and The One bent his head to snatch at bits of grass. Only when Daisy moved her arms did he start in alarm. That he thought she might have a whip almost broke her heart.

The sun was fast losing heat. Though The One had his rug, Daisy became worried that he would catch cold. Underneath the rug, too, his dried sweat must be itchy. What could she do to make him comfortable? Dragging herself to her feet, she overbalanced and sat down on something hard. Her crutches. She scrambled up and whipped round, glaring, suspecting Skelton. There was nobody there.

She picked some tender grass shoots. The One stretched his nose towards her. After a while, he took the strands and chewed, turning the froth round his mouth pale green. When he had crunched out all the sweetness, he spat out the stalks, stretched his nose again and tentatively licked Daisy's palms. He moved closer, needing the salt. With great care, Daisy put her arms round his neck. He allowed her to do this. She began to cry.

In time, she undid the buckle and rolled the rug back. The One's flanks were criss-crossed with a tracery of raised welts, fine as the veins on a leaf, only these were blood red and clashed with the copper of his coat. Daisy tore off her petticoat and dipped it into the stream to make a sponge. Delicately, she wiped the sweat from the welts, trickling cooling water from cupped hands. The One shuddered. He lowered his head and began to paw the ground again. 'What is it?' asked Daisy, fearful. He buckled suddenly, first his front end, then his back. Daisy had to jump out of the way. The rug slid off. The horse collapsed entirely, rubbing his neck and one side of his face into the bracken. Finally, he kicked out and rolled clean over. Again and again he rolled, over and over, over and over, luxuriating in the soft prickle of the bracken, which scratched in just the right places. When he had quite finished, he heaved himself up and shook himself violently. Finally, with his mane and tail a woody tangle, he moseyed over to the stream, plunged his nose in and began to drink.

Daisy's heart lightened. The One would not have rolled with Skelton. He certainly would not have rolled with Grint. He might not even have rolled with Garth. Yet he was still happy to expose his soft underbelly and be entirely defenceless with her. She felt a little dizzy. She did not deserve this; she would just accept it as the miracle it was. She waited until he had drunk his fill before picking up the rein. 'We'll have to go back to the stables,' she said. 'You need proper food, and I promise, The One, I *absolutely* promise that nobody with a whip is ever going to ride you again.'

'That's the truth,' came a voice from beside her. In her fright, Daisy lurched, almost falling again. For one extraordinary moment, she thought The One had spoken but the arms that caught her were human enough. She twisted. 'Garth? *Garth?*'

Garth steadied her, then let go. 'Did you think I'd let you do this on your own?'

'But how . . . where . . .'

'I travelled on the roofs of the trains,' Garth said proudly.

'The tunnels!' Daisy could hardly believe her eyes.

'I wasn't by myself,' Garth said. 'I think lots of people travel like that, and anyway, I climbed into the horse vans once the train had started. I've kept The One company the whole way.' He went to the horse. His face tightened when he saw the welts. 'I think he liked me being there.' The One snorted.

'Oh, Garth! Garth! It was so awful. Did you see?'

'I was on the top of the stand.'

'It'll never happen again,' Daisy said at once.

'No, it won't,' Garth said. 'His next jockey won't have a whip.'

'There'll be no next jockey,' Daisy said. 'It's enough.'

'Don't be silly, Daisy. You've got this far. You can't give up now.'

'Don't you see? I have to give up. The One can't go through that again, not even for Hartslove. I can't ride him myself, and who else could I trust?'

Garth gave her a look both terrified and fierce. 'Me. You could trust me.'

All Daisy's relief at Garth's presence dissolved. She could

243

not cope with this again. 'You've tried. You've tried very hard. It didn't work.'

Garth stood his ground. He had felt Grint's whip, felt every sting, every cut, every lash, once for The One, once for Daisy. He must speak quickly. 'Listen to me, Daisy. Please listen.' He touched The One's shoulder. 'It's got to be me. I see that now – well, I saw it before, even though I couldn't do it. This time, I swear by the Resting Place, the Dead Girl and the whole of Hartslove, I'll ride The One and I won't chicken out.'

His voice rang with a sincerity that Daisy could not doubt. But sincerity would not sit in the saddle. Sincerity would not rise in the stirrups. Sincerity would not ask The One to gallop. Sincerity would not win the Derby. She let Garth talk on. It was useless trying to stop him. She led The One back across the heath to the stalls. The One seemed more cheerful. Daisy's heart was in her boots.

21

At Hartslove, spring had taken very firm hold. The tombstones warmed. Sprouting leaves had made the 'for sale' sign almost invisible. The girls and Mrs Snipper stopped listening out for carriage wheels.

Lily was concerned about Garth. 'He had no money for a ticket,' she worried. 'He must have stolen a ride. Can you be transported for that, or even hanged?' She fiddled with her birds until Rose took the cage from her. 'They get upset if you're upset,' she said, 'and there's no need. Garth can look after himself.'

She was not as sure as she sounded. She wondered again and again how she could have possibly allowed Daisy to go off without her. Skelton was hardly a fitting companion, and Garth did things his own way, which was not always the right one. 'I don't even know if she remembered her crutches,' Rose fretted to Mrs Snipper.

Mrs Snipper was unconcerned. 'Miss Daisy will be

Perfectly All Right,' she said, removing the knife with which Rose was supposed to be peeling potatoes. 'Where are those twins? They had no breakfast this morning.'

She was right. The twins had had no breakfast. They were in danger of having no lunch either for they were struggling with an enormous package they had had delivered to the stable yard, intending to secrete it in one of the empty stables. The package was a disappointment. They had hoped for something else.

Ten days before Daisy and The One had set off, Clover and Columbine had been sent by Mrs Snipper to the library with a tray of tea for their father. They were happy to go for they needed a fresh supply of newspapers. They argued on the way. Clover thought they should try *The Times* for a change. Columbine thought they should finish all the *Manchester Guardian*s first. They stopped arguing before they opened the door, both hoping to find Charles asleep. He was unlikely to object to them taking newspapers. Nevertheless, if he was awake they would have to ask him, and since Gryffed's death they never spoke to him if they could help it. Luckily, Charles was asleep, and heavily so. Putting down the tray, they quickly skimmed the papers. They were surprised to find that the top copies of *The Times* were not at all recent; the very top one was from the previous decade. Much thumbed, it offered a graphic account of the war in the Crimea together with lists of the dead, for some of whom there were long obituaries written in heroic prose. Clover and Columbine grinned. Treasure trove. The *Guardian* could wait. Clutching a dozen copies of *The Times* under their arms and stuffing more into skirts already stained with newsprint, they tiptoed out and, once safely in their room, began to sift. Inside the Crimea report they found a pair of reading glasses which they took turns to wear on the end of their noses. Later, tucked into a folded page that recounted the slaughter of the Light Brigade, they found a sealed envelope addressed to their father. For two days they fingered the envelope. On the third day, they opened it, read it and made a decision.

Three days before the Derby, they told Rose and Lily about the parcel. They all went to the stable. Rose stared. The parcel was still untouched. 'What's inside?' she asked.

'We don't know,' said Clover or Columbine truthfully.

'Where did it come from?'

The twins exchanged glances. 'We think it's come from Aunt Barbara.'

Rose sat down with a crash. 'Oh no,' she said. 'Oh no. Pa's done it, hasn't he? He's sold up and Aunt Barbara's sent us – I don't know – sent us something – packing cases – travelling cloaks – something . . .' She bowed her head. 'I know The One's not really going to win the Derby, but Pa might have waited until it was over. Daisy and Garth coming back to this?' She gestured at the package as though it was filled with snakes. 'How could he?'

Clover or Columbine tried to interrupt.

'It *is* Aunt Barbara's writing,' Lily said, wringing her hands.

'It might as well be the hangman's!' The writing made Rose weepy. She had not seen her aunt's hand since before their mother left.

'Oh, will you both LISTEN?!' shouted Clover and Columbine together. They had expected Rose to be angry, not to weep. And what did a hangman have to do with anything? Defensive, they gabbled. 'We found a letter from Aunt Barbara with the Light Brigade. The writing was hard to read, but the address was printed on the top and it seems that Ma must have gone to her when she left and we wrote to Aunt Barbara's address because we thought she might still be there – Ma, that is, not Aunt Barbara – of course Aunt Barbara would be there. Anyway, we told her – Ma, that is, though obviously she wasn't there – that The One was going to win the Derby and that everything would be all right after, so she could come home, and we thought – we thought . . . well, we thought she might at least write back. Then this came.'

Rose had only picked up one sentence. She stopped weeping. '*You* wrote to Aunt Barbara?'

The twins nodded. Rose could shout at them now and that was fine. They were used to it. It was better than her weeping.

'When did you write?'

'Can't remember exactly. A bit before Daisy went.'

'And who sent the letters for you?'

The twins touched shoulders. Rose suddenly realised that they had got quite tall and that their dresses were far too short. 'Father Nameless,' they said together and clasped their hands. 'Please, Rose, don't be angry with him. He didn't seem to mind, and we checked all our spelling in the letter against the spelling in the newspaper.'

Rose looked from them to the package. The same thought occurred to them all. The twins gasped. Of course! Aunt Barbara had written the address, but that did not mean there would not be another letter inside. They crept nearer to the parcel, eyeing it up. 'You open it, Lily,' said Rose.

Lily put out a finger and touched the paper. The package was well wrapped for something of its size. The string required three sharp tugs to undo it. Lily slowly pulled away the paper, revealing a large box with a lid. They all crept further forwards. There was no letter on top of the lid. Lily dragged the lid off and dropped it on to the floor. There was tissue, but still no letter. She removed the top layer of tissue. Under it, stacked together, their ribbons neatly pinned, were five hats: pink, white, yellow, red and blue. Lily took out the hats. More tissue. Still no letter. Lily handed the hats to Clover or Columbine. She removed the next layer of tissue. Five dresses, beautifully rolled so as not to crease, in colours matching the hats. Five sets of ruffled petticoats were under the dresses, with five pairs of gloves and lastly four pairs of open-work stockings and four pairs of cloth boots, the tongues lined in pink, white, red and blue, laced on the inside and with leather heels. Beneath them was a pair of special stockings and boots with thickened heels for callipers. Right at the bottom was another, separate, package, and inside this was a cotton shirt with a crossover collar, a tan leather waistcoat and a pair of worsted stockings tucked into a pair of long black leather boots. Slowly, Lily tipped the whole box upside down. A card fell out. She leaned down, picked it up and offered it to Rose. Rose shook her head. 'Good luck at the Derby. With love from Aunt Barbara,' Lily read. She passed the card to Rose, who passed it on to the twins without looking at it.

Clover and Columbine dropped the card. Rather dazed, they picked up the cloth boots to measure against their feet. 'They're the right size,' they said. They picked up the white dress and held it against Lily, and the pink against Rose. 'The dresses fit too.' They unwrapped each hat, inspected every ribbon and finally took deep breaths and set up a clamour. 'They're Derby dresses, Rose! She's sent them for us to wear for the race! Can we go? We must go! Please?'

'Don't be absurd. Of course we can't go,' said Rose, blinking. 'Aunt Barbara didn't send any money for tickets, and I don't even know where Epsom is except that it's miles away.'

'Couldn't we drive Tinker?'

Rose shook her head. She touched the clothes. They seemed a little unreal. 'Even if Tinker was a post-horse rather than a pony, and even if we set out now, we'd not make it in time.' She began to put the clothes back into the box. She did not know what else to do. Lily helped her, and after a while Clover and Columbine helped too. They dragged the box to the castle.

It took quite something to surprise Mrs Snipper, but she was genuinely surprised about the dresses. It was she who made the children put them on, the twins surreptitiously swapping when they were given the wrong one. 'Should we show Pa?' asked Columbine, loving the swish of the blue.

'No, dearie,' said Mrs Snipper at once. 'Don't do that.' As each girl took her dress off, she hung the dress up.

In the early evening, their spirits very low, the four drifted down to the Resting Place and it was there that Arthur Rose found them. Rose, who had been lying on the flat stone, blinked as the shadow of his cob fell over her. She sat up at once.

'Hello,' Arthur said, dismounting. 'Don't move.' He loosed his cob to graze.

'The One's gone,' Rose said. She knew she was blushing and wished she would not.

'Yes,' said Arthur easily.

'We haven't heard anything.'

'No. That doesn't matter. It's not The One I've come for. It's you – I mean, you all,' he added hastily.

'We're not animals and we're not ill,' said Clover or Columbine.

'Of course not!' Arthur Rose said. 'I've come to ask if you want to go to the Derby.'

A second's pause. 'Of course we want to go,' said Clover or Columbine uncertainly.

'Then we'll go together.'

'What?'

'Don't you want to go?'

'Of course we want to go, only it costs money and Aunt Barbara didn't send any, only dresses and boots.'

Arthur did not seek an explanation about Aunt Barbara or the dresses and boots. 'So we can all go together.'

'Do you mean it?'

'Of course I mean it!' He flashed them a bashful smile.

At once, the twins seized Arthur's hands and began to dance him around the chestnut tree. 'The Derby! The Derby! We're going to the Derby!' they chanted. Arthur could not help laughing, though he was nervous that Rose would find him silly. He extricated himself.

'It's very kind of you, but we can't go.' Rose rose, squinting a little in the sun.

'Rose, Rose,' Arthur said, tucking her arm under his and walking her round the chestnut tree. 'Remember the day The One was sound again?' She nodded. 'Well, I promised Daisy then that I'd be at Epsom and I'm not going to break that promise.' He gave her a very direct look. 'I can go alone, but I think it's important that you're there too because I think she's going to be . . .'

'Disappointed?'

'Distraught,' Arthur said because it was time for truth. 'I don't think she has any idea what The One's up against. She's going to need her sisters around her. For her sake, let me take you all with me.'

'Garth's there already.'

He looked into her eyes. 'Garth's not her sisters,' he said.

'No,' she said.

'Then we'll set off tomorrow on the train.'

'But where will we stay?' Rose had to ask. 'How will we –'

'Leave all that to me,' Arthur said gently. 'It will be my pleasure.' He would not allow her to ask any more. Instead, he walked her back to the flat stone, recaught his cob and mounted. 'I'll be in the courtyard at eight o'clock.' He pressed his legs into the cob's sides.

'No,' called Rose suddenly. He turned. 'I mean, don't come to the courtyard. We'll meet you at the stables.'

He understood at once. She did not want their father to see them going. 'To the stables,' he said. 'I'll not be late.'

Columbine and Clover ran back to the castle. Rose and Lily followed. They first spoke to Mrs Snipper, then took down their dresses and tried on their boots before packing them away with Garth's and Daisy's clothes. In

253

the morning, though they had not asked her, Mrs Snipper pushed a hamper of food over to the yard in a wheelbarrow.

Arthur arrived half an hour early in a hired trap. Everything and everybody was quickly settled. Arthur picked up the reins. Rose leaned out, suddenly uneasy. 'What will you tell Pa, Mrs Snips? I should have said something.'

'Indeed You Shouldn't,' said Mrs Snipper. 'You Look After Yourselves, That Horse, Master Garth and Miss Daisy. Leave Your Father to Me.'

'Are you sure?'

'Sure as the Nose on My Face.' Mrs Snipper waited until the trap was through the arch before she wiped the Nose on her Face on her apron. She missed the old days. She missed Lady de Granville. She missed her son. Now she would miss the children. She leaned for a moment against the castle wall. 'Hey Ho,' she said, before picking up Lily's birdcage and going back to the kitchen to prepare a breakfast she knew Charles would not eat.

22

Garth had not hidden himself back at the Newmarket stables. Skelton was not pleased to see him, but at least Garth supported him as he argued with Daisy the morning after the Two Thousand Guineas.

'We're going home,' Daisy said.

'Don't be silly,' Skelton rasped. 'This is the moment we've – you've been waiting for. If the horse can be runner-up in the Guineas wearing heavy shoes, imagine what he'll do when we get to Epsom and we put the racing plates on. Everything's arranged.'

Daisy did not seem to hear.

'Daisy!' said Garth, disconcerted. 'You can't take him home now!'

'We're going home.'

'No,' said Skelton and Garth together.

Daisy pursed her lips and began to pack The One's brushes.

'Daisy!' Garth put his hand on her arm. 'Didn't you hear me before? You won't have to worry about whips if I ride.'

Skelton knew he and Garth should stick together, but this was too much. 'Come off it, Master Garth. You can't even sit on the horse – on any horse. You certainly can't ride The One in the Derby.'

'I'm going to ride him,' Garth said with some spirit, 'and I'm going to ride him better than that toothless streak of vomit you employed. Look what he's done!' He gestured at The One's welts.

Skelton barely glanced over. 'Blame me for those, eh? Well, tell me this: who didn't teach the horse to start? Who's treated it like a domestic pet? Who can't even get himself into the saddle? If you want to win the Derby, sonny, you've got to do a bit more than quiver.'

'That's it,' said Daisy. 'We're leaving right now.'

Skelton put his hand across the doorway. 'Now, look here. I thought the idea was to win, so I did what I had to do, and at my own expense. If your idea was to come last, you should have said so.'

'He whipped him!' said Daisy without any expression. 'He whipped him!'

'For the love of Christ! Did you want the horse to be laughed off the track? Grint brought him home second!' Skelton was livid. To have his plans ruined when they were so close to fruition! He wanted to kill Garth and shake all

Daisy's teeth out. 'The horse knows how to win better than you do. What a shame. What a crying shame for him and for Hartslove.'

'We *are* going to the Derby,' Garth said.

'Not according to Miss Daisy, Master Garth,' Skelton sneered.

'We are, and I *am* going to ride. I swear it.'

Skelton's laugh was harsh. 'For the love of God. Then we really might as well go home. With you on board, the horse couldn't win a donkey derby.'

'Daisy!' cried Garth. 'You believe I can do it, don't you? Please, Daisy! You must tell him!'

Skelton began to throw the brushes into the basket. 'It's over then. I agree with you, Miss Daisy. No point in taking the horse to Epsom to be ridden by coward.'

Daisy was torn in two. She pressed close to The One. She could not bear this. Garth was not a coward – or only about riding. But she could not let Garth think she agreed with Skelton. She could not. She wanted to shout at them both to leave her and The One alone. She could not do that either. Instead she found herself saying, 'Garth can do it. It's Garth or nobody.' She twisted her horsehair bracelet. She slumped.

Skelton slammed the basket down. 'To think I've tried to help you. To think I've paid the entry.'

'You go home,' Daisy said to him wearily. 'Garth and I will pay you back the fifty sovereigns after the race.'

'Will you just! And how, pray, will you pay for all the other expenses?'

'That's our business.'

Skelton left them. This was impossible. Garth could not ride the horse at Epsom. He paced about, dreaming up a thousand plans, from kidnapping Garth, to injuring him, to pulling him off at the start of the Derby and whizzing another jockey on in his place. All these plans were hopeless. Skelton had to accept that if Garth did not ride the horse, the horse would not run, and if the horse did not run, there was no possibility at all of Skelton owning Hartslove. And the horse could win. After his Guineas performance, there could be no doubt about that. *But only with the right jockey, riding under Skelton's instructions.* Skelton sat on a milk pail and began to refocus. He sat for a long time before his eyes widened. What a fool he was! The answer was staring straight at him. There were many sorts of courage, and like father, like son! The boy could probably manage to ride in the Derby if his veins were filled with something a bit sparkier than his own blood. Brandy, for instance. Brandy had put Charles entirely under Skelton's thumb; surely it would do the same for Garth.

He got up and walked about again. They had eighteen days until the Derby. Much could be done with brandy in eighteen days, and on the day of the race itself, a jockey filled with brandy would do many things a sober jockey would never consider. Skelton made a quick decision. He would go back to Daisy and apologise. He would say that he had been precipitate. He would say that despite his reservations, she was in charge of the horse. He would not be friendly to Garth. That would be too obvious. He would, though, through the silent offering of the bottle, become as crucial to the boy as he was to his father. It was not an ideal plan but it could work, and the more Skelton thought about it, the more he liked it. 'You're a genius,' he told himself as he walked back to The One's stall, 'and one day the whole world will know it.' When he apologised to Daisy, he felt he almost meant it.

23

They arrived at Epsom fifteen days before the Derby. The One's welts were healing though they were not forgotten: Grint had known just how to strike for maximum hurt and minimum lasting physical injury. Skelton found good stables in the town and decent rooms for Garth and Daisy. 'If Master Garth can get himself into the saddle, he'll need to keep his strength up.' He did not stint on the malice: he felt barbed comments would lower Garth's suspicions.

Despite Skelton's apology and help, Daisy could not like him any better, and to avoid him she took the horse on to the downs very early and waited for Garth to find her. She was dreading it, but he was less white than she expected. She did not look at him again. Instead, she concentrated on keeping her voice low and even. She had no idea what to say so she spoke about the weather and the state of the ground, all the while hoping that The One did not look too powerful and eager beside her.

Garth, for his part, noticed how thin Daisy had got and how her face was stamped with worry. *She's only twelve*, he thought. *It's not fair.* He was very aware of the effort Daisy had to make to keep her voice so easy. He tried not to keep looking at the empty saddle or to acknowledge the fear in his mouth or to think of The One's long, strong neck soon to be stretched out in front of him. He tried and, for the first time in his life, he succeeded, because today he had a weapon he was not going to share with Daisy. At the bottom of his stomach a warmth was beginning to spread. Soon it would surge through his veins, rush up his spine and into the back of his head. Garth did not just hope the rush would come; he knew it would come because before he had set out across the downs, he had drunk a third of a bottle of brandy.

It was not the first drink Garth had had since the Two Thousand Guineas. He had found the bottle in the pocket of his coat after Skelton had apologised to Daisy. It was clearly some kind of peace offering and, as such, Garth had been inclined to smash it in Skelton's face. Instead, though he knew he should not, Garth had taken one sip, then another. It tasted better than he remembered. He had corked the bottle and enjoyed the small fiery buzz. Skelton probably thought he would drink the lot and disgrace himself. Well, he would show him. He was not like his father. He could take the stuff or leave it. He had taken only a few more sips, just enough to make him feel like the boy who flipped on the ruins, the boy who rode the Cannibal, the boy who could shoot a pistol at his own head. Just enough to make him feel like the boy who could ride a Derby winner.

Skelton had grinned when he saw the seal broken. Moneyless Garth could not purchase the drink himself. He would rely on Skelton for the next bottle, and the next one after that. All Skelton had to do was keep him topped up. This morning, Garth had a bottle safely tucked into his coat. The thought made him warm inside.

When she could not justify walking any further, Daisy made The One halt. 'All right, Garth?' she said matter-of-factly. 'I think this is a good place.'

Garth threw off his coat and hesitated only momentarily. The rush came just in time. He vaulted on, fumbling his feet into the stirrups and gathering up the reins. He would pretend he was a centaur: that The One was part of himself as he seemed to be part of Daisy. The horse moved. Garth grabbed a piece of mane. 'Woah, woah,' shushed Daisy. The horse did not want to woah. He began to walk. Daisy waited for the inevitable – for Garth to jump off. Garth did not. He sat a little straighter. The One walked a little faster. Garth grabbed more mane. The horse was huge. His strides were huge. The downs were huge. There would be no stopping him if he set off. Daisy glanced up. Garth's face was set. 'He wants to trot,' Daisy said. 'I can't keep up if he trots.'

Garth swallowed. Deep in his bowels, the brandy

swirled. Garth concentrated on the swirl. 'Let go, then,' he said. 'Let go now.'

Daisy let go. The One trotted smartly away. Garth swayed and lurched. The grass was miles below. The One's neck was miles long. The reins were just ribbons against the horse's strength. He closed his eyes. No – that was bad. He opened them. The One was slowing, returning to Daisy. He halted. Daisy could hardly believe it. A smile flickered across her face. Garth beamed down. Suddenly, she was beaming back.

'I've done it!' Garth said.

Daisy's hands were trembling. 'You've done it!' she echoed. 'You've really done it!'

'I can do it again.' It was half an hour before Garth vaulted off and handed the horse to Daisy. He returned to his coat, took a surreptitious swig, then got on again. This time, he cantered. Skelton watched for a few moments more. When he heard Garth laugh, he linked his thumbs behind his braces and swaggered back to the yard.

Over the following week, Daisy could not hide her astonishment. This was Garth as she dreamed he would be. For three consecutive mornings he trotted away, and though he did not exactly push forward into canter, when The One did canter, Garth crouched lightly in the saddle, no longer grabbing at either the reins or the mane. On the fourth day, finding his jockey agreeable and the turf springy, The One stretched out a little, and when a rabbit started from a hawthorn bush, he shied. Daisy gasped. Garth was unmoved. Not so The One, who launched off at full tilt. Daisy thought she might cry when she saw Garth rising in his stirrups like a professional and The One's ears prick, his stride strong and relaxed. Both horse and rider were enjoying themselves. Everything was possible again.

After the gallop, Garth tumbled off, flushed and unusually garrulous, laughing and dancing about. Daisy laughed too, putting this miracle down to the heady mix of determination and adrenalin. They walked back to the stables, The One snorting and prancing like a true racehorse. 'You make the perfect team, just perfect,' Daisy said, addressing both Garth and The One. She loved Garth's theatrical bow.

Seven days before the race, the real truth hit Daisy like a hammer blow. She was standing on a small hump of stones, where, conveniently, she had found her crutches, and she was holding a cloth in the air for the second time. They had been trying to regularise The One's starting technique by making him automatically launch forward after the count of three. This morning, they had had three successful and two unsuccessful attempts. It was after the fourth success that Daisy realised she was looking at something horribly familiar, namely that the smile plastered all over Garth's face was not actually Garth's smile at all: it was their father's brandy-smile. At first she thought she must be mistaken.

Garth would not be such a fool. But deep in her heart she knew there was no mistake. She was stunned, then furious with herself at her blindness. She could see it all now. Of course Garth could never have managed to ride The One on his own. She could not believe she had ever believed it. Feeling like a sneak, she riffled through Garth's belongings when he was washing under the pump. He had not hidden the bottle – it was his third – very well. When he returned, he paled. 'What are you doing, going through my things?'

'Who gave this to you?' Daisy held the bottle up.

'None of your business,' Garth said, snatching it back.

'Oh, Garth,' said Daisy, all the joy of the past days seeping out through her toes.

Garth was unrepentant. 'Look, it's not as if I need it. It just makes me ride better. Don't you see that?'

'But –'

'But nothing.'

'You'll end up like Pa!' Daisy said flatly.

Garth's face darkened. 'Rubbish. I know what I'm doing.'

'Pa thinks he does too.'

'Well, he's wrong and I'm right.' Garth scowled as though she was his enemy. 'I'm riding well. Isn't that what you wanted?'

'Not like this.'

'You mean you'd prefer Grint to ride The One?'

'Of course not! Don't twist things. I wanted to take The One home.'

'And lose Hartslove?' There was silence. Garth softened. 'Look. Think of it this way. I'm using the brandy like medicine, and as soon as the race is over, I'll give it up.'

Garth was so logical, so plausible. Daisy also knew he was quite wrong, because now that he no longer bothered to disguise it, she could see nothing but their father's look in her brother's eye and hear their father's bravado in his voice. He even smelled like Charles, and just like Charles would have an answer for everything. She asked only one question. 'Where did you get it?'

'I don't know,' Garth lied. 'It's like your crutches. It just appears.' He was pleased with this.

'It's not like my crutches. I need my crutches because there's something wrong with me.' She kicked some straw, then burst out, 'Garth! You're not a coward. You could ride without the brandy. I think you'd even ride better.'

Her voice smote him. But she was not right. He knew that, even if she did not.

The following morning, Daisy left Garth to brush the horse and walked down the main street of the town, tormented by a dilemma. Should she leave Garth to drink until after the Derby or should she do something to stop him? The first option was the easier, although it felt to Daisy like the coward's way out. Moreover, if Garth, drunk, won the Derby, drink would always be the friend he would

266

turn to when faced with a challenge. And soon he would not even need a challenge. After all, their father, who must have started to drink for some reason Daisy did not know, now needed a drink just to face the day. She pictured Garth a desiccated wreck standing by a library fireplace. She pictured him sitting in a pictureless dining room, his children tiptoeing past with pitying glances. She pictured him lying face down on his bed, a daughter pulling off his boots. She could not be even the tiniest bit responsible for that. She came to an apothecary's shop, went in, and after some discussion with the proprietor, emerged with a bottle of her own. She returned at once to the stables and, when Garth was fetching water, found his bottle, tipped out a good quantity of brandy and replaced it with the mixture she had been given. 'I just can't bear it,' she told The One. 'Everything's jinxed. Except you, of course.' He sniffed her hands and wrinkled his lip.

The next day, Garth was a little quieter but still climbed easily on to The One. He was surprised that Daisy let him: surprised and grateful. As they walked to the downs, Daisy engaged him in detailed conversations about how the Derby might go. 'Some say that you should take The One slowly at first and pick up speed in the last quarter-mile. The course is much hillier than it looks, so you've got to keep enough in reserve to put on an extra uphill spurt. He'll have different shoes on – did you know that? Racing plates instead of these heavy ones. Those will help.' The more Garth had to remember, the less he would notice the diminishing rush of the diluted brandy.

Every day for the next five days, Daisy tampered with Garth's bottle, sometimes nervous that she had gone too far. However, Garth's old terrors did not seem to return. She supposed, rightly, that this was partly because he no longer expected them. She did not try to analyse any more. It was enough that Garth was riding almost sober, and that when the race was over and he learned that he had ridden without drink, he would know that he was not a coward; that he was, indeed, as brave – braver – than she was. 'Just two more days,' she whispered to The One. 'Just two.'

Sitting on a chair in his hostel room, Skelton was holding a whip. There was a problem – a big problem. Though he had now supplied at least five bottles of brandy, it was clear that for some reason he could not fathom Garth was no longer drunk, and if Garth was not drunk, he would not be fuddled enough to take the whip, and if he did not take the whip, he would not beat the horse, and if he did not beat the horse, the horse was very likely to go his own sweet way, and horses that went their own sweet way did not win the Derby.

Skelton got out the piece of paper on which Charles's promise was written and laid it on the rickety table. Occasionally, he rose and cracked the whip hard across it. The table rocked. In the end, he folded the paper and put it back in his inside pocket. He would not be thwarted. He would not. He pulled on his coat and made his way to the racetrack. Five or six jockeys were hanging about, gossiping about their Derby prospects. They called Skelton over. He was going to refuse until they waved a bottle of whisky. It winked at him, and after a moment's reflection, he stuck the whip into his boot and walked across to join them.

24

O n the morning of the Derby, Daisy was up before dawn. Not that there was anything to do apart from keep The One calm, and getting up early was unlikely to help with that. To soothe her own nerves, she walked into the waking town. In ones and twos, the carriages were arriving and small clumps of people were trickling out of the railway station. In an hour, the carriages would be arriving in tens, twenties and finally in their hundreds until it was impossible to cross the street, and the small clumps of railway travellers would balloon into vast crowds, pouring on to the downs, chattering, quarrelling, pontificating and predicting as they jostled to get a good spot from which to view one of the greatest races on earth.

Garth was draining a new bottle when Daisy got back to the stables. He needed so much more of the stuff now. Never mind. He dropped the bottle when he saw Daisy, expecting a row. But Daisy only said, 'Promise me just one thing, Garth – that you'll stick to the brandy and not drink anything else.'

Garth found it easy to promise. They did not speak of the drink again, only of how he would ride – not getting in front too early if he could manage. 'Don't worry, though,' Daisy reassured, 'The One knows what to do, and he can out-gallop anything. Just make sure he starts properly and sit tight.' She touched Garth's arm. 'You can do it, you and The One.'

The morning was endless, broken only by the arrival of the farrier to nail on the racing plates. Daisy stood close to The One's head as the man bent to his work, Skelton fussing and checking. When the shoeing was finished, The One raised his weightless feet like a cat on a hot roof. It was a comical sight. Skelton laughed. Daisy and Garth did not.

At lunchtime, they walked The One from his stable to the racetrack and took up a place near the Rubbing House. Finding her crutches leaning against the corner of one of the refreshment booths, and so as not to stress the horse by her twitching, Daisy left The One with Garth. Even with the swelling crowds, the crescendo of noise and the endless cry of 'Get your Derby souvenirs here!' it was still hard to believe that the day she had dreamed of, argued for and imagined for so long had actually arrived. She had expected to feel – what had she expected to feel? She was not sure, only that what she did feel was nothing like it. Several times she had to pinch herself. Hardly realising what she was doing, she kept leaning down to pick up the bits of rubbish a brisk wind was tossing about. Nothing must distract The One.

As she was making her way back to Garth, a hired carriage swerved towards her. She stepped aside. There were cries. The carriage stopped and out poured Rose, Lily, Clover and Columbine, with Arthur holding back slightly. Clover or Columbine was waving a newspaper in which was a report of the Two Thousand Guineas. 'Daisy! Daisy!' they called. Until she saw her sisters, Daisy did not realise how much she had missed them or just how much she needed them today. She did not ask how they had come. She did not smile. She did not say their names. She simply seized the side of the cart and clung to it. Arthur Rose patted her shoulder. Dear Arthur Rose! He had kept his promise. She should have known he would.

Words tumbled out. 'Skelton's taken away The One's water because he says it's bad to drink before the race. Is that right? He says we should get to the paddock late so that The One doesn't get excited. What do you think? '

'I'd say he's right on both counts, absolutely right,' Arthur said. 'Trust him on this, Daisy. He knows what he's doing.'

Lily gestured at their clothes. 'From Aunt Barbara,' she said.

'What?' It was the first time Daisy noticed what her sisters were wearing.

Lily did not say more. She simply drew Daisy into the carriage. 'There are clothes for you.'

'No time,' Daisy said.

'Yes, you've time,' Lily countered gently. 'You've a runner in the Derby. The One looks the part and so must you.' Daisy bit her lip, and as Arthur directed the carriage to the horse-booths, she allowed Lily to dress her and tidy her hair, the twins forming a screen. She climbed down directly afterwards. She must rush back to The One. She must rush back to Garth.

Arthur and her sisters came with her. They nodded to Skelton, smiled nervously at Garth and wished The One good luck. Arthur shook Garth's hand, then Daisy's, then ushered the other girls away.

Garth was nervous, more nervous than he could have imagined, not about climbing on to The One – he felt the brandy must kick in today, surely. He was suddenly absolutely terrified of riding badly and losing. He fidgeted and fretted and nearly drove Daisy mad. About an hour before the race, three jockeys approached. 'Got your silks?' one asked. Garth nodded.

'Anxious?' Garth nodded.

'Always hard for a green jockey. Stick with us. We'll get you through. Come to the weighing room. It's a steadying place before a big race.'

Garth looked at Daisy. She was very uncertain. 'It's a bit early,' she said.

'As you like,' said the oldest of the jockeys. 'Everybody has their own way of coping. Just trying to help. You can learn a lot from old-timers when the pre-race nerves bite. If you don't want to, though . . .' He and his friends began to walk off.

'I wonder if I should go with them,' Garth said to Daisy. 'I think it *would* help to be with other jockeys.' Daisy was still uncertain. Garth was picking at his nails. His nerves were terrible. Daisy relented. It seemed mean. What could be the harm?

'Go,' she said.

'Really?'

'Of course,' she said, and she forced herself to smile. 'You're the jockey.'

Garth stopped picking his nails. 'Yes,' he said, 'I am.'

'Just be careful.'

'I'll be careful.'

Daisy stayed with The One.

'Ah, Miss Daisy,' Skelton said, his eyes darting about. 'Master Garth not with you?'

'He's gone to the weighing room with some of the other jockeys. He'll meet us in the paddock.'

'Good idea,' said Skelton at once. 'The other jockeys'll look after him.' Something in his voice was not reassuring. Daisy wished the race would start.

Garth caught up with the jockeys and sat with them under the pegs in the changing room. One produced a bottle of whisky. 'Horses have a purge; we have a dram,' he said, and pulled out the cork. He offered it to Garth. 'New blood first.' Garth shook his head. The jockeys did not press him. They took a small pull each – a pity to waste what Skelton had provided. One of the older jockeys wiped his mouth. 'Well, young man,' he said. 'You're lucky to be with us. Stacker here's won two Derbys.'

'Aye,' Stacker said, 'and never without a tot of whisky.' He pretended to take another pull. 'The thing about whisky, lad, is that it's not like other drinks. Whisky really clears the head, and a clear head's vital in a race like this.'

'My head's quite clear,' Garth said, and thought it horribly true. His head was far too clear. He could feel no brandy rush.

'Six add six!' said Stacker suddenly.

'What?'

'Head not that clear, boy!' Stacker laughed softly. 'It'll need to be clearer.' Still he did not press the drink. Instead, he and his fellows, as instructed by Skelton, began to swap stories of falls they had had. 'Worse on the flat, boy,' Stacker mused. 'So easy to slip, and those hooves . . . Hit you in the wrong place and – poof – your legs are gone. Only last week I visited a friend. Hasn't walked for – oh, it must be fifteen years.'

Garth's stomach heaved. When the bottle came round again, he took a swig. When it came again, he took another. After four rounds he felt brave. After five, he felt braver.

After six, he felt on the edge of something extraordinary. When the time came, he sat in his silks on the weighing chair in a trance. Only when the saddling bell sounded and he stood up, clutching his weight cloth, did the world topple and spin. He heard the other jockeys laughing. He tried to laugh himself, then realised with horror that they were not laughing with him but at him. 'Drunk!' Stacker said softly. 'You poor booby!'

Two jockeys took his arms and steered him out. Garth could not speak. Everything was floating, everything but one fact that he could neither face nor deny: he was drunker than he had ever been in his life and there was nothing he could do about it. In one cold corner of his mind he remembered his father's gun. He wished he could use it now. Skelton appeared and took the weight cloth from him. When the groom returned to Daisy and slung it over The One's back, his expression was inscrutable. 'Master Garth'll meet us in the paddock,' he said.

Daisy was checking the girth. She would check it again in the paddock, and again after Garth was mounted. Nothing should be left to chance. She attached a lead-rein to The One's bit. The horse seemed interested though largely unmoved by all the activity around him. Whilst the horse nearby lathered and fretted, he ate a feather from Daisy's hat. She removed it from his mouth. 'Not today,' she said. Her crutches were ready for her but she did not want them. This was it. She swallowed hard. 'Let's go,' she said.

Pressed from all sides by punters wanting to get a good look at The One, Daisy found the short journey to the paddock the most alarming of her life. Several times she was nearly crushed. In the paddock itself things eased a little and she was able to find a space in which to stand still. She searched anxiously for Garth. The One was almost too relaxed. A large knot formed in Daisy's throat. She saw her sisters and Arthur pressing against the rail. She could not acknowledge them.

The jockeys arrived in a gaggle, Garth amongst them. 'Garth!' Daisy whispered. 'Garth!' But Skelton took charge, shoving Daisy out of the way as he gave Garth a leg-up. It all happened so quickly. Daisy did not have time for any last-minute instructions. She did not even have time to say, 'Good luck.' Skelton checked the girth. Skelton pressed Garth's feet into the stirrups. Skelton, Skelton, Skelton. 'To the start,' the clerk of the course shouted. 'Get a move on there!' Garth was facing away from her as Daisy unclipped the lead-rein. Then Skelton was urging The One out of the paddock and in an instant the great tide of humans and horses had surged off, leaving Daisy almost alone. Arthur hurried to her. 'Quickly,' he said, and chivvied all the girls back to the carriage, helping them up so that they could stand above the crowd.

Garth was crouched in the saddle, his feet slipping in and out of the stirrups. His legs belonged to somebody else; his tongue was thick; his cap too tight on his head. He thought

Daisy was beside him. 'I should have refused! I couldn't refuse! I tried but I couldn't!' The words did not matter because no one was listening. The One was a precarious rock in an alien sea. Garth tried to focus. There seemed to be three chestnut necks in front of him, each with three sets of ears. The crowd was not a crowd but an open mouth ready to swallow him up and spit him out. The sun was not the sun but a fat yellow finger, wagging and pointing and chanting, 'You fool, you fool . . .' The wrestlers, the prostitutes, the three-card tricksters were dissolving into a coloured sea of smocks, shawls and scarves, and he, Garth, was falling, falling, falling into a black hole at the bottom of which lay all Daisy's dreams.

Garth might never have made it to the start at all had Skelton not been loping beside him. In the end, Garth fixed on him as the only steady thing. At the start itself, Skelton seized his moment. 'You've got one chance, Master Garth, and one only. Do you understand?' He had his hand on the rein.

Garth sagged. Skelton forced him to sit up. 'My God, boy!' he said, in mock horror. 'You're drunk. *Drunk!* On this day of all days! I can't believe it.' Garth did not even try to answer. Skelton pressed on. 'Can you use your legs?' Garth stared dumbly at him. 'For the love of God!' Skelton shouted. Some of the other jockeys looked round. Skelton came very close. 'You've blown it, you coward. You've blown all Miss Daisy's hopes. You've blown the future of Hartslove. You're going to lose. You're a scoundrel.'

Garth tried to move his tongue. 'No – no!'

'Yes, yes. *A drunken scoundrel!*'

'What – do? Help me.' Garth was beyond pride, beyond any place he knew.

Skelton seemed to hesitate.

'Help.'

As though very unwilling, Skelton held up something long and thin, careful to keep it out of The One's line of vision.

Something sparked. Garth pushed the whip away. 'Won't,' he slurred.

Skelton dug his nails right through Garth's cotton breeches. There was nothing friendly about him now. 'Do you want to win this damned race?'

'Yes.'

'Then take this whip and use it.'

'No – Daisy –'

Skelton fingers were a vice. 'You think Miss Daisy wants you to lose the race?'

'No, but –'

'Don't be a fool. She's depending on you. Everybody's depending on you and you're drunk. If you've any sense of honour, you'll just do as you're told.'

Everything seemed far away. Only Skelton's voice drove through the fog like a dart. 'Do as you're told, boy, and everything will be fine.'

'Can't –'

'You can, boy. You must.' Skelton thrust the whip at him again, less carefully this time. 'The horse'd have come nowhere in the Guineas without the whip. You know that. Take it and use it and burn it afterwards for all I care. Just damned well win this race, d'ye hear me? *Just damned well win.*'

Skelton's face swam. The bobbing heads around Garth swam. The sky swam. All Garth could see clearly was the whip. All he could feel was that his legs would not work. Then the whip was in his hands and Skelton was gone and The One was engulfed in the barge and crash of other horses fighting for their heads.

The starter, hemmed in and jostled by the throng, was calling the runners into line. The other horses thrust their noses forward, their jockeys hunched. The One did not like the jostling and was dallying, his nose stuck in the air, always on the lookout for Daisy. The other horses shivered and jibbed. The One spied an apple core and determined to eat it.

The rough hands of the starter's boys seized his bridle, forcing him to face the front. He did not like that either. Again he looked for Daisy and listened for her voice. 'Let them go, McGeorge!' 'Get them away, McGeorge!' The horse was quite aware of Garth perched in the saddle, and cocked an ear back. Garth was silent. When the flag dropped and the other horses leaped off, The One sneezed and continued to chew the apple core.

Garth knew he had to say something to get The One

to start. He knew they had practised it. He could not remember what it was. He wanted to close his eyes and die, but people were bawling at him, and in desperation, as though obeying an order from outside, he raised the long, thin whip and flashed it down. He heard the hum. He felt the vicious swish. He was vaguely aware that a man with a coxcomb of red hair had darted out and taken the full force of the lash across his face. Garth dropped the whip. The One, still chewing his apple core, gave a small skip to the side. From their carriage, Rose, Lily, Clover, Columbine and Arthur cried out in unison. Daisy jumped down and began to hobble as fast as she could to the track.

From his place on the hill, Skelton saw the whip drop and The One still chewing as the other horses rocketed away. He was at first disbelieving, then beyond wild, his veins foaming purple. He punched his fists together, shouting and screaming. He would kill Garth. He would crush his neck between his palms. He would roast him over an open fire. As for the man with the red coxcomb, Skelton would beat him to a pulp.

Snipe shuddered when the whip sliced his skin, but there was something more to do. As the blood began to drip he sang, 'One, two, three, GO,' in his foxy voice. At 'one', The One stiffened. At 'two', he pricked his ears; at 'three', he threw up his head; and at 'GO' he dropped the apple core and galloped.

He galloped alone for three-quarters of a minute, then

caught the back markers, two of whom had lost precious time swerving around a stray dog. The middle group was banked together along the slight right-handed rise. The One was happy enough behind them until the course swung left and he found himself on the outside, with a clear view. He could feel Garth swaying and rocking. The other horses were clustered together along the rail, their jockeys anxious for the shortest route. The One stretched out, enjoying the freedom of galloping alone. Round Tattenham Corner, the course dipped. The One shortened his stride and shied at a fluttering piece of paper. Garth flew sideways, only luck crashing him back into the saddle. The wallop jolted The One and now he thrust forward using the full power of his hindquarters, the light shoes adding a glorious spring. Along the straight he streamed, revelling in his own strength. This was fun! This was it! Garth, shaken about like a rag in the wind, the red jacket billowing, dropped the reins completely and wound his hands into The One's red mane. The One hesitated. Perhaps he would stop now. Over on the rail, only two horses were ahead of him. No, perhaps he would keep going. The ground was uneven so he veered over to join them.

In the stand, Skelton was frozen mid-curse. Around him, the crowd was on its feet and bellowing. 'Good God! Will you look at that?!' Only when The One passed the two-furlong marker did Skelton find his voice again. 'Go on! Go on! Go ON, you brute! GO ON!'

The One was still behind Stacker on the leader. One furlong out, he spied a figure in yellow beyond the finish line. Daisy! He hurtled towards her. Hearing the crescendo in the crowd, Stacker turned his head. He saw a cloud of spittle and a red haze approaching the level of his boot. Raising his whip, he made as if to strike his own horse, but at the last moment changed the angle of the whip and brought it down sharply on The One's nose. For a moment, The One could not breathe. It was moment enough. Stacker's horse drew ahead. The Derby was lost by a whisker.

25

Daisy stood quite still as the winning horse thundered past her. She even stood still as The One slithered to an ungraceful halt and Garth tumbled face down on to the grass. She was still when Skelton ran over, howling that the grinning Stacker had clearly breached the rules. It was Skelton, not Daisy, who objected violently when Stacker's supporters, to the fury of The One's, denied wrongdoing.

The One himself was blowing hard. He had exerted himself quite considerably. However, unlike the winning horse, who was shivering and panting and almost dead on his feet, The One was not distressed. He wiped his foamy mouth on Garth's prone back and nudged Daisy, who clung to him. Rose, Lily, Columbine and Clover fought their way through, still holding hands. Behind, looking out for Lily, was Snipe, the welt across his face raw as a dagger wound.

Still drunk, but acutely conscious, Garth curled himself into a ball. Lily ran to him and dropped to her knees.

'Garth! Are you hurt? Please tell me!' Garth rolled himself tighter. He could never unroll. He should be picked up just as he was and dropped into the sea. He had not won the race. Worse, had it not been for the red coxcomb man, he would have been no better than Grint. Daisy had trained The One brilliantly. The One had run the race of his life. It was Garth who had failed everybody and everything, including himself. His guts dissolved.

Arthur Rose was trying to calm Skelton. 'For God's sake, man!' It was a bittersweet result for the young vet himself, for if the Derby was lost perhaps Rose could marry him. Still, he owed it to Daisy to do the right thing. He went to The One. He inspected the horse's nose, prised Daisy gently away, took the reins and walked The One over to the chief steward. 'Look,' he commanded in a clear and carrying voice. 'A jockey might strike a horse up alongside by mistake. But he could not strike at this angle.'

The steward peered at The One. The crowd packed around him. The angle of the cut was described loudly by everybody who could see it. 'For shame!' somebody shouted. 'For shame!' the chant was taken up. The bookmakers began to shout too. The chief steward, nervous for his safety, sent a boy scurrying off. A flag was raised. There would be an inquiry. Both jockeys would be required to give their accounts. The chief steward would ask the race judge to preside.

Lily pleaded with Garth. 'Garth! Get up! You've got to

go to the stewards' tent.' Garth hunched tighter and tighter. 'Garth!' urged Rose. 'Please! Get up!'

'Get up, Garth!' echoed Clover and Columbine. 'Tell him, Daisy!'

A brisk female voice cut through. 'Let us pass, please! At once, please!'

Rose and Lily's heads snapped round. A woman in a sensible brown dress and a small veiled hat elbowed a passage through the crowd. 'Aunt Barbara!' Rose exclaimed, then stopped breathing. Next to her aunt was somebody else, and it was this somebody else who ran to Garth and knelt down beside him.

'I tried to prevent her,' said Aunt Barbara. 'But here we are.' Lily, Daisy, Clover and Columbine stopped breathing too.

A bellow came from the judge's tent. 'Will the other jockey come forward? If he doesn't, we'll have no choice but to award the race to Mr Stacker.'

Arthur handed The One's rein to a boy. 'The jockey's coming,' he shouted into the tent. 'He's coming right away.' He ran back to Garth, saw a woman bending over him and halted in his tracks.

The woman looked up. 'I'm his mother,' said Clara de Granville. Arthur had no idea what to reply. Clara bent over her son. 'Garth,' she said. 'Garth, can you hear me?' There was an almost imperceptible tremor. Very slowly, Clara uncurled him. His face was blotched, his cap squashed down one side. Taking off her gloves, Lady de Granville sat him up, straightened the cap, took out a lace handkerchief and wiped his cheeks.

Garth truly believed he was dreaming, or perhaps he really was dead. 'I failed,' he said to this apparition. 'I've failed.'

'We'll see,' the apparition replied. 'Come, we'll go together.'

Garth, still in his dream, put out both his hands, and taking them in both of hers, his mother helped him to walk.

The inquiry was brisk. The One's injury was examined. Mr Stacker tried to bluff. Garth managed to remain upright and Arthur Rose spoke on his behalf. He did not waste words. Mr Stacker had broken the code of jockeys and gentlemen. He was a disgrace to his profession. Trainers should strike him off their lists. When Garth's dazed condition was questioned, Arthur declared that the boy had been concussed when he fell off and that he had not fallen off until after crossing the finishing line. Arthur spoke well and with the conviction of the just. The junior stewards conferred. The chief steward hopped from foot to foot. The judge deliberated, and when it was announced that the winner of the 1861 Derby was The One, ridden by Garth de Granville and trained by his sister Daisy, not just the racecourse but the whole town could hear the cheers.

Blinking as he realised he was neither dead nor dreaming, Garth gazed wildly about. 'Ma –' he began to call. His mother was no longer beside him. It was Skelton, sweating with excitement. In the moments since the race was called for The One, the groom had lost count of the number of times he had checked that Charles's signed promise was safe in his pocket. He would not show it now. The moment to flourish it would be at Hartslove itself. His triumph and relief made him almost as drunk as Garth. 'Now then, boy!' he chortled. 'Get back up on that horse and enjoy yourself!' Garth was given no option.

Two lines formed, and Daisy found herself, Skelton and The One, with Garth back in the saddle, pushed between them. The cheering was deafening and her shoulders were quickly bruised from being enthusiastically patted. This was the moment she had dreamed of, but all she could think of was her mother. Everybody, it seemed, was trying to snatch hairs from The One's tail. The horse did not like it. He pressed close to Daisy and she pressed close to him. She was so hot. She was so confused. She could not hear the applause. She could not hear anything clearly. She was going to faint.

'Air! Give them air!' somebody shouted. An important man – Daisy had no idea who – stepped forward to present the prize money. 'Now, let me see. We've taken off a hundred sovereigns for the policing of the course. We've taken off the hundred sovereigns you've got to give the second-prize winner and fifty sovereigns for the judge. That leaves you with 6,100 sovereigns.' The bag was so heavy

Daisy could hardly hold it. Skelton helpfully held it for her.

Immediately afterwards, agents stepped forward with offers to buy The One. Daisy supposed she must have rejected them, though she never heard her own voice. She concentrated on breathing slowly and deeply. She was not going to faint. She was going to look straight ahead and brace herself because the lady she had seen before could not possibly be her mother. That must have been an illusion. She looked up and found she was quite wrong. Her mother was standing within two arms' length. She was standing next to Aunt Barbara. She was clapping. Aunt Barbara was clapping. Rose, Lily, Clover and Columbine were clapping. It was only then that Daisy allowed herself to believe that her mother really was there; that The One – brave, quirky, brilliant The One – really had won the Derby; that Hartslove really was safe. She also believed something else. She believed with her whole heart that this was the best day in the world and that nothing could spoil it.

26

It was not the best day in the world for Garth. When he came to more properly, he lurched off The One, elbowed past the pie sellers and cavorting dragoons, the exultant winners and the despondent losers, and staggered back to the stables in the town. Daisy knew he had been drunk. His mother knew he had been drunk. Worst of all, Skelton knew he had been drunk. He lay in the straw, his head splitting. It was nearly an hour before he felt well enough to gather his things. He would vanish. That was best. He took off the red silks and was leaving when Daisy and The One returned. 'Garth!' Daisy said with a dazzling smile. 'It's over. Nothing matters now. Ma came! *Ma came!*'

Garth's nerves seemed to be on the outside of his skin. The very air burned and stung. 'I was drunk, Daisy, and I hit him.' He gestured at the horse.

'Nearly hit him,' Daisy corrected, stroking The One's neck.

'I hit a man who was trying to be kind. What's the difference? I couldn't remember what to do. God, Daisy. I couldn't even count to three – and don't deny it,' Garth burst out, seeing that Daisy was about to do just that. 'Don't treat me like a child. I took the whip from Skelton. *I asked HIM to help me.* And I couldn't even count to three.'

'All right, it's true,' Daisy agreed. 'You didn't start properly and you hit someone.' Her voice hardened. 'And you were drunk.'

'I drank whisky,' Garth said. 'I drank it because I was frightened.'

'It was wrong, Garth.'

'You think I don't know that?' His eyes were pools of distress.

The One took Daisy's sleeve between his teeth. Daisy removed it. 'It's finished now. Finished, do you hear?'

'Finished for you.'

'No, Garth. Finished for all of us. Something new's starting. Ma came.' She stopped, suddenly anxious. 'You do remember seeing her, don't you?' She could see that he did. 'The others are with her. We'll see her again very soon.'

'She'll leave us. She'll leave because of Pa and me.'

'Perhaps she will leave,' said Daisy, 'but it won't be because of you.'

He ignored this. 'And the man . . . his face –'

'Yes. We should find him.'

'He wasn't a stranger,' Garth said.

'No?'

'We were both on the top of the trains on the way down here.'

'Are you sure it was the same man?'

'Certain.'

Daisy found this thought comforting. 'Stay, Garth,' she said. 'Stay for me.'

Garth gave a hopeless gesture but put down his pack.

Aunt Barbara came a little later. When she had admired The One and Daisy had made him comfortable and the stable manager had promised on his life to let nobody near him, they made their way to a hotel on the town's main street. In a stuffy room, Rose, Lily, Columbine and Clover were perched on hard hotel chairs, ready to leap up and catch their mother if she showed any sign of flying off. Arthur Rose was hovering outside, wanting to be helpful yet not wanting to intrude.

Clara de Granville rose when Daisy and Garth came in. Daisy wanted to run to her but her legs locked. At the racecourse, Clara had been just their mother. Here, she seemed more unfamiliar. Her face was older; her hair not pinned quite as Daisy remembered; her clothes reflecting Aunt Barbara's taste rather than her own. And there was something else. This lady was no longer a cobweb. Something missing had been filled in, and it made her both more their mother and less. Daisy's legs remained locked until she heard her name. The voice had not changed at all. Then she ran forward so fast that she would have fallen had her mother not caught her and hugged her, a living, breathing, solid hug, the hug of a person as thrilled to see Daisy as Daisy was to see her.

The embrace finally over, Clara de Granville kept hold of Daisy's hand. Garth remained by the door. There was an awkward silence. Garth could not break it. His heart hurt much more than his head.

His mother regarded him. He began to curl up. She spoke directly. 'Garth, can you forgive me?'

The question was so unexpected that Garth stopped curling. 'Forgive you, Ma? What for?'

'For leaving you.'

'Why shouldn't you leave me?' His throat was still rough from the whisky. 'I wasn't worth staying for.'

'Is that what you think?'

'It's the truth.'

'No, Garth. That's just what you believe.' Clara de Granville let go of Daisy's hand. Daisy sat down. 'You sit too,' Clara said. Garth sank on to his haunches.

Slowly, and with some pauses, their mother tried to explain. 'I left because I had a sickness in the head that was nothing to do with any of you. The doctors couldn't help. At times, nobody could help. It's strange that sometimes sickness in the head can cripple as badly as sickness in the body. Anyhow, when I couldn't bear it any more, I went to Aunt Barbara and slowly I felt better.' She stopped.

'Couldn't we have made you better?' asked Clover or Columbine.

'No, Clover, you couldn't.'

'Did we make you worse?'

'No, Columbine, you didn't make me worse. You couldn't have done that.'

'So what did Aunt Barbara do?'

'I don't know,' said their mother. 'Sometimes, when you're in a muddle, you just need a place where – I don't know how best to describe it – a place where your mind can go to sleep for a bit. That's what we do with our bodies after all. When we're ill, we sleep. Do you understand?'

Garth closed his eyes. He could refuse to understand or he could try to understand. Refuse. Try. Refuse. Try. He opened his eyes. Daisy was staring straight at him. 'Try,' she said as though reading his mind. She would not allow him to look away.

Clover sighed.

'What is it, Clover?' her mother asked.

'I hope you're going to stay, because you're the only person who calls Columbine and me by our right names,' Clover told her. 'If you disappear again, even we may forget which one of us is which.'

Lady de Granville exchanged looks with all her children. She exchanged the longest look of all with Rose, whose face so resembled her own.

'We didn't know how to get you back,' Rose whispered. 'We were frightened.'

'I was frightened too,' Lady de Granville said.

'And are you still frightened, Ma? Are you?'

Daisy had to speak, though she dreaded the effect. 'Before you answer, Ma, you should know that Pa's still drinking and Gryffed's dead and everybody's left except for Mrs Snips and Skelton. If things were frightening before, they're not much different now – except that The One's won us some money.'

Rose was shocked. 'Daisy! We don't have to—'

'Yes, Rose, we do,' said Daisy.

Their mother got up and stood by the window. Six pairs of eyes followed her. Lady de Granville turned. 'How did you know The One would win the Derby, Daisy?'

'I don't know.' Daisy struggled to be honest. 'I didn't know all the time. But I did know something. I knew that he made me feel so . . . so . . .' She frowned, searching for the right word, and at last she found it. 'He made me feel so hopeful,' she said.

Their mother's eyes danced. 'Hopeful,' she said. 'That's exactly the word. Hopeful's what you children make me feel. I don't know why I couldn't see it before. I think hope must have been smothered by your father's –' a tremor, a breath – 'by other things.'

The last of Garth's strength seeped away. He slowly keeled over. He was asleep. His mother took a cushion from the sofa and placed it carefully under his lolling head. 'I see hopefulness very clearly now,' she said. She moved amongst them, settling one of Rose's curls, touching Lily's cheek, stroking Daisy's hand and kissing Clover and Columbine's foreheads. 'Though none of you have four legs and a snip, you're each my The One. Help me never to forget that again.'

27

Skelton found it harder than he imagined to keep his secret. He bitterly resented being obliged to doff his cap to Lady de Granville and having to stand like a schoolboy when Daisy told him that on account of the whip he was never, ever to go near The One again. He sloped off to make his own way home. His revenge would be the sweeter the longer the de Granvilles imagined their troubles were over.

Daisy was delighted to see him go. She saw to the horse's every need, and when she could not manage, Garth helped her. He was subdued, not cowed. Daisy understood the distinction very well. She never asked what was said in the long hours Garth spent alone with their mother once his hangover wore off. It was enough that when Garth came to find her he was walking on his hands, wordlessly showing her two things: first, he was happier; and second, there was no bottle in his pocket.

Lady de Granville, Rose, Lily, Columbine and Clover travelled back to Hartslove together, Arthur acting as baggage handler, guide and guard. Their journey was quick. Daisy, Garth and The One's journey took a little longer. Not that it was hard. Nobody could do enough to ease the passage of the Derby winner: the train companies gave him the most comfortable box; his rack was filled with the best hay; well-wishers left small presents of oats and carrots. Garth and Daisy stayed with him day and night.

The whole of Manchester, or so it seemed, turned out to greet them. Amongst the first well-wishers was Mr Snaffler, set on making a great show of checking that apart from his bruised nose, The One was undamaged by his experience. Daisy was chilly. 'Arthur Rose is the only vet The One needs,' she said, 'and don't worry, we'll pay all your bills tomorrow.' Snaffler blustered. Daisy swept past him. The One, not caring for the crush, kept the scarred nose that had achieved so much fame tucked into Daisy's elbow.

After the stationmaster expressed himself delighted to send on their baggage, Garth and Daisy began to walk The One down the long road to Hartslove, Daisy in the saddle. After a mile or two, the townsfolk thinned out until there was just the three of them. They did not hurry. When, hours later, they climbed up on to the familiar moor, Daisy was amazed to see her crutches tucked neatly into a crag. 'I used to think it was you who collected these and put them where I could find them,' she said to Garth. 'Help me off.'

Garth helped her out of the saddle. She swung her crutches. 'It's not you, though, is it?'

Garth shook his head. 'I don't know who it can be.'

'The Dead Girl?'

'I don't think she ever leaves the castle.' Something else was bothering him. 'Daisy?'

'Yes?'

'We never found the coxcomb man I hit.'

'A red saviour for a red horse,' said Daisy.

Garth gave her a sideways look. 'You'll be writing poetry next.'

Daisy giggled and poked him in the ribs. 'We didn't find him, but I'm sure if he needs to, he'll find us.'

'You really think that? What if he doesn't know where we live?'

'Garth! We've got the most famous horse in the world today! We've got The One! Everybody knows where we live!'

The One was surprised by how loudly two human beings can laugh. Daisy mounted again. Garth hitched her crutches over his shoulder. Over the moor and down into the Hartslove valley they strode. At Hartslove's rusting gates, Garth stopped. 'Do a lap of honour round the Resting Place,' he said.

'The One's probably tired,' Daisy answered, but her eyes were alight.

'He's the winner of the Derby.'

'I don't know —'

'He'll look after you,' Garth said. 'Just hold tight.'

'I'm holding!'

'One, two, three, GO!'

The One, happy to be home, launched himself off, galloping where he chose. At first Daisy was too busy clinging to the saddle to enjoy herself, but the rhythm was so secure and The One's movements so fluid that when he leaped over the flat stone and swept around the chestnut tree, she was steady in the saddle. She threw back her head. Now she could hear applause, and it was not the fickle applause of the Epsom crowd. Nor was it Garth clapping her on. What Daisy heard was the deep, sustained and endless applause of Hartslove itself. As she galloped her winner over the drawbridge, Father Nameless's bell rang out and at its peal Daisy threw a victorious fist into the air and let out one wild whoop of utter delight.

Charles had barely set foot out of the library since his children had left, and Mrs Snipper's meals – strange ones, since she had no provisions from Snipe – had remained largely uneaten. Often, he locked the door. Equally often, using a key Charles did not know she had, Mrs Snipper crept in and removed the inevitably empty bottles. If Charles was sleeping, she covered him with a blanket. It was Mrs Snipper who brought him the news of The One's victory, news that had been delivered to her by Snipe along with a bag which Mrs Snipper secreted in a cupboard in the dining room. Snipe volunteered no information about the wound on his face, and Mrs Snipper did not press him. Snipe's business was his business unless it was her business. She cleaned his face and gave him an extra helping of soup.

At first, Charles was astounded by the Derby news. 'Won? He WON? Are you certain it was The One?' When Mrs Snipper said that indeed she was certain, and that the whole of Manchester was preparing for the horse's triumphant return, Charles shrank as though she had announced an outbreak of plague. 'But he was lame! He was going to break down! He – he –'

'I don't care what he was going to do,' said Mrs Snipper. 'I'm just telling you What He Did.'

Later that day, the hired carriage drew up and Mrs Snipper ran to greet it. Arthur Rose got out first, pulled down the carriage steps and handed out, in turn, Clover, Columbine, Lily and Rose. There was a pause. With a sudden premonition, Mrs Snipper's heart skipped a beat. A neatly shod foot appeared on the step, followed by the clack of crinoline under silk, and then, with a slight hesitation, the rest of the person Mrs Snipper longed to see quite as much as the children. 'Oh,' she cried. 'Oh my! Oh My Lady!'

Clara de Granville held out her hands. 'Mrs Snips!' she said. 'I'm so glad to be home.'

Charles heard the carriage. He was in a fever. His contract with Skelton had been a joke, right? They had both agreed it was a joke. Skelton would already have torn it up. But he knew in his heart that Skelton would have done no such thing. He knew it as certainly as he knew that if he did not stop drinking he would soon be dead. He swallowed three gulps of brandy very quickly and placed the bottle on top of the newspapers. A deathly calm overtook him. He stood in the middle of the room like a condemned man waiting for the executioner. He watched the door handle. Any second now. Any second. Any . . .

It was Rose's step he thought he heard, though with the acuity that sometimes accompanies drunkenness, he actually understood, the moment he heard it, that it was not Rose's step. The door handle turned. He braced himself.

Clara de Granville was framed in the doorway. Charles was motionless. His wife removed her hat slowly. She saw the bottle on the newspapers. She saw her husband's soldier's stiffness. She saw Gryffed's empty bed. It struck her that she could walk towards Charles, or away from him, but that if she walked towards him she could never walk away from him again. She thought of her children. She thought of The One. She walked forward carefully, though without hesitation. It took both herself and Charles a long time to speak, and their actual words were much less important than the fact that they spoke at all.

When, in due course, they emerged from the library, they found Rose, Lily, Clover and Columbine in the drawing room recounting every detail of the tumultuous week to

Mrs Snipper and discussing a celebration dinner for Daisy and Garth when they returned. Charles allowed them to exclaim and beam. He could not tell them now; they were too excited. Nor could he tell them when they pulled him with them to take their mother upstairs; they were too happy. Nor could he tell them as they rushed in and out with armfuls of fresh flowers and helped Mrs Snipper throw open the windows of his wife's room, bringing it back to life. That would be too cruel. Nor could he say anything when Daisy and The One swept over the drawbridge with Garth performing cartwheels behind. Charles knew that Skelton was in his house and could appear at any moment, but as long as Skelton did not appear, he could remain silent.

They garlanded The One and turned him loose at the Resting Place to roll and sneeze and graze. Eventually, Charles slunk away, and Garth, missing him, went in search. His mother had told him much about his father that he wished he had known before. Still, he knew it now and, in exchange, he would tell his father the truth about himself and the race, a truth Daisy was sure to gloss over. He found Charles leaning against the fireplace in the library, his hands knotted behind his back. Charles had finished the brandy, wanting his head to be foggy; it was still clear as clear.

Garth spoke quickly. 'I got drunk before the race, Pa. I got so drunk I could hardly stay on. The One didn't know when to start, and I couldn't remember what we'd practised – Daisy and me, that is. Skelton wanted me to use a whip, like Grint did in the Guineas, and I did use it, only a man got in the way and I hit him instead. Ma told me about the war. I understand now.' He tailed off.

Charles unknotted his hands. 'Oh, Garth,' he said sadly, 'drink has made fools of us both.' Garth moved towards him. Charles shook his head. 'It's time,' he said, and walking swiftly past Garth, he made his way to the stables. Garth followed.

Skelton was waiting in the doorway of his house. He welcomed Charles heartily. 'Well, Sir Charles,' he said, 'I believe you've come to honour your bargain.'

Charles swallowed. 'It was a joke, Skelton. You said it was a joke.'

'Saying's saying. I don't believe a judge will find this a joke.' He produced the contract and waved it in front of Charles's nose. 'Written and signed by yourself.'

'Skelton –'

'*Mister* Skelton.'

'Mr Skelton,' mumbled Charles, 'you and I know it was a joke. I was drunk. You *know* I was drunk. And though you might want to take Hartslove and The One away from me, you can't want to destroy the children – for God's sake, man – the children.'

Skelton unrolled the paper. 'The writing's very careful,' he observed cruelly, 'and your signature's very straight. Poor old Sir Charles. You can't even do drunk properly.'

Charles stood as straight as he could. 'I'm begging you, Skelton,' he said. 'Tear up that wretched contract.'

'I won't,' said Skelton and closed the door in Charles's face. Charles turned. Garth had heard every word. 'Garth!' Charles stuttered. But Garth was already running back to the castle, leaving Charles to stumble behind.

Arthur Rose had arrived at Hartslove, invited by Lady de Granville to be thanked properly for looking after her girls. Charles barely saw him. 'All of you, come to the dining room,' he said, 'and bring Mrs Snipper.'

Surprised rather than alarmed, they all gathered. Garth's expression was blank as a waxwork's. In honour of Arthur, Rose was wearing her Derby clothes and had her hair up, which caused Arthur some pain. Hartslove was stirring. Rose would soon be off. He made to leave. Charles waved him in. 'You might as well stay,' he said. 'You'll hear soon enough.'

Charles sat, then stood, then sat, then stood again. He coughed. 'Just after The One had his accident, I got drunk in Skelton's house and we made a joke. If The One won the Derby, I would give the horse, the winnings and Hartslove to him. The One has won the Derby.' He stopped.

'So?' said Rose. 'A joke's a joke.'

'Not quite. You see, I wrote it down,' Charles said in a great rush. 'And I signed it. Skelton has the paper and insists that it's not a joke, it's a contract, and the contract must be honoured.'

305

'But a joke's *not* a contract,' said Daisy. She refused to understand. 'You laugh at a joke.'

'It doesn't look like a joke,' Charles said. 'That's just what we called it. We didn't laugh – or perhaps we did. Doesn't matter.'

'But if Skelton *knows* it was a joke—'

'*Mister* Skelton knows nothing of the sort,' a voice boomed from the door, and the man himself appeared. 'And nor does the county judge. Don't think I haven't had the contract checked and verified.'

'You're a scoundrel,' said Charles.

'And you're a soak, which is lucky for me.'

'It can't be true,' shrilled Daisy. She still tried to block it out. 'The One won the Derby so that we could keep Hartslove.'

'A contract's a contract.'

'But The One!' She felt physically sick. 'You can't have him! You can't!'

'It's a pity your father didn't have your faith.' Skelton rocked on shiny boots. He held out his hand to Mrs Snipper. 'I'll have the keys.'

Mrs. Snipper reversed. 'You'll get nothing from me.'

'I'll get everything, one way or another.'

'No!' shouted Daisy. 'No!'

Arthur moved between Skelton and Mrs Snipper. 'Hold on. If Sir Charles is, as you say, a soak, then he's not competent to make a contract,' he said.

'That's right. Oh, that's right!' Rose was smiling again.

'Oh really,' sneered Skelton. He had not realised until now that Arthur was in the room. Not that it mattered. 'The writing's very careful. Very careful indeed. Not drunken writing, not at all.' He smirked. 'Bad luck, young man. There's no heiress for you here.'

Rose went white.

'Mr Skelton,' Lady de Granville said, rising up, 'you can't mean to deprive us of our home.'

'Well, your ladyship –' he rolled her title round as though it were a sour plum – 'homes come and homes go, and you'll not miss the place, having been away so long.'

Daisy banged her fist on the table. 'We'll give you the Derby winnings.'

'Not enough.' Skelton sat down and splayed his legs. 'I want what I'm entitled to.'

'Skelton,' said Mrs Snipper.

'*Mister* Skelton.'

'Skelton,' she repeated, 'I'll buy the place off you.'

'You?!' He laughed out loud. 'What with? Your wages?'

'Now that's a proper joke,' Mrs Snipper said. 'I don't have wages. No, I want to buy the place – and the horse of course – with money.'

'Would that be money you've baked in a pie?' jibed Skelton.

'You don't bake money in a pie. I'd like to buy it with this.' From under the sideboard Mrs Snipper produced the bag Snipe had brought home. 'There's nearly twenty thousand pounds in here,' she said. Skelton gaped. They all gaped. 'Why the gaping?' said Mrs Snipper. 'I had a bet on The One, that's all. I told you I would.'

'But how on earth did you win so much?'

'I put a bet on the day you left and got Very Good Odds.' She looked around. 'Really, I don't know why you're amazed. I've always betted on Sir Charles's The Ones. I knew it was bound to Work In The End.'

Skelton recovered himself and calculated. 'You can have the castle for all that, but not the horse.'

Daisy gasped.

'I'll have both or none,' Mrs Snipper countered. She opened the bag.

Skelton put his feet on the table. 'I'm not giving up the horse.'

'Well then,' said Mrs Snipper, 'no deal.'

Daisy slumped. 'I won't believe it,' she whispered. '*I won't believe it.*'

Skelton tossed the contract to her. 'Perhaps this will help.'

Arthur caught it. 'May I?'

He held it up. He read it to himself, then he read it aloud. 'I, Charles Gavin de Granville, promise that if The One, who can't walk at the moment, manages by some miracle to gallop, and by a further miracle actually manages to gallop first past the winning post in the Derby of 1861,

I really don't see how, but anyhow if the horse does, I'll give it, the horse, I mean, the prize money and Hartslove Castle to my groom, Skelton. Signed, Charles Gavin de Granville and Arnold John Skelton.'

Charles put his head in his hands.

'I'm going to read it again,' Arthur said.

Rose was appalled. 'Don't torture us, Arthur.'

'I'm going to read it again.'

'As often as you like,' said Skelton.

When he had finished, Arthur did not hand the paper back. Skelton was unmoved. 'Don't think destroying that'll make any difference. I've a certified copy.'

'Good,' said Arthur, 'because if you don't have one, I'll make one.'

'What on earth do you mean?'

'Haven't any of you been listening?' asked Arthur. He was quite calm. 'This contract says quite specifically that the horse should be first past the post, and he wasn't.'

'Don't be such a jobsworth,' growled Skelton, snatching the contract back. 'Everybody knows what this contract means. The other horse was disqualified. He didn't count.'

'Contracts mean what they say. That's the nature of contracts,' said Arthur.

'That wasn't the judge's opinion.'

'I don't suppose you told him how The One won?'

'I told him what he needed to know.' Skelton's voice was rising. 'This place and the horse are mine. They're mine. I paid the Derby entry fee. I paid for the transport. I paid for the oats.' He wagged a finger at Charles. 'I paid for the *drink*.'

Daisy struggled to her feet. 'You paid for Pa's drink? You wicked, wicked man!'

Skelton realised he had made a mistake. 'You think he could live without drink? He couldn't even tie a bootlace without a bottle of brandy. You're beholden to me, you silly little girl, BEHOLDEN, do you understand?'

Mrs Snipper interrupted. She had been counting out money. 'There,' she said. 'It's not quite as much as my first offer, but it'll Cover Your Outlays.'

'I'm not leaving! This place is mine! The One's mine,' shouted Skelton, lurching to his feet.

'Not according to this contract,' said Arthur. 'I'm happy to fetch the judge, if you'd like. Perhaps two or three would be better. We could tell them about the drink, too.'

Daisy was staring at the contract in horrified wonder. 'That's why you helped with the haunting when the Entwhistles were here. I was grateful. *Grateful!* How could I have been such a dupe?'

'It wasn't me who helped you. I didn't help you at all!'

'Liar! You were helping yourself!'

'It wasn't me!'

Nobody believed him, and Arthur Rose had something more important on his mind. He looked at the date on the contract and took a guess. 'The One's knee,' he said. 'What do you know about that?' He clenched his fists. 'My God, man!'

Skelton could take no more. That oaf, Sir Charles! That drunken oaf! Couldn't even write a proper contract! He launched himself at Arthur, head lowered. 'I'll have you, you interfering bastard. You'll regret making a fool of me.' He caught Arthur above the eye. Arthur barely flinched. His fists were ready and they were keen. They fought with deadly intent, Arthur silently and Skelton with much swearing and cursing until Garth pitched in and Skelton was finally driven like a mad dog through the hall and into the courtyard. Daisy found her crutches tucked under the arms of the Furious Boy. She ran outside too, and it was she, who, having chosen her moment, delivered the final, terminating blow directly across Skelton's right knee.

28

A very special light emanates from a place in which hope has triumphed over despair. At Hartslove, this light was not the glow from the windows of Lady de Granville's reoccupied rooms in the north-west wing. Nor was it the light from the lantern that Daisy hung in the chestnut tree at the Resting Place. Nor was it the result of some grand cleaning and renovation of the castle. There was no cleaning or renovation. The Furious Boy's arm was mended; a few leaks in the roof were fixed; the kitchen lift handle was oiled; the sold portraits and furniture that could be found were bought back, including Sir Thomas and the dining-room table. Otherwise, Hartslove remained just as it was, its gates rusty and its dust undisturbed. The new light that emanated was not a physical light: it was the light of a place whose pulse is strong again.

Charles did not stop drinking at once. He had bad days, better days and good days. But the return of his wife and the success of The One had lit a touchpaper. When he drank, it was no longer the drinking of the desperate. Often, of an evening, having drunk nothing at all, he would go to the stables and gaze at the Red Horse of Hartslove, as the crowd of admirers that flowed up the drive had christened him, though Daisy never called him anything but The One. Often he found Garth at his shoulder.

Garth never attempted to ride again. Riding was for Daisy, not for him. His fear was inexplicable. He never conquered it. The most difficult part was trying not to waste time convincing himself even now that if only he could find the right remedy, he would be able to leap fearlessly into the saddle. Accepting that this was never going to happen was hard. Occasionally, as he and Charles were leaving the stable yard, Garth would still spit, bang his heel three times and whisper, 'Hartslove luck!' This, though, was not some lingering fantasy about riding; this was to show his father that Garth never again wanted to be distant from him. And Charles always responded with a smile, though for many months, perhaps even a year, the smile was rather wan.

Lady de Granville was soon busy with the bittersweet task of repairing her wedding dress for Rose to wear. Rose had not waited for Arthur to propose: she had taken her courage in both hands, walked him down to the Resting Place and proposed herself. He heard her out without interruption, then slowly and carefully outlined his concerns about the differences between them in birth and expectation. 'You could have everything,' he said in the end.

'I already have everything,' Rose said.

'You belong here.'

Rose stroked the chestnut tree. 'This place is at the root of me,' she said, 'and the root's so deep it can never be uprooted. But I don't choose to live here, not like Daisy does, or Lily. I choose to carry Hartslove away with me and return to it from elsewhere. I don't want to be free of it – not at all. It doesn't weigh me down, though I once thought it did, with the Dead Girl and Father Nameless and all. But I want to be me as well as Rose de Granville. Do you see?'

Arthur was not reassured. 'What happens if you find you want to be Rose de Granville more than Rose Rose?'

'Rose Rose,' she said dreamily. 'It's a lovely name.'

'It doesn't answer my question.'

'Oh, Arthur,' she said. 'Haven't you noticed?'

'Noticed what?'

'We're done with doubt here. It's all out of fashion.' He tried to stay serious. With Rose skipping round the chestnut tree, it was impossible.

The return of their mother and the saving of Hartslove helped Lily bear the imminent loss of Rose. She was also helped by Snipe's renewed, though still secret, attentions. Her dove-cage was soon replaced by an aviary. A pair of swans appeared on the river. Two white kittens were left in a basket by her bedroom fire. This strange, one-sided courtship endured for decades, tacitly encouraged by Mrs Snipper and puzzled over but unquestioned by both Charles and Clara de Granville. Lily believed her suitor to be a ghost, and that pleased her. When she became a ghost herself they would meet, and that was enough.

The twins were bridesmaids at Rose and Arthur's wedding. Aunt Barbara came and stayed for weeks afterwards, helping Clara to take up domestic reins she had never fully grasped. Clover and Columbine disliked this arrangement, particularly when Aunt Barbara, disapproving of their passion for newspaper obituaries, suggested a governess. Yet all was well. The first governess lasted only a month, the next one a week, the third only a day. The One grew used to being woken at midnight, whitewashed and ridden around the courtyard by Daisy as Father Nameless tolled a bell. If the governess was particularly stubborn, Garth would perform backflips along the ruins or fold himself up until he had no head.

The Dead Girl and Clara de Granville watched these antics from an upstairs window. Neither interfered. Both agreed that though Barbara understood many things, she never understood that Hartslove would teach the twins all they needed to know.

All this time, over the wedding preparations and long after, Clara and Charles hovered about each other like two uncertain birds. At mealtimes, Clara sat in her old place under her portrait and Charles hardly sat at all, picking up his fork, putting it down, walking swiftly to the fireplace, fiddling with the logs, then walking back and sitting, before doing the same all over again. The children watched him, and watched their mother, and watched their mother watching him. Both before her wedding, and when she visited afterwards, Rose took to nervously chattering, trying to make everything seem quite normal, and the others joined in to help her. When the dining-room candles were snuffed out, they all leaped up to relight them.

One evening the candles did not go out, and much later that night, Clara found Charles between her and the Dead Girl as they observed The One on his ghostly, governess-frightening parade. After a while, the Dead Girl faded and Clara discovered she was leaning against Charles. He expected her to draw away when she realised what she was doing. She did not, and when he rested his chin in her hair she sighed. They heard the governess scream as The One galloped off in a white flourish. They heard her drag her suitcases across the floor. They smiled at each other when, night-time or not, Clover could be heard offering the services of the new carriage. They remained quietly together after the carriage drew up and drew away again. It was very late indeed by the time Charles walked his wife back to her room, and it was almost dawn when, instead of murmuring, 'Goodnight,' she drew him in and closed the door.

*

At sunset on the anniversary of the Derby triumph, Daisy went to the stables. Her crutches were leaning against The One's door. 'Come,' she said softly. The horse followed as she swung out of the yard, along the drive and over the grass to the Resting Place. Although everything else was still, shadows danced on the tombstones. The One scratched his neck against the chestnut tree and nibbled the buttercups that covered Gryffed's grave. Daisy watched him for a bit, then dropped her crutches and lay face down on the flat stone. It was still warm from the day's heat. Beneath it she imagined the wheel of Hartslove's history turning. She rolled on to her back. In his own time, the horse ambled over and lowered his head, his forelock tickling Daisy's face and his long blaze shining like painted moonlight. If Daisy had put up a hand, she could have felt the tiny scar on his snip. But she did not put up her hand. She put out both arms. It was a broad embrace, the broadest she could manage. It took in The One and all the previous The Ones. It took in everything that belonged to Hartslove, both what Daisy could see and what she could not. 'Who'll be here in a hundred years?' she asked as the horse licked the stone beside her ear, curling his lip at the fuzziness of the lichen. The question was needless; Daisy already knew the answer. She rolled on to her stomach. In a hundred years, the castle would still be here, the ghosts of Hartslove still racing across the valley in a smoky tumult. The One hovered over her. 'And our ghosts will be here too,' she said, 'yours and mine. Don't you think, The One? We'll be the ghosts of Hartslove.' The One raised his head. He knew nothing about ghosts, but he did know about Daisy, and whatever she said, he agreed.

If you liked *Hartslove*,
turn the page for more thrilling titles
by K.M. Grant

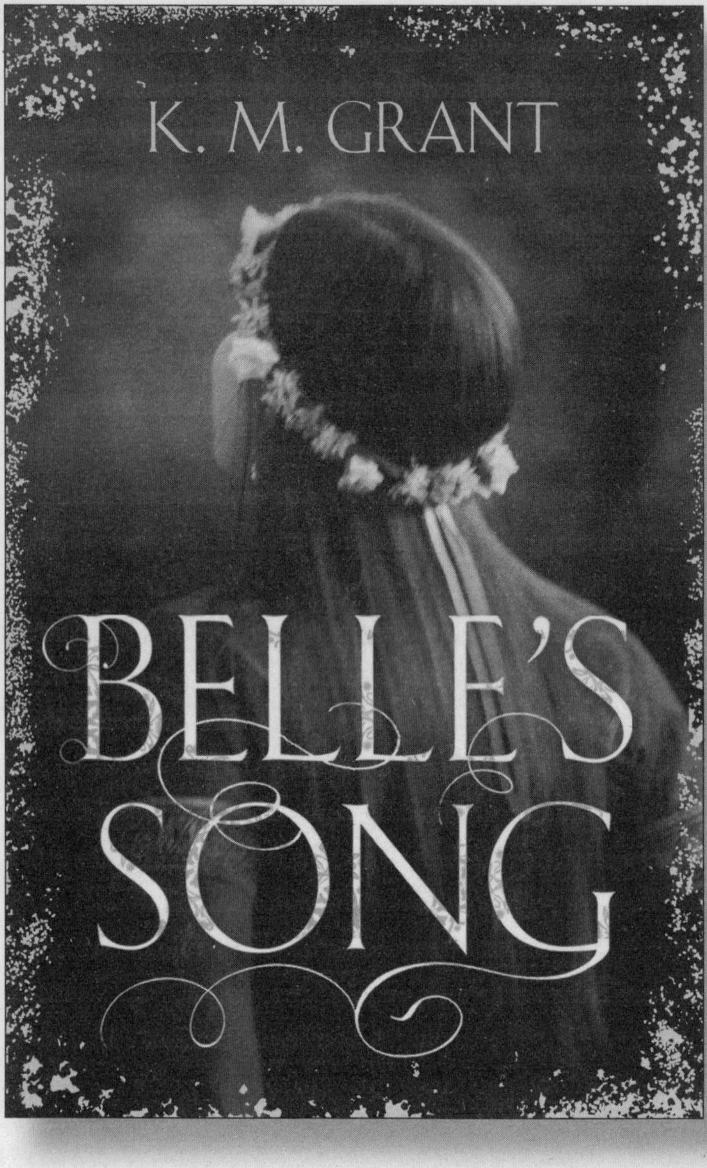
K. M. GRANT
BELLE'S
SONG

Belle's Song

When Belle meets Luke, son of an alchemist and Scribe to the famous poet Chaucer, she is determined to travel with him to Canterbury on a pilgrimage. She hopes for a miracle: that her father will walk again.

It is a time of unrest across the country, and the young King Richard II is just hanging on to his throne. A malign character on the pilgrimage suspects Chaucer of treason and slowly winds Belle into a political intrigue. At the same time, the impulsive Belle is drawn towards both Luke and Walter, the wealthy son of a knight. But Walter himself is guarding his own romantic secret.

As the uprising against the king starts to gain pace and the web of intrigue around Belle and Chaucer tightens, Belle and her friends must risk everything to save their country and themselves . . .

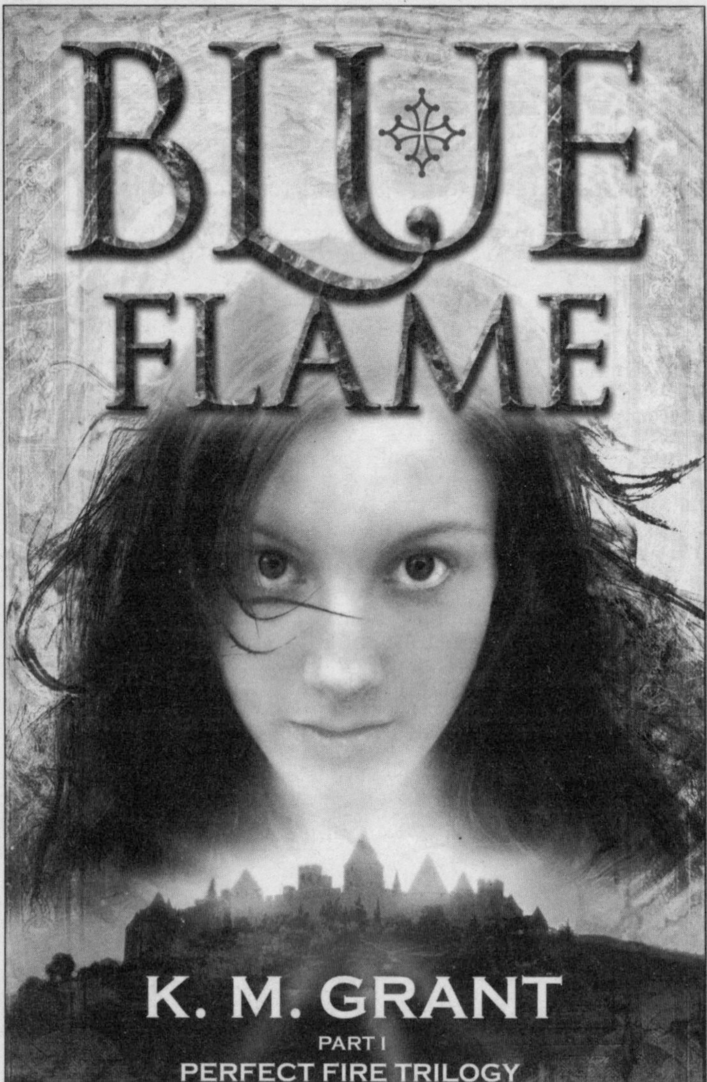
BLUE
FLAME
K. M. GRANT
PART I
PERFECT FIRE TRILOGY

Blue Flame

PART I OF THE PERFECT FIRE TRILOGY

Chalus Chabrol, 1199. The Occitanian knights battle for their lives against Richard the Lionheart. They are guarding the Blue Flame under which all Occitanians must unite to resist invasion. But the knights cannot survive and so it falls to Parsifal, young son of the knight Bernard, to travel on alone and find the true keeper of the flame. Yet when Parsifal returns home, the Occitan is ablaze. Catholic Inquisitors and Cathar heretics, far from uniting, are fighting each other for the soul of the land and its people. To which sect does the Blue Flame belong?

Parsifal's path intertwines with that of Raimon, son of a Cathar weaver, and Yolanda, daughter of a Catholic count. They are falling in love. But in a time of hate, love is never left in peace. With family against family, north against south and Catholic against Cathar, Raimon must help Parsifal find the Blue Flame's true meaning before the Occitan is destroyed.

'She has woven such a gripping plot that I shall certainly be lining up to read book two. I hope she doesn't keep us waiting too long' *Guardian*

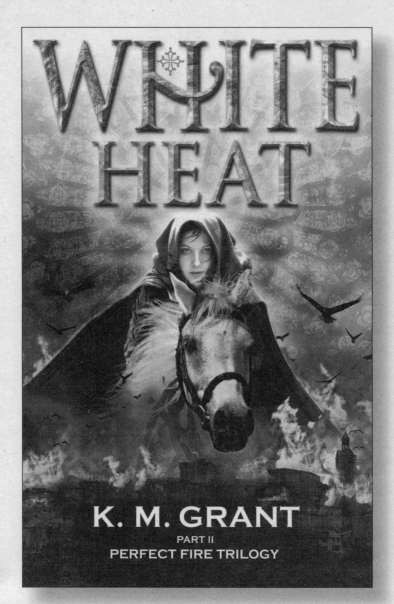

WHITE HEAT

K. M. GRANT

PART II
PERFECT FIRE TRILOGY

White Heat

PART II OF THE PERFECT FIRE TRILOGY

Will Raimon's and Yolanda's love survive the ravages of a siege, her enforced betrothal to Raimon's enemy and the growing divisions within their beloved Occitan?

Raimon has escaped the pyre and carried the Blue Flame, the true spirit of the Occitan, to the mountains above Castelneuf. But there he is besieged by the Catholic Aimery and the Cathar White Wolf. In Paris, Yolanda, believing Raimon is dead, resists marriage to Sir Hugh, who is building a war train to topple Raimon and bring the flame and the Occitan under the rule of the French king . . .

In a blazing finale, as Castelneuf burns, all sides are forced to reconsider what they are willing to sacrifice for the Occitan, for power and ultimately for love.

'For all the book's political and emotional complexity, the pace is breakneck . . . Volume three in this tricolore trilogy, *Paradise Red*, cannot appear too soon' *Financial Times*

PARADISE RED

K. M. GRANT

PART III
PERFECT FIRE TRILOGY

Paradise Red

PART III OF THE PERFECT FIRE TRILOGY

As Yolanda's lover Raimon and her brother Aimery set off to regain the flame and the heart of the Occitan, Hugh prepares to lay siege to the Cathar stronghold where the flame burns. Unbeknown to him, his wife Yolanda flees his castle into the freezing snow.

What is Yolanda running from? What underhand game is Aimery about to bring into play? And will Raimon's passion for the flame cause him to lose Yolanda and even himself?

K. M. Grant's spectacular novel weaves together the friendship, love and bitter rivalry of her wonderfully evoked characters in a finale to a superb trilogy of romance and adventure.

'K.M. Grant provides a top-notch tale of star-crossed lovers, court intrigue, twisted religious hatreds and the mystical power of landscape'
Financial Times